I0700968

ALSO BY AMINAH FOX

## MOURNERS
*The Mourners: The Deadly Elite*
*The Harlots: The Devoutly Corrupt*

## ALL THE OTHER GODS
*The Eleventh Hour*

## CRUSADERVERSE
*Where the Stars Sing*

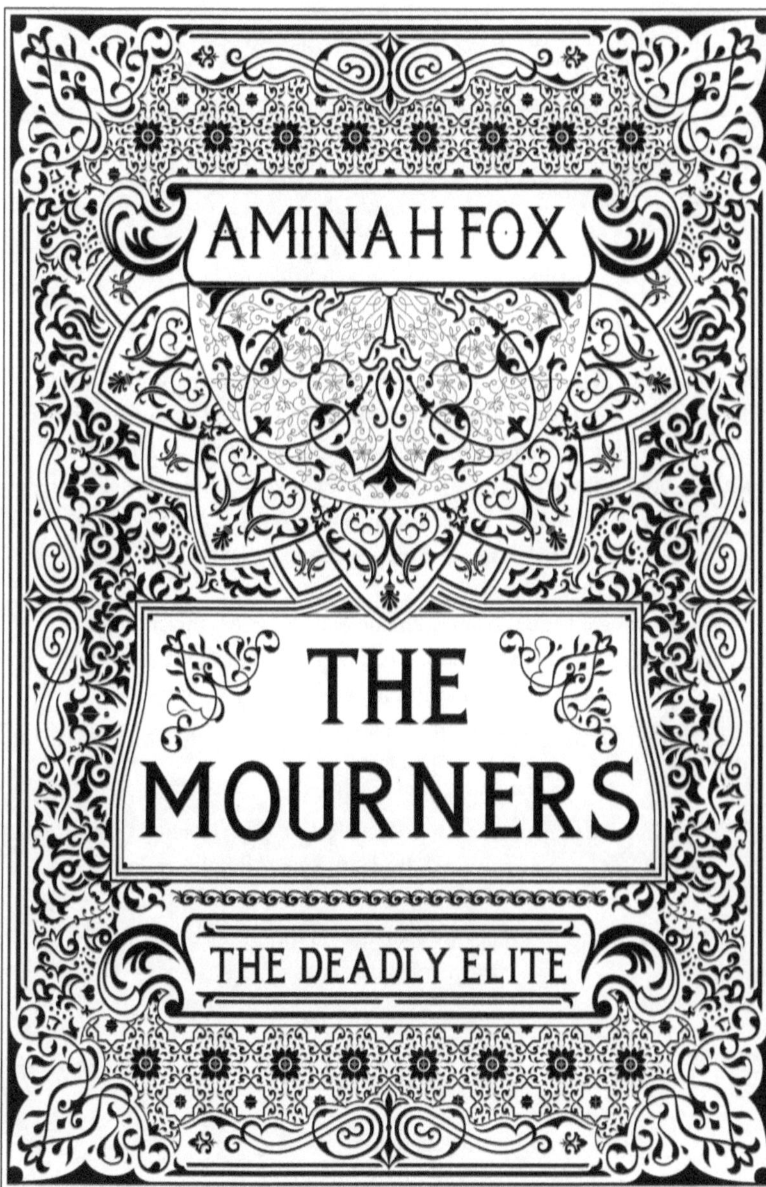

AMINAH FOX
THE MOURNERS
THE DEADLY ELITE

*For my brothers,*
*Kevin and Stephen*

# Prologue
## Cyrus

The search team had been dwindling for several months, the hunt for the harlots had surpassed average commuting distance by fourteen miles, and they had been forced to set up camp approximately forty-nine paces south of where he stood now. Cyrus Coin, who had lived all his life being the least attentive of his siblings and rarely remembered passages of Holy Writ, never expected to find proof of Him in an angel number, but seven was everywhere. In the fingers of sunlight that woke him in the mornings spent in his tent to the omens of death that clung to the trees, tarred and feathered during their searches at night. He was a God-fearing, Christ-haunted man as all Seekers were trained to be, though Cyrus could not have had worse luck; he had been the one to find the harlots.

"A moment longer," Cyrus urged as the sky grew darker above them. "The harlots are dead ahead."

"Does a harlot's bosom frighten you?" Ezra asked with a slight chuckle.

Cyrus didn't entertain the jab at his character. He was younger, entering his late twenties, and he had once heard Ezra shriek when a branch touched his shoulder.

"Harlots are harlots," he said. "We are all purveyors of sin if we learn nothing from it."

"You empathize with them?" Ezra asked. "With those who tempt men from their proper houses? Is that not treason?"

"Cyrus would never commit treason," Jakob said softly. "If he empathizes with them, then it's due to him being the son of a reverend elder."

Cyrus had intended to be silent on the final day of the search. He meant to pray for the harlots the night before as once they were captured, they were to be auctioned to the bawds without trial—Apostate's orders.

"My father would vote in favor of them getting a proper trial," Cyrus added lowly.

"My uncle would wish for the same in his old age, Cyrus," Ezra replied. "Though he's not as sharp as he used to be, and he's not the head of state. There are men meant to enforce the law and men meant to abide by it. And women follow men in doing so."

"We've waited long enough," Jakob said. "I want to be home before tomorrow night, maybe morning. Where is the page whistle?"

Cyrus watched as Jakob searched his pack for it, his brow knitted tightly together above his weary eyes. Jakob was twenty years his senior, far more accustomed to the ways of the Seekers than himself and had married lower than his station. A humble man with more to lose. Paired with a fool and a youth, neither with enough sense to remember a page whistle. Under suppressed anger, Cyrus could sense a manner of urgency in the man. It permeated off him.

Cyrus bore the weight of it. He had spent all his life in Texas, but this was his sixth year as a Seeker. His first time near the border.

The harlots were a mere twenty minutes from freedom, all they had to do was cross, but they slept around a fire, huddled together. He had counted them, young and middle-aged women, all would be convicted the same. For years Cyrus had been plagued with watching executions a thousand times over, and there was no new guilt for men like him. Or so he thought.

"Here, I've brought a light," Ezra said, offering Jakob a flashlight. "The old ways serve us just as well."

Jakob took it. "Aye, they do," he said, using the light to cast a signal south.

Cyrus watched as the signal was repeated by another Seeker, and then they waited.

"We've done our part," Ezra said with a yawn. "The men will load up the horses and file out before long, only a matter of time. There's no need to watch, boy. You'll only frighten yourself. I remember the first time I saw them do it, still thought of them as women then. But that's the trick. Demons possess the body, they sneak up on you quieter than any mouse, Cyrus, and at first, you sneeze, and you may shiver and try to run from it and tell yourself it's a bad dream. But once it gets inside you, it makes you feel warm like your mother's love until you begin to burn. You'll think it's fever, but no, and you'll start to drown in it. Struggle as you might, you won't have the strength to fight it. Before long, you'll slip away, thinking you're in pleasure, begging for more, but you're in pain. Though you don't know it yet, and you start tempting others to sin as well, and then you're sinking into a pit of darkness. Weak and weary."

"Don't frighten the boy, Ezra," Jakob said apathetically. "Those harlots can't be helped unless they find it in their hearts to repent."

"When have you heard of a harlot rebuking her demons?" Ezra said, stretching out and propping his head up on his pack. "They're out all night dancing with them. Selling what's not theirs to give."

Jakob grimaced. "Don't speak in such a way, or the lord will judge you as harshly."

Ezra shook his head and yawned again. "I only speak the truth, Jakob, they'll have them soon enough, and we'll all be on our way back in time for breakfast, I hope."

Within moments of Ezra speaking aloud, the Disciples rode out, bearing the Apostate's famed raven on their war flags, set forth by rage and driven by the will of the lord to see the women apprehended and justice executed. Forty in total, moving two by two across the glen, their horses' hooves roaring like thunder, and as they descended on the harlots, shrill screams rose into the night.

# 1

## Elide

"I, Hansel Hester, violated the sanctity of my marriage bed and that of Reverend Elijah Stone, knowingly, foolishly, and regretfully," Hansel said, lifting his eyes to meet those of the reverend elders. "And I have come to make amends."

Hansel stood like a soldier, and the loyal follower of God's law could have been one, had he not retired those dreams years ago upon her birth. Their ancient laws had served the Maleficarum family for ten generations, as had the Hester family. Growing up in Texas, as part of the Apolitian commune, Hansel had faced temptation often, thinking the men of their family were plagued more than all others. Elide knew little of the temptations men faced, only that her own were few and far between. At the moment all she wanted was her winter coat as the courtroom was exceptionally chilly.

The elders' heavy black robes protected them from the cold, though each of their brows were furrowed due to

Hansel's request. Reverend Warner, the eldest reverend and overseer of Baptiste, looked irate by the request. The old man's jaw was clenched so tightly, Elide thought it might snap. Last week the floors of the church shook when he'd read Juliette's penalty for adultery. Elide had been shaken as well, concerning those around her, and she'd hoped to never be on the other end of his wrath.

"Juliette has already faced the penalty for your co-conspiracy," Reverend Elijah said, grimly. "Her auction is sanctioned for October."

Hansel winced at the statement. "And what of my penalty?"

Elide's instincts were telling her to grab her brother, but she didn't move. She didn't want to dishonor him by interrupting his act of repentance. No matter what her instincts told her.

"Of your what?" Reverend Warner stated.

Hansel took a deep breath. "Forgive me, I—"

"All is already forgiven," Reverend Warner interrupted, clasping his hands together. "You have sought for something you've already earned, Hansel. A man needn't seek a gift that has already been given. Tell me, has your wife's retraining not been going well?"

"It's going well, but—"

"Would you rather be rewed, perhaps to a lina or baroness instead?"

"No, I—"

"Then there is nothing more this council can do to serve you," Reverend Warner said.

Elide could hear the warning in his voice and reached

for her brother's arm, hoping not to vex them further. Hansel pulled his arm away.

"Is there no penalty I must face?" Hansel shouted.

The council looked among each other, communicating wordlessly and coming to the same conclusion.

"Young man, there's no need to fuss," Reverend Coin stated, as he appeared to be the most levelheaded among the reverend elders. "You have made a mistake, as many of us do, and as head of your household, I would expect you to be relieved. It is the decision of this council that your guilty conscience should suffice and there is no need to ruin two futures with our verdict."

Hansel didn't speak. For three days, he had paced the length of Elide's living room plagued with guilt, declaring his sorrows to her, and this was their conclusion. No matter what he had felt or did feel now or how long it had taken the search committee to find Juliette beforehand. The hunt for her was over, their standing in the commune remained intact, and regardless of the morbidity of the circumstances, Hansel was forgiven by everyone but himself.

Elide watched as Hansel nodded obediently, accepting the verdict.

"Your sister is approaching her assignment year, is she not?" Reverend Coin asked with a smile.

Hansel nodded, glancing at Elide.

"Dear girl, where is it you hope to be assigned?" Reverend Coin asked, turning to her.

Elide hesitated. She often wished to be among the more scholarly linas, walking the aisles of Library Decaturian in Blackburn, exploring their peerless selection of books on a winter's day. But, at times, she was drawn to dreams of being a baroness, living off an endowed fortune in Hickory, on her own property, surrounded by the arts, and able to select her future husband. She could have a library built for her, she reasoned. There were no foreseeable issues—or more accurately, Elide would have to get a high score on the LAT to make either option available to her. There was one application, therefore, one chance at happiness.

"Elide is mute sir," Hansel said.

"Oh, my apologies, Elide," Reverend Coin said kindly. "I'm afraid my ability to sign is rather lacking."

Elide gave him a small smile.

"Very well then," Reverend Warner stated. "This meeting is adjourned. You are dismissed, Hansel."

Hansel bowed lowly, and Elide was relieved. Then she had the oddest feeling that someone was staring at her, and in the corner of the courtroom, perhaps they were. Three spectators in black veils and dark, long-sleeved dresses stood like shadows along the wall; the eldest clutched a cane with both hands.

"Mourners," Hansel whispered, guiding Elide out of the courtroom with a hand on her upper back. "Never look them directly in the eye. I hear they can smell fear."

Elide swatted her brother the moment they stood outside the courthouse.

"Ow! It was only a joke, Elide," Hansel said, trying to flag down a carriage.

"What if they'd heard?" Elide signed, gesturing back at the courthouse. "What then?"

Hansel sighed. "I wouldn't let anything happen to you," he said softly. "Hell, you wouldn't be staying at the house—*your* house—alone if it were up to me."

"It's not my house," Elide signed. "It's Dad's."

"Well, Dad left it to you."

"Reverend Warner says—"

"It doesn't matter what Warner says," Hansel said. "Dad left it to you, and that's that. He can't overrule another reverend's will, even a dead one. And if he tries, I won't let him. Okay?"

Elide rose to her toes and hugged Hansel.

She knew he meant it and that he meant well, but in protecting her, he would bedevil the council again, and she couldn't let that happen. Hansel was struggling with newlywed life; Elide knew he wouldn't have selected Lilah of his own volition. Their grandfather had matched them a week after their father's death, and as the patriarch of the family, he had final say in most things, including who they wed.

"We should get you home; it'll be dark out soon," Hansel said, holding her at arm's length.

He flagged down a horse-drawn carriage with a pug-faced driver that grumbled as he stopped.

"Thanks for stopping, Fred," Hansel said with a hint of a smile.

The old man grumbled. "Least I could do for you getting that Timber boy to fix my wheel," Fred said with a chuckle. "Though I would've preferred he'd matched it with the set, bit odd for my customers to see one black wheel. Some have joked that it's an omen."

Elide couldn't agree more. The newer metal wheel gleamed brightly in contrast to the duller silver wheels. She imagined it would have made a fine set of four, but the black wheel made the others look shoddy.

"Then let's hope it's a harbinger of good luck," Hansel said, eliciting a raspy laugh from Fred as her brother helped her into the carriage.

"Where you headed then?" Fred asked.

"The only place that's ever brought me peace, 42 Mansfield Street in Baptiste," Hansel answered before stepping into the carriage himself.

# 2

## Mansfield Street, Baptiste, Texas

Half an hour after their departure from the courthouse, they traded the large red brick buildings of Central Prospero for the small, overcrowded houses of Baptiste. Most families had lived in the area for generations and were nestled within a few streets of each other, allowing their children to wander freely between houses for meals and baths. Parents could work while children stayed with aunts or grandparents. Whether work was near or far, they could get by with horse-drawn carriages, which were plentiful. In Texas, there were no cars because cars were too modern, and modern amenities that were deemed as overt luxuries went against the faith—as did initiating war.

But war was scarcely spoken about in pleasant conversation, though men went off daily to fight it, to protect them from the outsiders who wished to rob them of their faith. The bombings hit southern Baptiste the worst, leaving behind burned balconies and buildings half standing, half fallen. Their family was one of the lucky ones. Their homes hadn't been robbed from them; they would rest their heads on pillows tonight, not dirt.

Elide sighed as they passed another pub. She looked away the moment she saw staggering men, because they reminded her too much of their late father, who was a long time dead but had left quite an impression. She never wished to wed a man that struggled as he did. When they were some distance away, she braved another look out the window and smiled when she saw her home roll into view.

"All right, out we go," Hansel said, getting out and helping her out of the carriage as he always did.

As soon as they were out, Fred took off without another word, the carriage kicking up dirt behind it.

"Well, Fred was in a hurry," Hansel said. "You can come over for dinner if you'd like."

Elide smiled. "I'm going to stay in tonight," she signed. "They're allowing a new film to air at six."

"Really? I hadn't heard, though with everything going on, it's a bit hard to keep up with recreational activities. I wish I had more time," Hansel said with a sigh. "You sure I can't convince you to come have dinner with us?"

"I'm going to study after the film," Elide signed.

"Oh, right, the LAT. When is that?" Hansel asked.

"Tomorrow," Elide signed.

"Wow, that's right," Hansel said lowly. "Twenty-one's the year. It's always the year. I swear my head is in the clouds today. I still remember teaching you how to tie your shoes. I forget some days how much older we are now."

"Speak for yourself," Elide signed with a hint of a smile.

Hansel laughed. "Oh, very funny, mock your poor brother," he said, hugging her goodbye. "I love you, and good luck on your exam."

She hugged him tightly to assure him that the feeling was mutual, and then the two went their separate ways. She into 42 Mansfield Street, their childhood home, and him into 41.

Elide stepped on three letters upon entering her home, so the first she looked at had mud caked onto it. It was the smallest of them and was from her friend Fiona, who lived several streets away, but typically used all seventy-two hours of designated cellphone time within the first week of the month. Perhaps calling Gabriel Timber, who was six months their senior and engaged to Fiona when they were both eighteen with her parents' permission. Elide was not envious of her friend; she was happy for Fiona. Having never experienced true love herself, Elide knew nothing of the trials or temptations that came with it. Sometimes she wondered if she, too, would falter and use her entire monthly allowance of cellphone time on one man. For her, there were only two contacts: Hansel and Fiona. Though she rarely had a reason to use her phone, as she never had any critical emergencies, nor did she need her brother to chaperone a date. Men who had pursued her in the past were of unsavory character and curious—or more specifically, questioning what it was like to have sex with a mute woman.

She attributed it to the area. There weren't many hopeless romantics in Baptiste aside from herself. Most were easily paired off. But it didn't upset her because she would make a life for herself through the examination. The Livelihood Assessment Test was her ticket out, as it was for most people that lived there. Gone were the days that they'd have to continue to live in squalor, living from check to check, rather than having vacations as those higher up could afford. The aptitude test would measure her skillset as it had those before her. Score too low and she'd likely stay in Baptiste and work as a scrubber, subjugated to clean up after others, or be a packer, packing and shipping packages throughout Texas. Neither job fit her. Though the employment rate in those jobs was high, wages were low. She would need a particularly high score to be either a baroness or lina, but she was confident in her abilities. Or at least her ability to study. Her brother was lucky to have inherited the title of Mart from their father; he received monthly stipends from the commune as a leader of the people. He covered his household's expenses and hers.

That, however, hadn't prevented him from risking his position over the temptation that drove him to bed Juliette in 41 Mansfield Street. Elide questioned whether it had been cupid's arrow or foolishness that had struck him, though she was sympathetic for both parties. She couldn't reconcile why their grandfather hadn't selected Juliette to be Hansel's wife. The ways of men were a mystery that she, a woman, had no right to question. Or, more so, questioning them aloud would sooner cause her tongue to be cut out. Faith was against her in that instance. Though, she was one of the lucky ones. God had given her the gift of being speechless on the day of her operation. But God had also given her Hansel, and he, common as he was, had often given answers to her questions that no man had to give a woman as deemed by the faith.

3

The night was filled with nightmarish sounds. Most nights, Elide slept through them; she never had the urge to check the source of them, sensing her fear was unfounded, but mostly because she was already anxious. The first bang in the walls could have been a demon or merely the water shifting through the pipes. The same way the creaking floors were the house settling as the old house did every night—rather than a burglar lurking around the house. Today was the most important day of her life, so it was only right for her to be nervous about it. The weight of it was dreadful to think about.

Her morning was no less wild. The first four hours she'd been awake were chaotic, to say the least, and she was short on time.

Elide had placed her flashcards on the kitchen counter in a plastic index card holder, which she had been gifted on her twentieth birthday. She had set the holder beside the toaster. She was positive she had. Today it wasn't there.

She opened all the cabinets in her kitchen, even the cereal cabinet, and hadn't found it there. She was checking under the dining room table when the front door opened, startling her, and causing her to bang her head on the table.

"What happened here?" Hansel asked. "It looks like a tornado's gone through the place."

Elide got up and rubbed her head, trying to alleviate the pain.

"I can't find my flashcards," Elide signed. "They were by the toaster."

"Well, Lilah had said she'd popped in last night," Hansel said. "Perhaps she moved them."

Elide shook her head and flung her bag over her shoulder. "I have to go, or I'll be late," she signed, growing increasingly angry by his response.

"Sorry, Elide. I know, boundaries," Hansel said. "I'll tell her not to touch the key from here on out."

Elide nodded as she grabbed hold of her coat and binder and quickly left the house before she could lose her temper. She flagged down a carriage and handed him a note with her destination. Elide tucked her phone into the coat and zipped the pocket to keep it safe. Her chauffeur wasn't concerned with her not speaking, though he wasn't her usual driver. Most people didn't speak to drivers outside of giving them money. In some ways, this was beneficial for her as it didn't indicate any difference between herself and anyone else, though she wouldn't have minded having a conversation with him.

Inside the carriage, there was nothing but silence to keep her company. Outside, a storm had started with gossiping clouds, speaking in dark tones and flashing like camera bulbs. But the most talkative was the rain rushing down the carriage window that showed no sign of slackening.

After they'd ridden a few miles on the dirt roads, she stepped out onto the sidewalk in front of Miller Hall. Elide had studied here all her life, taking numerous classes and testing often. She'd even had her height measured here when she was six, but today would decide the rest of her life; whether she would be trapped in Baptiste or would thrive in Prospero. She covered her head with her binder and rushed inside the building so eagerly that she crashed into someone and landed on her back on the floor.

Elide gathered up her binder and went to mouth an apology, but when she looked up, a hand was waiting for her. It was a Seeker man that didn't look nearly as angry by the error as the four fellows he was with.

The Seeker men wore brown suits with black ties—Seeker formal attire. There to collect early initiates and begin their training as apparently being taught to search and protect took priority—if this was what Second Class soldiers looked like, she was afraid to see First Class.

Elide took his hand, and he helped her to her feet while saying, "Easy," as though she was a skittish horse.

"Sorry," Elide signed.

She blushed and then mouthed the word.

"It's all right," he said aloud while signing back. "I know some from my time in the west."

"Watch where you're walking, girl," a larger Seeker beside him stated harshly.

The Seeker man turned to him. "No need to be uncivil, Ezra," he said. "Accidents happen, don't they."

He gave Elide a warm smile that made her cheeks grow warmer.

She was almost certain she recognized him from a photo in Hansel's yearbook. He had distinct features; his dark hair and pointed nose were both familiar though his green eyes couldn't be captured in a black-and-white photo. His jaw was sharper now than it was then, but she couldn't remember the name beneath it.

"Cyrus, making friends, I see," a voice coming from behind Ezra said, and Elide pulled away her hand.

"Reverend Coin," Ezra said, quickly bowing his head to the reverend elder. "We weren't told you would be making an appearance today."

"Well, it's quite rare that a man my age gets to see his son and he's not on his deathbed," Reverend Coin said.

"I had been meaning to visit," the Seeker beside Elide told the reverend elder. "But we've been rather—"

"*Busy*, tracking those harlots," Ezra finished for him. "That your boy managed to find all on his own."

Reverend Coin smiled with pride as though he had made the discovery himself and patted his son on the shoulder. Elide tensed as she felt immediately out of place. And yet she couldn't think of a way of excusing herself, but she didn't mind it. She would likely never step foot in this building again after today—once they were assigned, everything else would fall into place.

She would miss sitting in classes together with Fiona, they would be trading that for morning tea and brunches soon, which was difficult to envision, but the easiest pill to swallow. Her anxiety was the least of her worries now.

"Excuse me! Excuse me!" someone said in a melodic tone, her voice growing louder as she pushed through the crowd. "There you are! I've been looking all over for you," Fiona said.

Her best friend, Fiona, stood in her best dress, holding a binder close to her chest as though it was a shield. Her blond bob was curled, and her small nose wrinkled at the sudden realization of the men around Elide. There was a hint of nervousness in her green eyes, and she let out a nervous laugh. When they were younger, Fiona looked like a porcelain doll, but now she looked much more like the plastic dolls women bought their daughters in stores. If she wasn't already promised to Gabriel, she would have another suitor waiting for her among these men.

"Sorry, if you'll just excuse me and Elide. We need to have a little last-minute review for our tests," Fiona told them, quickly hooking her arm into Elide's and pulling them far away from the Seekers and Reverend Coin.

When they were a few feet from the exam door and well out of earshot of the Seekers, she stopped in her tracks.

"Okay, spill! Tell me absolutely everything immediately, Elide," Fiona said giddily.

Elide stared at her blankly.

"Oh, come on, Pansy wouldn't shut up about how you

were talking to Cyrus Coin of all people," Fiona said, cocking a brow.

"I bumped into him," Elide signed. "It was an accident. What's the big deal?"

"The big deal is that he's basically a celebrity," Fiona answered, sighing. "If I weren't already spoken for, I'd go for him."

"Reverend Warner says we're all equal and—"

"Yeah, yeah, no celebrities," Fiona said, rolling her eyes. "You know I heard on the radio that the lands across the water have celebrities. We ought to go visit someday if you ever get a passport."

"I'm working on it," Elide signed and Fiona laughed.

"I'm only teasing," Fiona said with a giggle, hooking their arms together again. "You worry too much. Soon we'll take the test and be up in Prospero together. Gabriel will be a tom, messing with all those fancy doctor's instruments and I'll be married to him as a baroness, and you'll be right there with me, even if you choose to be a lina. Best friends forever. No exceptions."

Elide smiled at her friend's candor. There were often days she wished that she was nearly as bold as Fiona. Elide was honest but had never been able to openly express feelings, though she was sincere whenever she declared them.

"All right, everyone," Tutor Mackenzie said, clapping her perfectly manicured hands together. "Time to line up and remember what we say is nearly as important as what we do. Your oral test will be worth forty percent of your score. For those requiring different testing procedures, your proctor has been made aware. Any questions?"

She waited a moment. "Yes, Mr. Anderson?"

"Is it true what they're saying about the North End?" he asked.

And the students stirred, whispering frantically about a rumor that hadn't reached Elide's ears. The North End was a trade route built by construction workers from Baptiste who'd volunteered to travel north with military protection to establish trade with the lands across the water. They started in the center of what was once called Houston—now called Prospero—and planned several other routes bridging from Texas to other trade routes until they stopped working on them. There weren't any trade routes in Baptiste, there were plenty of dirt roads, and the city may as well have been left to rot after the first civil war.

"Mr. Anderson, keep all questions not pertaining to the test for the end, please. And I assure the rest of you that there is no need to panic about the North End. We are well protected within our great state," Tutor Mackenzie said confidently. Instilling confidence in many around Elide, including Fiona. "Now, what do we say?"

"Our fate is not our own to decide," they all recited in unison—all who weren't mute.

Tutors passed out numbers to students. Then they were told to go down one of twelve hallways. Fiona was sent down Hall 2 as a man directed Elide to go down Hall 3. When she stopped, she stood silently against the wall. Her neighbor across from her, Lorraine, was sweating and pale.

Lorraine was always nervous, though she typically received high marks in everything: her eyesight, her hearing, her mathematics tests—her results were exemplary— and yet she was shaking. Perhaps she feared the idea of abandoning her family, or she feared them finding out it was what she wanted. Though she was likely projecting as she had failed to tell her brother her hopes for the future.

The proctors were paid volunteers, mostly from Baptiste—their uniforms were all white—women in dresses, men in dress shirts and dress pants. There were three Scout women—they were Seekers, but the name changed with gender—and they had tattoos on their wrists. Soldiers were the only ones allowed to have tattoos; the swallow meant they saved someone, but no one told Elide what a mouse meant.

"Lorraine Hoss and Elide Hester," a volunteer said sharply.

The volunteer who called Elide was from Prospero— his shoes were too nice for him to be from Baptiste. She couldn't be tested by someone from Baptiste because it went against the rules and would nullify her result. If she were put in a room with a Baptiste proctor, she would have to ask them to move her.

Elide stepped forward obediently, walking behind Lorraine into the room he pointed to.

Inside, the room was halved by two offices built from stanium, a white metal that neutralized sound—they used it in buildings in Baptiste so people couldn't hear their neighbors.

Lorraine looked back at Elide, gave her a small smile,

and went into the first office and shut the door behind her. Elide was frozen to the spot. Her breath caught in her chest. She had half expected them to take the oral test last and wasn't sure what she would say. She'd not practiced any form of pitch for herself, though Tutor Mackenzie had never spoken of what the subject of the pitch would be.

The second office's door creaked open, and a woman with round glasses poked her head out. She was thin with brown skin and curly hair that was in a tight bun and wore a white pantsuit—it was the first time Elide had ever seen a woman in a suit—and tall shoes. She signaled Elide to come to her, and Elide obeyed. Then she quickly got Elide into the office and shut the door behind them.

"You've really got to be careful," the woman said, "it is bad enough to have liberty men take notice of you, but it is worse to not be able to speak if they do something."

It took Elide a moment to register the insult and another for her to realize the woman was a lina. A lina's stagecoach had broken down by a pub when Elide was seven. The woman was wearing "kitten" heels and a tweed dress. She stuck out like a sore thumb among the Baptiste women. Calling someone from Prospero a "liberty" was an insult that held a lot of weight, because it was undefined, at least to a Baptiste woman like her.

The woman took a deep breath.

"My name is Angelique, and I'll be your proctor for the oral test," she said calmly. "Your multiple-choice test will be taken in another room."

"What do I have to do for the exam?" Elide signed.

The room was empty aside from the desk and the two

chairs that accompanied it, hardly an effective testing environment, Elide thought.

"You'll take one of these," Angelique said taking a seat and setting a bottle on the desk. "And then we'll begin."

Elide eyed the two pills in the bottle curiously. They were the same color. Angelique pulled out a blank sheet of paper and a pen.

Elide looked at the pills again. There were no obvious differences between them, aside from their shape. The weight of the bottle seemed about even. Perhaps the test itself was whether she would pollute her body with drugs. Or the test was literal, and, therefore, she had to select a pill as instructed. She could feel her heartbeat in her chest. Elide had never taken drugs. Hansel was the adventurous one, and he'd chosen to stay in Baptiste.

"What happens when I take it?" Elide signed. "Do I have to take one?"

"Yes, either of them. Neither will harm you."

Elide's mouth felt dry, and she swallowed hard. She took the bottle, opened it, but hesitated and set it down.

"What's the difference?" Elide signed.

"Both will take you places, but only one will take you where you want to go," Angelique said. "Choose whichever one calls to you."

Elide took a deep breath and looked between the two pills again. And then pulled out the circular pill and swallowed it.

Testing had lasted all afternoon. Now it was growing colder and darker, and Elide couldn't remember the LAT at all. All those weeks she'd spent studying, and she couldn't remember a word from her oral test or the multiple-choice test, though she had taken both or at least been told that she had. Elide had taken a seat at a cafeteria table outside the testing room, in front of Hall 2. Her head was throbbing, likely a side effect from not having eaten this morning—or the pill. Either way, she'd be home soon. It was getting dark out, and she and Fiona were supposed to head back to Baptiste together.

"My proctor thinks I'm a shoo-in for baroness," Fiona bragged as she took a seat beside Elide. "What's wrong? Are you worried about your score?"

Elide groaned. She felt as though she would faint if she stood back up.

"I think that pill gave me a headache," Elide signed.

"I'd rather have a headache than fishy burps," Fiona said. "Which one did you take?"

"Hey," Gabriel said happily. "What's wrong?"

Elide looked up at him. He had dark hair, brown skin, and brown eyes and was wearing a dress shirt with jeans.

"Those pills are what's wrong," Fiona answered.

"What pills?" Gabriel asked, looking between the two women.

Fiona sighed and rolled her eyes. "Figures, the guys would get off easy," she said, then she toyed with a strand of her hair. "We had an oral test, and apparently, the women had to take pills, which they completely failed to mention in the LAT prep book. And I nearly slept through half the multiple-choice test. It's a miracle I finished in time."

*I'd rather be tired than nauseous any day,* Elide thought to herself.

Gabriel laughed. "Well, neither of you could have done worse than Lorraine Hoss. I heard she vomited during the oral test, and they had to escort her out."

Elide was sure it was meant to make her feel better, but it didn't. She could only imagine how having her LAT score slip through her fingers would've felt. Elide felt a pang of guilt in her chest—she couldn't even remember leaving Angelique or the office—but she wasn't sure how much of a test those pills were. They were just pills.

"Well, I've got something that'll take the edge off," Gabriel said lowly to Fiona. "Some of the others and I are thinking of heading into the woods for a little celebration. Nothing impure, honest."

Elide was skeptical of the offer, but Fiona looked giddy.

"Come on," Fiona begged. "It'll help you relax. And tomorrow, we'll find out our scores and be spending the rest of our days in Prospero."

Elide sighed. She was tired, but she could feel her head clearing.

She wouldn't mind spending time with a few of her classmates before they likely never crossed paths again. So, she nodded in agreement, and Fiona hugged her tightly.

By the time they'd reached the forest, the party had already started, and Elide's head was clear. Gabriel paid off the stagecoach's driver, and he agreed to wait for seven hours, but no more.

"Don't worry," Gabriel told Elide. "Everything will be fine. If any Seekers show up, Rob here will text me, and we'll be out of here before you know it."

"She can't help but worry," Fiona said teasingly. "Elide was raised to be a proper young woman with good morals and sound judgment. And I would've been too if I wasn't engaged to you, Gabriel Timber."

"Oh, hush," Gabriel said, kissing Fiona's forehead. "Come on, I see the guys over there."

Elide followed them and took a seat on a log where a few boys were playing cards. Neither looked up when they arrived.

"Hey, what are you two playing, James?" Gabriel said, sitting down across from Elide with Fiona beside him.

"Don't know what it's called," the younger boy answered. "Just know I have to put the numbers in order and empty my hand."

Elide could count on one hand the number of times she'd heard James Anderson talk while his twin brother talked much more. Ryder was the older of the two. He had blond hair like his father, with his mother's silver eyes and pale skin. He always wore clothing to emphasize that he was from Prospero, preferring to stand out in a crowd. He had no interest in being a tom, and though he didn't declare it, Elide would guess he had his eye on becoming a Disciple while James wanted to be a Seeker.

Disciples were the personal guard of the head of state, the Apostate, who led the First and Second Class armies that stood for freedom above all else. The Disciples were all male and wore black from head to toe with a gold crest of a raven embroidered on their uniform's breast pocket.

"So, how's everyone feeling about the test," Ryder asked as he set down another card.

"Great, I'm sure my mother will be pleased," Fiona said. "I studied day and night, and it finally paid off."

"I'm just glad it's over. If I knew it was going to be that easy, I would've taken more breaks," Gabriel said. "At least we're done with high school."

"How about you, Elide?" Ryder asked with a hint of a smile.

"Good enough," Elide signed.

"She says—"

"I don't need you to translate, Fiona. I've been working on it," Ryder said. He let out a laugh. "I'm sure Elide crushed it like she always does."

Elide blushed. Ryder was being kinder to her today, perhaps he was in a better mood than usual, or it was simply because he was beating his little brother at the card game.

"No fair, Ryder, you cheated!" James shouted as Ryder set his last card down.

Ryder laughed. "Come on, James, don't be a sore loser," he said playfully.

After a few hours, more partygoers showed up in the forest with wine and beer to drink, and some began exchanging more than words. Elide knew kissing wasn't against any laws if it didn't lead to sinful behaviors, but she still felt it was a slippery slope. Fiona and Gabriel were relatively careful. They'd left to kiss and fool around at a lake nearby. They always avoided being seen, unlike some others present. Public gambling, however, went against a few laws, though James was in high spirits now that he was winning card games.

"You want a drink, Elide?" Ryder asked, shoving a beer into her clumsy hands.

Elide rarely drank wine. And if she drank anything it was usually with Hansel and his wife. She didn't want to drink.

"What? You think I put something in it," Ryder said accusingly.

Elide shook her head. And while she didn't want to offend her friend, she set it down.

"I don't want any, but thanks," Elide signed.

Ryder shrugged and said, "Whatever." He drank his beer before downing Elide's too.

Elide pinched her lips together. She was tired and wanted to go home, so she grabbed her coat and waved goodbye to Ryder. Elide had to walk up the hill before she could reach the parked stagecoaches, all the while hoping one of them could bring her back to Miller Hall so she could contact Hansel to pick her up. But as she walked, she had the strangest feeling she was being followed. And the more she tried to ignore it, the more anxious she was.

She didn't hear anyone behind her but could feel her heart pounding in her chest. *Everything is fine*, she told herself. *Everything is fine.* But she couldn't shake the feeling. She sped up, rushing with her coat in her arms, and made it a few feet before she fell forward.

"You all right, Elide? You took quite a tumble," Ryder said, helping her up.

Elide nodded and turned to go, but Ryder didn't let go of her arm. She felt her stomach turn. She was sure that she'd left him by the campfire.

"Aye, what's the rush?" Ryder said. "The party isn't even over yet."

She was taken aback by his statement. She tried to pull away again and sent them both tumbling back down the hill. When they stopped rolling, he was on top of her, and she tried to shove him off.

"Damn, Elide, just relax," Ryder said. "I'm not going to hurt you."

But he didn't get off her. He just looked at her, and as she looked at his face, she saw something that looked worryingly like desire. His pupils were dilated as he stared down at her, panting heavily, each breath reeking of beer. She flinched and instinctively hit his chest, but like a man possessed, he ignored her. Then he grabbed one of her arms and used his free hand to slide up her dress, and for a moment, all she could hear was the sound of his breathing. His fingers traveled her inner thigh, and then, "You. Come here!"

The voice was gruff and angry as Ryder was lifted off her by two men in black. Elide's heart pounded in her chest as she saw the crests on their coats—Disciples. *Thank God*, she thought. She sat up and was immediately pulled up onto her feet.

"You two are under arrest for attempted fornication and eliciting temptation," the Disciple said angrily.

"I didn't do anything, it was all her," Ryder stated.

She couldn't believe what she was hearing. He was blaming her? Elide shook her head furiously.

"All right, then what's the story," a brawny Disciple asked, signaling the Disciple to release her.

He waited a few moments. Elide fidgeted, but her hands were bound behind her back. She tried to mouth "him," but neither man seemed to understand. After two more attempts, the brawny Disciple ordered, "Take her away."

# 4

The Disciples led Elide over the hill and into a carriage. As they rode off, they passed other partygoers, each looking frightened and powerless as they were forced into the back of carriages by brutish-looking Disciples. Elide also felt powerless, growing increasingly aware that the two Disciples in the carriage with her had their guns pointed at her as though she were a wild animal about to charge. And then it dawned on her—she had tried to get out of her restraints and wasn't able to speak—they thought she was possessed.

Temptation often was linked to possession. Therefore, if they believed that Ryder was possessed, then in their eyes, she was as well. If she struggled more in her restraints, they may see it as thrashing, or *convulsing*, another symptom of possession. So it was in her best interest to sit still, no matter how difficult that may be.

When the carriage stopped again, they were in Central Prospero. But neither man showed any desire to speak to her. "Watch her, Seamus. I'll see if they're ready," the elder Disciple said tersely.

"Yes, Sergeant," Seamus said.

Then the sergeant stepped out of the carriage, leaving her with Seamus. Elide didn't move.

Seamus scowled at her. "You're the Hester girl, aren't you?"

Elide nodded slowly.

"Why aren't you talking then? Your brother's a mart, and you have a right to a call. Don't you know that?" he asked angrily.

Elide nodded again.

"Then why aren't you talking?"

She tilted her head, trying to move her hair from her neck, acutely aware of the gun beginning to shake in his hands as she did so. Elide felt her hair brush away from her neck, but she wasn't sure if he could see the scar from her surgery. But then she felt his fingers graze her neck and push the hair back the rest of the way.

"You can't, can you?" Seamus said softly. His finger traced the scar.

Elide shook her head no, and he took his hand away from her neck. Then she saw something in his eyes that looked almost like pity.

"Diaboli?" he asked.

Elide nodded at the mention of the pneumonia strain. Diaboli, a strain gifted by the devil himself, affected countless lives in Scopus. It was commonly misdiagnosed, and late diagnosis led to surgeries that were lifesaving but could be botched and leave the patient mute.

Seamus went to say something, but before he could speak, the carriage door swung open.

"You," the elder Disciple said harshly. "Let's go."

She went to step out of the carriage, but a hand grabbed her restraints.

"Seamus, what on earth are you doing?" the elder Disciple shouted.

"I don't think she can speak, Sergeant Patts," Seamus said. "She's got a diaboli scar on her neck. I think that's what she was trying to show you earlier."

Sergeant Patts observed her for a moment and said, "Very well then, Seamus, uncuff her, but I'm holding you responsible if she gets loose."

"Yes, sir," Seamus agreed.

Elide felt the metal handcuffs slip off her wrists and gave Seamus a grateful smile. Sergeant Patts helped her out of the carriage, and though she was thankful, her heart sank in her chest as she realized where they were. The building somehow appeared larger tonight as she stood in its shadow and looked up into the starless sky.

The outside of the courthouse was lined with ceremonial banners representing each district, displaying different colors and symbols in line with their united faith. More Disciples stood at the entrance, each armed with a rifle and the ability to use it. Another carriage sat abandoned at the east corner of the building with two Seekers guarding it and frighteningly so. A military detail to this degree meant there were not only marts present in the courthouse tonight but the Apostate as well.

*Of course, the Representative Assembly,* Elide thought. Every fall, Texas's marts met with the Apostate to discuss the issues that impacted the cities they serve and vote on legislation and media and entertainment allowed to enter the state. All thirteen states of Scopus had assemblies throughout the year to prove their devotion to the Apolitian people. There could be no greater shame than being brought before the court amid such important proceedings. Elide imagined she would be receiving a harsher punishment now. Harsher than Hansel, perhaps harsher than Juliette.

She gulped. But what could she do? She couldn't run. Even if she wanted to, there were guards everywhere. And how would Hansel feel when he saw her brought in for a crime? Elide never so much as considered stealing a stick of gum in all the years she'd been alive. Stealing was a sin that went against God. And she may not have been perfect, but she'd never intentionally go against God.

Sergeant Patts conferred with the Disciples manning the doors and proceeded to knock twice, then Seamus led Elide inside at gunpoint. She rubbed her wrists, trying to soothe the leftover pain from the handcuffs while ignoring the men staring at her as she passed. Disciples were the Apostate's personal guard. They trained the *Enoch,* the elite soldiers that fought for the Apolitian people's freedom and protected them from enemy forces. Enoch wore green uniforms, and there were several in the courthouse when she entered, so someone was going to be punished.

After passing door after door, Sergeant Patts led them into the courtroom. Seamus still held the gun to her back, and Elide had to force herself to walk normally, finding that she feared embarrassing her family more by falling than being shot. Depending on the charges, she could be punished by being sent to the brothels, a labor camp, or if they were feeling generous, death by execution. Possession was a serious crime. Possessed individuals usually had a lapse in faith that was to such an extent they could not be redeemed. She tried to appear confident, thinking this could be her last moment in Prospero. And it was quite a place to die.

The courtroom was a large room with high ceilings and walls draped with scarlet and gold banners representing the colors of Texas's flag. Overhead the bright lights made the beige marble floors appear brighter, and Elide could almost see her reflection in it.

Disciples were sitting in the seats normally reserved for spectators, and there was a long table for the accused to stand at, where Ryder was being held by two Enochs. Violet-clad marts were clustered together, whispering in a corner of the courtroom, but her brother wasn't among them. Hansel stood with the reverend elders, arguing with Reverend Warner. At the head of the courtroom was a statue of an angry-looking raven with outstretched wings— the Apostate's sigil. *So this was the Apostate's courtroom,* Elide thought. She had heard stories of its grandeur, how convicts saw the last of Texas's beauty in this room.

As Seamus guided Elide down the aisle, she could feel her chest tighten as fear welled up inside her. By the time she stood beside Ryder, she felt hopeless, so much so that it eclipsed any relief she may have felt when the barrel of Seamus's gun was no longer in her back.

Then a man wearing all black entered the room and took his place at the center. Elide stared down at the table in front of her.

"Proceed," he said plainly.

Somewhere behind Elide, someone cleared their throat.

"Sergeant Patts of Prospero, my lord," Sergeant Patts said. "An hour before today's testing in Miller Hall commenced, we received an anonymous tip about a party taking place in Partisan Forest at nightfall. We sent six Seeker parties out to discover if there was any truth to the matter and found there were two being held. Public transport carriages were found on each scene, and drivers informed us of their employers' names and were released after questioning. Upon our arrival to the scene, youth were participating in all manners of debauchery—" The sergeant took a deep breath, and Elide looked up from the table to find he was looking directly at her, causing the Apostate to do the same. Sergeant Patts sighed and said, "Seamus Petrovsky and I found the young man on top of the young woman with his right hand up her skirt and his left holding onto her wrist."

The marts immediately began discussing the sergeant's story. Then an Enoch that had stood against the wall stepped forward.

"You accuse my son of touching such filth?" His voice was cold and hard.

He was paler than his son, but their resemblance was uncanny. His coat was dark green with a high collar, and his mutton chop beard was silver. And the hatred in his voice was fervent.

Hansel scoffed. "Filth? A daughter of a reverend elder compared to the son of a drunk, Cain?"

"Watch your mouth, boy," Cain said pointedly. "At least my stock doesn't come from questionable breeding."

"I've heard enough from both of you!" Reverend Warner shouted. "Race holds no standing in this crime, and presently we know both parties were willing participants."

Elide looked at Reverend Warner in shock. The idea that she would ever be a "willing participant" in any crime was ridiculous. But others in the courtroom immediately nodded in agreement.

She had spent weeks studying for the aptitude test, and she wouldn't throw away her future for sex. Juliette had been declared a harlot by the Apostate the moment she was discovered with Hansel and sentenced without trial. But she'd gone on the run instead of turning herself in. Now Juliette was being held in a cell somewhere and awaiting her auction to the brothels without anyone allowed to visit her. Adultery was hardly an offense worth committing but could be declared as Elide's crime at any moment—if her soulmate was considered to be someone other than Ryder.

"And in your own words, Elide Hester, can you please describe what happened?" the Apostate asked.

Elide jumped. He was looking at her, and the courtroom was silent. Ryder stood beside her, looking pale and reeking of beer, but to her surprise, he didn't speak in her stead. Elide understood this was her chance and hoped the Apostate understood her. "I was heading home, and Ryder stopped me," Elide signed. "He was trying to . . . *attack* me."

She felt "attack" was the better word to use. If he was able to understand her words at all.

"She said Ryder attacked her," Hansel said, quickly translating.

"Thank you, Mart. I'm well versed in sign language," the Apostate said calmly. "And I believe the word she should have used was *rape*. Which, if it was not already clear to your son, Cain, is a *punishable* offense."

"No disrespect, my lord, but the girl probably threw herself at him," Cain said. "Ryder attracts plenty of proper women. He doesn't have any need for one of them. Isn't that right, boy?"

"Yeah, she's lying," Ryder protested. "I would never do anything like that."

Hansel scoffed. "My sister wouldn't lie about that. He's lying. He's trying to save his own skin."

The crowd erupted into an argument.

Seamus moved Elide to the other side of him. His face was hard with anger and fatigue. The Disciple acted as a barrier between her and the two men intent on having her charged. His hand was hovering over his gun. Elide worried that there would be a reason for him to use it.

"Quiet!" Reverend Coin demanded.

And slowly, the crowd obeyed. "This court has yet to

be provided with sufficient evidence to convict," Reverend Coin said.

"Hasn't it?" Reverend Warner said, stepping forward. "The two were found in a compromising position, where adultery can be assumed."

"As I recall, Sergeant Patts indicated that Elide Hester's wrist was being held. I would insinuate in—"

"But we are not here to insinuate," Reverend Warner spat out, interrupting Reverend Coin. "We are to base our ruling on fact, and those facts provide sufficient evidence to convict both of *adultery*."

"Silence," The Apostate said in a stern but calm voice.

The reverend elders held their tongues, though they continued to glare at one another.

However, instead of reproaching either man's behavior, the Apostate approached Ryder and stood before him. Ryder hunched his back as if the gravity of his actions had now begun to weigh on him. The Apostate was taller than him and wore an all-black uniform, making Ryder's muddied clothing look lesser in comparison. His eyes were dark and focused on the blond twenty-one-year-old.

It was only when Elide noticed the raven on the Apostate's ring that she shuddered, a golden creature with scarlet eyes. For a moment, it was all she could focus on until the Apostate spoke again and said, "Now, what do you say?" Seemingly ignoring the fact that Ryder was shaking.

"She . . . I . . . I didn't mean to," Ryder said, and then he paled. "No, that's not what I meant. I—" He hesitated and looked to his father. Ryder looked confused as to what had come over him. "I hadn't had that much to drink. Or I didn't think I had."

"Thank you," the Apostate whispered.

Then he nodded at two Enochs, who grabbed hold of Ryder.

"Now, wait just a minute," Cain protested. "I won't stand for this!"

"You'll stay back, Cain, or be held in contempt," Sergeant Patts said, grabbing him.

"Proposed penalty?" the Apostate asked.

He directed his question to the reverend elders, who were in murmured discussion.

"We can send him to a labor camp for three years," Reverend Coin suggested.

Reverend Warner scoffed. "*Labor camp?* The crime was committed in Baptiste, which means his punishment is outside of your jurisdiction," Reverend Warner said.

"Be that as it may, the Anderson family are from Prospero, which is under *my* jurisdiction," Reverend Coin retorted. "And three years in a work camp will get the boy back on track."

Elide couldn't think clearly. She felt as though her heart had leapt to her throat. Fiona's father was an Enoch who patrolled the labor camps, and he rarely slept because of all the horrors he'd seen. Fiona had told her about the last time the reverend elders had sent a woman to a work camp, and she was stripped and sprayed down with a hose. If a worker didn't work, they were beaten until they bled or not given food for days on end.

"No, I have a better idea," Reverend Warner said with

a hint of a smile. "Matthew 5, verses 28 to 30. In short, if the boy looks at a woman lustfully, he's committed adultery. And if he touches her due to that lust, then he has given into temptation. And the scripture suggests that we remove the offending body part, as it's best to lose one part of the body than allow the whole to be corrupted."

The Apostate nodded.

"No, I won't have it!" Cain protested, rushing forward, but three Enochs restrained him.

Somewhere a door opened and shut in the room. And suddenly, Elide could only hear her own breathing as she watched Cain become more frantic, fighting against the other soldiers. Her brother moved beside her, though he was focused on the Apostate. The Disciples rushed forward to stop the four marts that were trying to interfere, and an Enoch reemerged from a room with a machete in his hand.

The armed Enoch passed by Elide, while two other Enochs grabbed hold of Ryder and held down his right arm. Elide could feel her heart hammering in her chest as the blade came down, and Ryder cried out.

**5**

Elide rubbed the cotton towel over her right cheek again. She knew the blood was gone before she looked into her hand mirror, but she could still feel it on her skin. The sound of the blade passing through Ryder's skin as it severed his hand, still echoed in her ears. She felt her stomach turn and swallowed down bile. *Breathe,* she told herself. She wouldn't vomit in the bathtub. She couldn't introduce anything toxic into a holy bath. Elide took a deep breath to calm her nerves. Her curly hair was wet from submerging herself under the bathwater earlier. She'd been trying to block out the noise. Lilah had prepared a bath for Elide on her brother's instructions, or more accurately, his conclusion that she'd had a *rough day.*

The water was mixed with oils, including a holy oil meant to cleanse impurities created by sin. Women were required to bathe in holy oil on two occasions; on the morning of their wedding day and on the off chance they were sinned against—or sexually assaulted by a lustful convict like Ryder Anderson. And she would have preferred the former.

Elide set down her hand mirror and pulled her knees into her chest. She felt like a naive little girl. In all twenty-one years of her life, she had never been touched sexually. Ryder had known that. They'd been friends for years. He had never shown any interest in having sex with her before. He had gone on dates and had lost his virginity in a brothel. He wasn't shy, not about his thoughts or his feelings. And when it came down to it, he had tried to take advantage of her. He had been on top of her and had to be pulled off by two Disciples. If they hadn't shown up when they had—well, she couldn't think about that.

Someone knocked on the bathroom door. Elide took a deep breath and stood up, wincing at the sight of the bruises on her legs from her tumble down the hill. She dried off her limbs with a cotton towel, wrapped herself in it, and answered the door. Lilah stood on the other side with her foot tapping, curlers in her brunette hair.

"I've left your dinner in a container on the kitchen counter," Lilah said, eyeing Elide from head to toe. "There's clean pajamas folded on your bed."

"Thank you," Elide signed.

Lilah smiled. "You're welcome," Lilah said sweetly. "Oh, and Hansel and I are going to bed early tonight. It's been a tough day for all of us, but at least Ryder was punished, and now he won't do the same to anyone else. I'll be downstairs cleaning the kitchen. Call if you need anything."

Lilah gave her a tight-lipped smile, then turned on her

heels and went back downstairs. Elide wasn't the least bit surprised by this. The two had spent very little time around each other, though she was sure that was how Lilah preferred it. Her understanding of sign language was minimal, which had led to an initial awkwardness when they'd first met that had lasted through the years as Lilah had more pressing concerns. Like keeping up with women in her social circle, who murmured conversations about topics such as homemaking, embroidery, and romantic movies.

Elide enjoyed the romantic movies she'd seen on television, and they taught her about a different kind of love that she couldn't help but want. There was something special about the unconditional love she found through those movie men.

But women in those movies didn't have scars. If they accidentally cut themselves with a kitchen knife, a handsome tom bandaged it. They didn't have a scar running along their neck *caused* by a doctor.

Elide snapped out of her thoughts as she heard voices coming from downstairs. She walked over to the stair banister, and the voices rose.

"You know, Adelaide's boy, Jack, he's just like your sister," Lilah said. "Mute after diaboli."

"Is he now?" Hansel said, sounding bored.

"Yes, and you know what I think? The Apostate should've demanded the toms come up with a solution by now. I mean, someone has to do the research. Children shouldn't be getting diaboli anymore—"

"You shouldn't speak that way about the Apostate," Hansel said, cutting her off. "Besides, what's done is done."

Lilah scoffed. "Well, I don't mean to sound spiteful, but even Fran thinks if they'd caught it earlier, he wouldn't have needed surgery," Lilah said. "And it's Fran of all people. The woman burns water."

"Stop!" Hansel said sharply. "I'll hear no more of this. You're the wife of a mart, Lilah. Start acting like one. You're supposed to set an example for other women and help promote peace and hope among the people of Baptiste," Hansel said. "And you can't do that if you walk around with shallow ideals and callous thoughts about our neighbors."

Lilah took a deep breath. "Forgive me, Hansel."

"Head back to the house. I'll be there shortly," Hansel told her.

Lilah didn't argue, and she left. Elide heard Hansel sigh. It was silent for a few minutes as if he were standing in the kitchen in quiet contemplation. Then she heard the rustling of a bag on the counter.

"I'll stop by to check on you tomorrow, Elide," Hansel shouted as if he knew she was listening.

She hesitated for a moment but then decided to knock on the wall beside her to signal that she'd heard.

"Goodnight," Hansel said softly.

Elide heard the front door open and then the familiar click of the lock after Hansel shut the door behind him.

She padded her way to her bedroom and lay back on the bed, where she had a perfect view of the digital clock by the television on her dresser: 12:00 a.m. Midnight, which meant her LAT scores should be in. She sat up and buttoned her nightshirt and pulled on the matching pajama pants. Even though she was alone, she didn't want to sit around in the nude all night.

Her phone was on the docking station, it'd been charging for quite some time, though the sixty-five hours she had left to use it was stagnant. The moment she took it from the docking station, the seconds began to count down, but she ignored them. A few seconds were eaten away as she waited for the Wi-Fi to connect on her phone, but not too many, and an email with a link to her LAT scores appeared on her phone. Elide sat back down on her bed. The website didn't take long to load, but the seconds felt like hours just before her score appeared. So she closed her eyes, wishing, or perhaps, *praying* that her score was high enough. The test was scored out of 3300. The lowest she could've gotten was 2200 to be a baroness or lina.

Elide slowly opened her eyes and nearly screamed: 3136. There it was, the first step in her dreams fulfilled. She sighed in relief. *Finally*, she thought, holding her phone close to her heart. She lowered her feet to the floor and turned on the radio in her room. The CD in the player was a birthday gift from Fiona, and its tracks were from the Outlands. One track in particular always made her heart sing. It was an older song called "All the Way," sung by a man named Frank Sinatra. And as he sang, Elide couldn't help but weave around the room, swept up in the sound of his voice and wrapped up in her daydreams.

6

E lide woke, gasping for air. She coughed and spluttered, hand on her chest as though it would make it stop. Her dream had been terrifying, but somehow, she remembered so little of it. Everything or, *almost* everything before her drowning was gone. In the dream, she woke with a start and came face-to-face with a frightened Hansel, but their conversation, and everything else between it and them trying to cross a river, was muddled. All she'd known was that they were running. Never what they were running from. It was terrifying—but it was still only a dream.

As she dressed, she couldn't help but wonder what the dream meant. Perhaps it was merely anxiety for Selection Day. She had selected both baroness and lina in her preference section on her application and had left the third spot blank. Now she had to hope one of the chairs bid her. Chairs were the head administrators for each career. There were normally three appointed per career, except for toms, who only had two because they were more selective than the others. Most medical careers were harder on their candidates.

Elide looked herself over in the mirror. She rarely wore dresses, but she hoped it would show both careers that she was a good candidate. White was a color that symbolized virtue, so it couldn't possibly send the wrong message, and to wear either of the other colors would be too bold. Baroness royal blue or lina canary yellow would be seen as making assumptions, and it would be embarrassing if she were bid on by the other career. White was her safest option.

After taking a deep breath, she nodded at her reflection and went down to her living room, where four people were waiting, two of which were strangers, both of whom wore Mourner uniforms—black veils, black gloves, and ankle-length, black coats. The black-clad women flanked Reverend Warner as her sister-in-law poured each of them a glass of water.

"Good morning, Elide. It's an honor to see you again," Reverend Warner said with a smile.

Elide nodded. "Is something wrong?" Elide signed.

"No," one of the Mourners said. "Nothing is wrong per se, as long as you come quietly."

Elide looked between Reverend Warner and the woman. Was this about the trial? She'd thought it was over.

The woman's eyes were hard behind her veil, and the other woman didn't show any emotion at all.

"Goodness, Ayla, there's no need to frighten her," Reverend Warner said, and the talkative Mourner's eyes narrowed toward Elide. "We're here about your score, Elide. It's quite rare, to say the least, and I'm honored to be the one to tell you that you've been selected as an initiate into the Mourners."

*What*, Elide thought. She knew she hadn't written them in her preferences. She knew she had filled in everything right, but for some reason, they were here.

"There's been a mistake," Elide signed. "I chose baroness and lina as my preferences."

"Well—"

Ayla cut Reverend Warner off. "You were bid on by Mother Superior, and she doesn't make mistakes," she said harshly.

"Precisely," Reverend Warner said with a nod. "You, my dear girl, are an anomaly, and I assumed you'd merely left your third preference vacant, and therefore a bid from the Mourners would be welcome given the circumstances."

"Then I refuse their offer," Elide signed.

Reverend Warner laughed and said, "I'm afraid that isn't an option, Ms. Hester. Within a day, perhaps even the next few hours, our enemies will know of your existence, and they will not rest until they find you and *kill* you. We need to get you to Prana, where you'll be surrounded by those who would risk life and limb to protect you. Lord knows you aren't able to protect yourself."

Elide started to sign, but she felt someone grab her arm. By the time she realized it was Ayla's hand, she believed her arm was frozen, or perhaps frostbitten. Icicles spread through her veins like wildfire, numbing her from the inside until the cold reached her heart, and she cried out. Slowly the world grew darker, and then she was falling, but someone caught her and braced her against their body.

"Damn it, Ayla!" shouted a new voice. It was close —*they* were close. And as her vision cleared, Elide saw it was the silent woman holding her up. "You could've killed her."

Ayla scoffed and practically spat out, "She's still conscious, Emma, and we need to move her. We're running out of time."

Elide felt her weight shifting but could do nothing to stop it. She was watching the world move through blurry eyes and was walking with her captor, but she wasn't in control of her legs. Once inside the carriage, Emma released her, and suddenly Elide had control over her body again. Her mind cleared, and whatever had possessed her was gone.

The carriage seats were cushioned and decorated more lavishly than any carriage Elide had ever been in. There was a large window in the back of the carriage where she could see the dirt road. People were walking by slowly, curious about the carriage but avoiding eye contact with the Enochs that guarded it. And then she saw Hansel coming up the road, and Elide waved her hands wildly, trying to get his attention. As her second captor settled into the cushioned seat beside Emma, she began to bang on the window.

"Well, what are you waiting for? Let's get a move on," Ayla shouted to the driver.

The Enochs got onto their horses, and the carriage

began to drive off. In that same moment, Hansel saw her and began to run after the carriage. Elide banged harder on the window, this time rattling it, and she saw Hansel shouting something at her, but she couldn't hear it. And when she banged on the window again, she felt something cold on her ankle, then the world went dark.

7

When she woke again, she was dizzy. The world was hazy, but she knew where she had been and where she was now. Elide looked at the two Mourners across from her. There were stories of Mourners manipulating the minds of bystanders to do their bidding and putting terrifying visions into criminals' minds. She had even heard people refer to them as witches, and maybe there was some truth to those old wives' tales. Maybe they were unnatural. But as she stared at them, all she could think was: *why?* Why her?

"This is a mistake. I'm not supposed to be here," Elide signed toward them.

Ayla rolled her eyes. She reached into a pack on the floor and tossed something burgundy out of it at Elide.

"You'll need that," Ayla said. "It's cold where we're going."

Elide pulled it on. The coat was warmer than it looked.

The warmest coat she'd owned was scratchy on the inside, but this was softer.

"Initiates traditionally wear burgundy," Emma said with a sweet smile.

Elide stared at her. Could she hear her thoughts? Was that even possible? Baptiste was a hub for chatter about other countries in Scopus, where to visit, and where the best careers were, but people rarely spoke of the Mourners, and when they did, it wasn't anything good. They were one of the oldest elite organizations in Scopus and the first to be made solely of women, and like the Disciples, they serve the Apostate. If the Disciples were the Apostate's right hand, then the Mourners were his left.

Elide looked out the window and realized that she must've been asleep for a very long time. Outside, the world was dark, and the only sound she could hear was the carriage wheels scraping against rocks as they rode on. She felt a pang of sadness in her heart. This morning, she'd been a nervous young woman on her way to a ceremony that would decide the rest of her life, but now she was being dragged God-knows-where. Her heart lurched at the thought of Baptiste. Hansel running after the carriage, trying to say something to her. And the more she thought of it, the only word she could make out was her name. Would he scorn Lilah for letting them in? Would he demand that Reverend Warner tell him where they'd taken her?

Elide rubbed her arms, sensing the goosebumps on her skin. They were far from Baptiste now. Baptiste was never this cold at night. She had to be trapped in a nightmare; this couldn't be happening to her. In a few minutes, she would wake up in her room and run next door to tell Hansel about it over breakfast.

The carriage jostled over something large and boulder-like, and the driver shouted an apology. Elide stared at the light in the carriage, the flat bulb was flickering, and when Ayla tapped it, it stopped. The two Mourners were preoccupied and had removed their veils. Emma had ginger hair, and freckles peppered her pale face. She was embroidering a picture on a piece of fabric with an embroidery hoop. Ayla was texting someone. Her black hair was in a bun, and her face was long and thin. And it only took a few seconds for her to notice Elide was staring at her, and she put her phone away.

"How long will it take to get there?" Elide signed.

Ayla scoffed.

"Why? So you can complain to Mother Superior? Tell her over and over again how your bid was a mistake?" Ayla said with a condescending smile. "It was foretold that there would be seven initiates this year—it's rare for us to even get four, but *seven*. That is a heavenly number, one of God's numbers. If you question the Mother Superior's selection, you question Him."

"I am not committing blasphemy," Elide signed.

"And yet you continue to argue," Ayla replied.

The coach jostled as it went over three large bumps.

"Leave her alone, Ayla," Emma said in a soft but stern voice. "She's young and scared, as we once were."

"Perhaps she should be *more* scared than we were," Ayla said harshly.

Elide stared at them.

"Scared of what?" Elide signed.

Emma leaned closer to her and said, "Well, during the Civil War in 1864, a few years before Scopus came to be and the Outlands became the Outlands, the army discovered the first of us—or women like us, anyway—among the slaves. Two of those women were Tellers, women with a power that was the key to discovering secrets behind enemy lines—and even *winning* the war. If you're really a Teller, then you're the most valuable initiate en route."

Elide shrunk back into the seat. What were they thinking? The Civil War was centuries ago—they couldn't possibly believe that she was like them, a witch, a mutant. Whatever they were, whatever genetic disease they carried—what would they do when they realized she wasn't one of them?

"It's not possible," Elide signed. "I'm no one."

For a moment, Emma looked confused, and then she laughed. "No one is no one," she said.

"Or she's right—she is no one," Ayla said sternly.

"I meant that I couldn't have that power. I would know if I had a power," Elide signed.

Did they think she was hiding it from them? That she wanted to live in the slums of Baptiste her whole life.

"Not necessarily," Emma said.

"Or we're wasting our time," Ayla said bitterly.

"The informant was quite sure of what she was," Emma replied.

"Informant?" Elide signed.

The two Mourners exchanged a look.

"Whoever they are, they're lying," Elide signed.

"They didn't," Ayla retorted.

"They could have," Elide signed.

"No, they couldn't have," Emma said. "The test never fails. Mother Superior selected the proctor herself—the informant wouldn't lie to her. The bids are never wrong."

"*Rarely* wrong," corrected Ayla.

Elide shook her head dismissively, feeling tired suddenly. She wanted nothing more than to sink into the seat and sleep, yet she couldn't. There was someone out there that strangely had declared that she was a mutant, a human with a genetic disease, an *anomaly*. Perhaps this was a form of revenge. She was scared to think of who it could be. But Elide knew she was right. She was no one, an orphan from Baptiste, the sister of a mart, a scrawny, mute woman still tripping over her own feet. She'd followed Emma mindlessly into the carriage and could only imagine how much trouble she was about to be in.

The coach went over another bump, slamming Elide against the window, and she gasped. *Those aren't rocks,* Elide thought.

Outside, the driver had lit a lantern, creating enough light to see the green-clad corpses lying on the grass along the road. She couldn't see more than a few feet outside the coach, but what she did see was enough. She'd heard stories of the war with the Outlands for a long time. How bloodthirsty the Outlanders were and the tales of them sustaining bullet wounds without injury, and how their numbers kept growing, and their soldiers kept coming. She felt nausea seize her stomach, and she took a deep breath to calm her nerves.

Then the coach stopped.

Emma and Ayla exchanged a look. Then the two Mourners looked out the coach windows.

"Someone's gotten through," Emma said to Ayla. "Stay here, I'll—"

A scream cut off her sentence. Emma stepped out of the carriage first, then there was a sound like a thunderclap, and she fell back into the carriage with blood leaking from her bullet wound. Her body shuddered, and she was gone. Elide's stomach seized as she stared down at the corpse, barely registering the sound of shots whizzing through the air as she vomited.

"Outlanders!" Ayla shouted to nearby Enochs, whose horses had begun to buck wildly.

Ayla and an Enoch moved Emma's corpse from the carriage and onto the ground.

"Here," Ayla said, shoving an electric cattle prod into Elide's hands. "Don't leave the coach," she said before shutting the door.

"Protect the novitiates," ordered an Enoch outside.

Instinctively, Elide sat down on the floor, curling herself into a ball, clutching the cattle prod tightly with tears welling up in her eyes. She could hear them fighting, their guns ringing out, bodies falling to the ground. She had never seen such horrors in all her life, and she felt worse for hiding from it.

Her heart was hammering in her chest as she sat up.

The door behind her flew open, and a tall bald man in tattered clothes glared down at her, brandishing a knife. Elide held out the cattle prod, pointing it at him in warning.

"Mutant scum," he said, raising a gun in response. "You die—"

But then he began coughing and spluttering. He gasped for air, then blood trickled from his mouth, and he fell forward.

Before Elide could react, another Mourner kicked the corpse out of the coach and slammed the door shut.

Then she banged on the side of the coach and shouted, "Let's move!"

The coach jostled forward and began to move quickly.

Once Elide had gathered the nerve to question this new stranger, she signed, "Who are you?"

"Mirana," she said. "And you must be the Hester girl."

"Elide," Elide signed, sitting back on the seat across from Mirana.

"Well, *Elide*, you should get some rest. We'll be in Prana in a few hours," Mirana told her.

Elide stared at her blankly.

"How did you do that?" Elide signed.

"Do what?"

"Kill that man," Elide signed.

Mirana thought a moment.

"The mind is a very powerful thing," Mirana said with a smile.

Elide stared at her. How could she do that with her mind? Why would anyone want to be able to do that?

"Now," Mirana said as she raised her hand. She snapped her fingers at the same moment she said the word, "Sleep."

And though Elide was sure her dreams would be nightmares as her fear gave way to exhaustion, she closed her eyes and fell asleep.

# 8

## Prana, Texas, Scopus

Elide had to shield her eyes when she woke. Somehow, she'd managed to fall asleep against the window. It was morning now, and their coach had stopped behind another coach waiting for the gate to open. Across from Elide, Mirana looked amused but said nothing, and instead got out of the carriage the instant their eyes met. She walked up to the guards at the gate and handed a stack of papers over to them.

After they'd verified that they weren't Outlanders who intended to kill Mother Superior, they signaled the first carriage to go through. Elide shuddered at the thought of committing murder. She knew the seven deadly sins by heart thanks to Professor Vera. She was a history professor in Miller Hall, and her lectures focused on them and occasionally on Outlanders. The Outlanders were violent soldiers, she'd said, uncivilized killers, rapists, and blasphemers. They committed atrocities like genocide and enslaved and sold their women to appease the demons they

62

bargained with. They consorted with the devil in dark rooms by lamplight, thinking God couldn't see them in dim light. Their leaders were sworn to President Ulysses Howe, known as the Servant-to-Pestilence. He ordered the attacks on Scopus's borders under the guise of freeing the Apolitian people, *her* people, and uniting the two lands under his rule.

Her disgust for President Ulysses Howe aside, Elide had to admit he was smart. Their religion emphasized the importance of unity through faith, and he promised them unity, but he failed to see their religion as freedom. The list of what their faith meant was long, but her favorite parts centered on equality and the availability of a better life for all, including a scrawny girl from Baptiste like herself. But Howe failed in other areas of his regime, as his idea of unity was narrower, and his stance on racism was question-able or *indifferent*. If he was against it, why were his people allowed to execute those who were different from them? In Scopus, racists were shunned and sent away to be retaught. Outside Scopus, someone like Elide wouldn't be safe.

Mirana got back in the coach before signaling the driver to go through the gates of Prana. The buildings were larger than those she'd seen before. Baptiste was mostly rundown townhomes, but here the buildings were more elaborate. The architecture reminded her of Prospero's churches, sprawling and gothic, and though they were the same age—as all career academies were—the masonry buildings here looked newer. Perhaps this type of stone was brighter but still beautiful.

Elide had heard stories of the different career academies during her school years. Campuses varied in size, but every campus was comprised of individual colleges. She was curious about what they specialized in here. There were at least three buildings that she could see in the front, two of which were built around quadrangles.

They were heading toward the center building that was so large it blocked out the sun when she stood in front of it.

"I'll escort you to your dorm suite," Mirana said. "Then you can get some rest before you're presented to Mother Superior with the other novitiates tonight."

The coach stopped in front of the building, and an Enoch opened the coach door. This Enoch looked less intense than the others and even smiled at Elide as he helped her out of the carriage.

"Evening, Taylor. I trust everything is in order?" Mirana said as though it was more a statement than a question.

The Enoch looked at her and said, "The dorms for the remaining novitiates are prepared. And Argus and his men are interrogating the Outlanders. Are you injured?"

"No, luckily. If you could inform Mother Superior that I've arrived safely, I would appreciate it," Mirana said.

"Mother Superior asked for you," Taylor said.

Behind him, two Enochs exchanged a look that said more than silence should ever allow.

Elide looked at Mirana, hoping for an explanation.

"Then send her my regrets as I've promised Ms. Hester that I would escort her to her room," Mirana said.

Taylor shook his head in a way that said she'd regret it. But he signaled the other two Enochs to follow him.

"I thought there wouldn't be any men here," Elide signed.

"Usually, there aren't," Mirana assured with a tight smile. "But someone must've gotten word to Mother Superior about the attack on the road, and she would've asked the Thanatos Institute to spare a few Enochs and Disciples in case the Outlanders reached the academy. So, we she probably get you inside."

Elide followed Mirana inside, and any fears she may have had about her current situation washed away. She sighed. There were statues with their heads bowed in various directions as they passed by closed doors and murals of battles on the ceiling.

They stopped at a great hall where Mirana spoke to two Enochs about security measures. In the dining hall, young Enochs and burgundy-clad women sat together, eating and socializing, reminiscent of Elide's days in Miller Hall. But cliques in Miller Hall were easier to spot. Here, though they sat in groups, they looked the same. A few of them stared at her, and some even whispered about her, but none of them approached her. Elide returned their stares and smiled at a few, trying not to show how anxious she was.

"Novitiates," Mirana told Elide, gesturing toward them. "The young women in burgundy, they haven't taken their vows yet—you'll wear the same throughout your studies."

"And when would that be?" Elide signed.

Mirana smiled and said, "Six years."

Mirana gestured for Elide to follow her and led her to a staircase a few feet from the hall. After they went upstairs and through a door, they entered a large common room with a large fireplace and scarlet couches, where several novitiates were giggling about something. Her escort waved to them, then led Elide down a long hallway with numbered doors and grim paintings lining the walls. They finally stopped at a door with a painting of a woman beside it and a label beneath it that gave her name, the artist's name, and the year the art was completed.

"Leta Rathmore. She was one of the first Mourners recorded by General Robert E. Lee," Mirana said. "It seemed only right to put her portrait in the first- and second-years' dormitory."

Mirana opened the door, and they stepped into a small common area. There were three bookcases against the wall, one was empty, while the others were filled with books. A television was sitting on a table beside them undisturbed, and the remote sat on a coffee table by the couch. And on Elide's left was a wall with a pass-through window, separating the kitchenette from the small living room.

"You have two roommates. They share that room over there," Mirana said, pointing toward a birch door on the right. "You'll be in this room over here."

Elide followed her to her new room. It wasn't a small room, though it wasn't particularly big either—thirteen feet by twelve feet. Furniture took up most of the space: a desk, a dresser and a wardrobe, a heater in the corner, a full-length mirror, and a queen-sized bed. The walls were white, but there was a large window near the foot of the bed with a view that looked out on a courtyard where novitiates were lying on the grass, socializing.

"Oh good, Starla brought in your uniform," Mirana said, handing Elide the folded uniform.

Elide unfolded it and looked at herself in the mirror. A floor-length burgundy dress that matched the other novitiates with fabric softer than any she'd ever felt.

"It's beautiful," Elide signed.

Her reflection reminded her that she was still her—long, dark curly hair, square, brown face, wide, round eyes, and a small nose. She was still Elide Hester from Baptiste, though she felt she couldn't be. The weeks she'd spent studying for the LAT meant nothing. Her career preferences had meant nothing. But there had to be a reason for it.

"All right," Mirana said as she set the room key on the dresser. She began to walk out the door but stopped suddenly. "The bathroom is there on your right so you can bathe. Oh, and you can decorate the walls if you'd like, whatever makes you feel at home."

Elide nodded.

"Well, I'm off then. When you see me around, feel free to say hello," Mirana said as she squeezed Elide's shoulder and left the room.

Elide stared at her reflection for a moment. She was trying not to imagine what home was like right now. She was worried about Hansel. He had chased after the coach and couldn't keep up. *He must be worried sick*, she thought, as something made her stomach churn. It was a strangely familiar feeling that she wasn't quick to brush away.

Today she had to bathe and dress to meet the Mother Superior, a woman she had never intended to meet, who would decide her fate. And tomorrow, after the decision was made, Elide might be praying before her execution for all she knew. What she did know was that she wasn't a Teller, whatever they were. And what would Mother Superior do when she discovered that her informant lied?

Elide thought over the possibilities as she showered. In a different world, the water streaming down her back would soothe her. But in this one, the only thing soothing her was the pomegranate bath soap and shower loofah her roommate Starla had left in the bathroom for her. *A gift for you, my new roommate, from Starla,* the card said. It was a sweet gesture.

Elide stepped out of the shower and toweled off her wet body. She padded back to her room in the towel and threw it off the moment she kicked her door closed. She put on fresh undergarments and dried her hair with the towel. When she finally stepped into the dress, she felt disoriented seeing herself in it. Elide rarely wore red. Red was the color for passion, lust, and love. And she avoided looking wanton in front of men. Though burgundy, especially this shade of burgundy, was beautiful.

Mother Superior's wrongful bid aside, she had to admit, the dress made her feel beautiful too. Elide always felt she was rather plain. But in this dress, she was beautiful. Perhaps she wasn't scrawny but lithe. Her cheekbones were high and pointed, and when she moved her hair to one side, her curls had a sheen that she'd never noticed. *Maybe the Mourners are witches,* she thought, and all she saw was a product of an enchantment placed on the dress.

Elide heard the dorm suite door open and two murmuring voices. She knew they belonged to her room-mates, but she was too tired to introduce herself. So she locked her door and fell onto the bed.

She dreamt she was back in Baptiste, slipping into a white nightgown to spend her weekend in. In a few hours, she would be whisked away to Prospero, and her training to be a proper baroness would begin. When she went down-stairs, Hansel was waiting for her, and she ran into his arms and hugged him tightly. Hansel smiled down at her; he was so happy for her that tears were in his eyes. She reminded him that he'd be able to visit her once she was deemed a baroness, seeing as choosing a career didn't mean she aban-doned her family. And after some convincing, he agreed to visit her. But then someone screamed. Lilah was gripping her stomach, her fingers coated in blood, and as she began to speak, blood trickled down her lips.

Elide bolted upright, panting, gasping for air, as she looked around the room and stopped on the scarlet curtains covering her window. The window was open. She groaned and got out of bed to close it.

Elide jumped when she saw someone staring up at her. Though it was only a group of Mourner novitiates sitting outside in the courtyard, eating and drinking. She sighed and shut the window. Then a knock came from the door.

She looked at it and checked herself in the mirror. Still her. Still in Prana. Still no clue what was going to happen to her.

"Hello, Elide, are you there?" a female voice called from the other side of the door.

Elide opened the door, and a tall woman with a glistening, white smile stood on the other side. She wore the novitiate uniform and had gold bracelets on both wrists. Her shoes were black and polished. Her hair was long and dark, and her brown eyes twinkled as she smiled; her skin was bronze and so smooth and unscarred that she looked as though she'd been born perfect.

"Hi," she said, "it's nice to meet you. I'm Starla—oh, you haven't unpacked."

Elide hesitated. She hadn't had the chance to pack in the first place, and if she had, there wouldn't have been much. Her family was poor; she was lucky her father had been able to leave her the house—though, in the eyes of Reverend Warner, as a woman she had no claim to it.

"I know how to sign, by the way," Starla said quickly. "My mother and I used to volunteer at the school of the deaf in Redwood. That's in Prospero—not that I'm assuming you don't know where Prospero is. And I know you aren't deaf—though I wouldn't have a problem with it if you were. I swear I'm not ignorant."

Elide smiled. "It's all right," Elide signed. "Thank you for the welcome gift."

"Of course!" Starla said. "It's not a problem at all. I'd

heard what happened on the ride here and immediately thought that if it was me, I'd want a nice hot bath after someone tried to kill me."

"How do you know what happened?" Elide signed.

Starla sighed and rolled her eyes as if the memory annoyed her more than the event itself. "Well, Pepper had heard from Isadora about it, and she'd heard it from her Enoch boyfriend. I swear the nonstop gossip that flows out of those two. We're not even supposed to fool around with Enochs, it's a rule, but the moment the Apostate comes to visit, all the professors are so focused on pleasing him that they hardly notice a bent rule here and there. Like, why do we even have rules?"

"Why can't we fraternize with Enochs?" Elide signed, and then she flushed red, realizing what she'd just asked.

Starla giggled.

"Oh, you and I are going to have fun," she said with a hint of a smile. "And it's because they're afraid of us losing our virtue. You know, purity stuff. We're supposed to be saving ourselves for a Disciple, if not the Apostate himself, but no one's good enough for the Apostate. I can't help but wonder how his ancestors managed to have children."

"The Apostate is here?" Elide signed.

Starla nodded, and suddenly her eyes widened. "Oh God, I almost forgot. I'm supposed to bring you to be presented to Mother Superior in the great hall," Starla said. "Second years have to be there, so I'll be watching. My presentation was last year, and the Apostate wasn't there. Thank God. I tripped in front of everyone. Oh, I can fetch you a pair of shoes if you like. You look about the same size as me."

"Why is the Apostate here?" Elide signed.

"I don't know, maybe the attack on the road, maybe to instill the fear of God into us," Starla said, sounding bored. "It's really anyone's guess with him," she said, pausing to nod at her own statement. Then saying, "Are you really a Teller?"

Elide's heart skipped a beat. She didn't know how to respond.

"Never mind. Don't tell me. I like surprises!" Starla said abruptly, and then she clapped her hands together. "Now, let's find you some shoes."

Surprisingly, they'd reached the bottom of the staircase on time. Elide had hardly looked at herself, but after she'd allowed her *welcoming* roommate to give her new shoes, Starla wanted to help her with her hair, and that meant perfectly coiled curls with two braids pinned at the back of her head to keep her hair from falling back over her ears. And Starla had even done "light" makeup on her. Elide had never seen makeup in Baptiste; their shops didn't hold luxury items. But Starla promised only to conceal her under-eye circles and apply mascara to her eyelashes, and she'd held to that promise. Afterward, Elide could hardly believe how pretty she looked. Starla was a miracle worker.

Six other novitiates were standing beside second years and didn't look nearly as nervous as she was. In fact, many looked confident and whispered and pointed in Elide's general direction. A few were giggling at whatever gossip they were spreading. All of them were standing in front of a pair of large double doors that went into the great hall. The doors themselves were flanked by hooded statues that gave off all the warmth of a cold winter afternoon.

"The girls are just excited, is all," Starla whispered. "And maybe a little jealous that I'm the one that gets to walk you in."

*Jealous of what*, Elide wondered. But before she could ask, the doors opened, and they filed in. The hall had several long tables that looked prepared for a feast. Six of the tables had a Mourner standing by them, each holding a flag with a sigil on it. For a moment, Elide couldn't read the words on the flags, but as they got closer, she could—Mirai, Leta, Rapha, Kedeh, Laska, and Hamle. The Apostate's men were seated at the seventh table. Whereas novitiates were sitting at the other six tables while most Enochs stood at attention against the walls.

Elide shuddered when she spotted the Disciples standing in front of a large dais that ran the width of the room, where elder Mourners sat in seats behind a table, and the Apostate sat in the center seat. His eyes were surveying the room as if he were searching for something.

Starla stopped suddenly and said, "All right, this is where we part ways."

Elide felt a surge of dread go through her.

"Don't worry, it'll be okay," Starla said, touching her arm. "You won't be walking up there alone."

Elide noticed that the other novitiates, or *first years*, were receiving a similar pep talk.

"What am I supposed to do?" Elide signed.

"Nothing," Starla said. "Trust me, you're already unique enough. I can sense it."

*Maybe I'm not*, Elide thought with a pang of guilt. She would've noticed if she was special. Wouldn't she? She felt as though this had to be an elaborate ruse. Any moment someone would jump out and tell her it was all a joke.

"I can't go up there," Elide signed. "I just can't. I don't even know what a Teller is."

Starla shot her a quizzical look, and then said, "Everything is going to be fine."

"Stop saying that," Elide signed.

Someone on the other side of the room clapped their hands.

"Ladies, leave your escorts and present yourselves," a female voice commanded.

Elide stared at the woman. She was tall and thin with platinum hair. She looked like a marble statue wearing a black gown.

Starla nodded and went to sit at the Hamle table as her fellow second years went to their respective tables. But Elide couldn't move. Luckily, neither did the other first years. Elide tried to calm down and nearly managed to until she noticed the Apostate staring at her. And suddenly, the white marble floors reminded her of the courtroom. *Except this time, there won't be a trial*, Elide thought, and her heart sank.

A hush fell as a novitiate took the first step toward the

dais, and then another followed, and somehow Elide managed to follow them, and before she knew it, they stood at the foot of the dais. All eyes were on them, and Elide was just glad she wasn't shaking.

"I am Professor Richie, my specialty is illusionary casting, and I look forward to teaching you in the future," the platinum-haired woman said. Her icy-blue eyes shimmered as she spoke. "And now, our Mother Superior will declare your appropriate orders."

An elderly woman came forward, her cane tapping as she walked, and Elide tensed. Without her veil, Elide almost hadn't recognized her, but the cane was all too familiar. Her skin was pale and wrinkly, and her eyes were cold and dark. Her forehead looked strained by the taut bun at the base of her head, and her black gown was dragging on the floor as she finally stopped in front of the first novitiate. Elide was the third and was nearly as frightened as the first.

The girl was taller than Mother Superior, but she shook all the same. Mother Superior looked her up and down and *tsked* three times.

"Sara Pickett—" Mother Superior said, and the girl's eyes widened. "You hold a common gift but no less worthy of being among us. You are Mirai."

Two tables of novitiates cheered, and the Mourner beside the banner smiled as well. Sara curtsied to the Mother Superior, who put something into the girl's hand. Then Sara went to take a seat at the Mirai table.

The room fell silent again as the Mother Superior approached the second novitiate. She looked at her in the same way but remained silent this time. Mother Superior narrowed her eyes, and the girl in front of her held her breath.

"Lucida Morgan," Mother Superior said, practically hissing the girl's name. "Your gift aids yourself and others, but I am sure you know that already. You are Rapha."

The Rapha table cheered. Lucida beamed at Mother Superior as she took something from her hand, though this time, Elide could see it. It was a pin with the Rapha crest on it: a brown stag on a blue background. Lucida went to the Rapha table, enthusiastically greeting another girl.

And Elide stared at the floor. *I can't do this,* she thought.

Her stomach clenched. She could feel the Apostate's eyes on her as Mother Superior stepped in front of her. Two fingers hooked under her chin, and Elide's eyes slowly met the elderly woman's gaze.

"Do I frighten you?" Mother Superior asked.

Elide shook her head no. But before she could explain further, Mother Superior turned to the Apostate.

"This was the one my informant spoke of," she told the Apostate. Then, turning back to Elide. "You should hold your head high, my dear. I can only see what is already there."

*But there's nothing there,* Elide thought with a pang of guilt. These people were all expecting something from her. She could imagine the disappointment they would feel when she could not deliver.

"You can't hide from a Kedeh any more than she can hide from you," the Apostate said as if they were speaking casually over brunch and not in front of an audience of at least a hundred.

Mother Superior stared at Elide.

For a moment, Elide thought about begging for her life, but then she felt something.

Elide's feet felt rooted to the floor. She couldn't move, and it was terrifying. But somehow, perhaps instinctively, she knew her body had fallen into a state of paralysis. However, she couldn't shake the feeling inside her. It surged from her stomach to her heart, beating to the same rhythm, and before she knew it, she was calm. As Mother Superior's eyes slid over her, she felt water wash over her, as if she were lying on the sand at the beach as the tide came in, and then something called to her. Or *it* rather. The thing inside her heard it and rose higher with every breath she took. Elide tried to fight it, sensing that whatever it was would take her. She squeezed her eyes shut, clenching her fists as she did so.

"Breathe," Mother Superior whispered to her.

Elide hesitated. Then she obeyed, and in that same moment, it came rushing forward.

She could feel it seeping through her pores, running through every nerve and revealing itself to Mother Superior. And the elderly woman smiled.

"Brilliant, Elide Hester," Mother Superior said with a nod. "Simply *brilliant*. You are like those that came before you, seeking truth and knowledge. But unlike your ancestors, you will find it," she said plainly and smiled again. "You are Teller."

The crowd erupted into cheers. People rose to their

feet, clapping and crying, in awe of her. The other first-year novitiates beside her were clapping as well. The Apostate had stood up and was applauding with a smirk on his face. Elide wondered if it meant he approved of her.

Elide turned to look at the other novitiates and felt as though she were no longer presenting herself to the Mother Superior but that she was being presented to her peers themselves.

"Welcome, Elide," the Apostate said.

She nearly jumped. She tried to hide her embarrassment at not noticing him approach her.

"You look better," he said, taking her hand for a moment.

Elide nodded and signed, "So do you."

He laughed at that. "Ah, the Hester cheek. I'm quite familiar with it. Your brother had a few choice words for me when he discovered where you were being taken."

Elide felt a surge of guilt.

Then he stepped away from her and returned to his seat.

"Take a seat where you feel most comfortable," Mother Superior told Elide.

Elide nodded and went to the Hamle table, where Starla was waiting to welcome her with open arms.

"See, I told you everything would be all right," Starla said. "I never doubted what you were. Mother Superior is never wrong."

Elide nodded slowly but couldn't look away from the Apostate. But he wasn't looking at her; he was watching the proceedings.

"I'm surprised she's sitting with us Hamles," said a pale girl with wavy brown hair, and Elide looked at her.

Starla rolled her eyes. "Well, she's not the judgmental type, are you Elide?"

But before Elide could respond, she was cut off by the pale girl.

"Everyone's just a little judgmental, Starla," the pale girl said. "Take me, for instance. I'm a third-generation Mourner and the second to get something other than canon-fodder over there. Hamle is more valuable than most, but we're not Teller."

"Yvette, don't talk about the Laska that way in front of her," said a girl with dark brown hair and two blond highlights framing her face.

Yvette scoffed, sticking her pointed nose in the air. "Oh *please*, Isadora. Everyone knows they're a dime a dozen; Mother Superior is just being nice about it. They can play soldier all they want, but we all know their gift is pretty much useless."

Elide tapped Starla on the shoulder.

"What's their gift?" Elide signed to her.

Starla hesitated. "Oh. Well, you know when you were a kid and you rubbed your feet on the carpet, and you could shock someone?" Starla said.

Yvette laughed, and a few other Hamle snickered. Starla ignored them.

"Well, they're a bit like that, but it's more painful. Believe me, I fought one in combat training," Starla said.

Elide glanced at Isadora, who nodded and then rolled her eyes at Yvette's expression.

"They're the best at hand-to-hand combat though," Isadora added.

A girl at the Kedeh table leaned over the aisle and said, "You must be joking. Laskas have a tactile disadvantage."

Elide glanced at Starla, who was still trying to win the argument with the other girls. And Elide couldn't help but smile at them. It felt like she was back in Miller Hall again, socializing and gossiping, joking around and laughing with each other. For a moment, she was home.

# 9

"Well, what do you think?" Starla asked as they stared into the box.

Admittedly, Elide half expected it to be another dress, but it wasn't.

They'd returned to their dorm immediately after the ceremony was over, and just as they were getting settled in, an Enoch delivered four more novitiate dresses and a pair of pointed boots for Elide along with her class schedule and textbooks, which she'd set on her bookshelf. Then an hour later, another knock had come from the door. This time, a Disciple stood in the doorway with a black dress box, but inside was a gray coat with a high neck that came with a silver raven pin.

"I don't need it," Elide signed, shaking her head.

Starla sighed. "It's not about *needing* it. It's a gift, Elide," Starla said, staring at the coat.

Elide laid her hand on the coat. It was made of high-quality fabric and would keep her warm in the winter weather, but the thought of wearing it overwhelmed her. She was grateful to know that she was a Teller. She had never thought of herself as unique, and yesterday had proven otherwise—but this was too much.

Elide had gotten through being presented to Mother Superior, clearly to the woman's approval. And she assumed she'd received the Apostate's approval as well, seeing as this gift was from him.

"I can't wear that," Elide signed as she looked down into the box again.

Starla gaped. Elide folded the tissue paper back over the coat, placed the lid on the box, and put it in her room. When she came back to the common area, Starla was still in shock.

"I'm already different enough. I don't need to draw more attention to it," Elide signed.

"You're not even going to wear the raven pin?" exclaimed Starla, clearly horrified.

"That's the Apostate's sigil," Elide signed.

Starla was flustered.

"And *clearly*, he's offering it to you until you have your own," Starla said. "He wouldn't give permission to just anyone to wear the raven."

"Then I'll thank him for it, but I can't wear it," Elide signed.

"Yes, you can! Don't you see? He's declaring you as his equal. No one wears the raven unless he gives them permission to."

"I've only just moved here! Not to mention, it was against my will, and I still have no idea what it means to be a Teller. So, no, Starla, I don't need a gift that makes me stand out more than I already do," Elide signed.

Starla took a deep breath. She sat quietly for a moment and then nodded.

"*Fine*, but don't give it back. That's rude," Starla told her.

Elide smiled, and the two relaxed on the couch. They were supposed to be waiting for Pepper and Isadora to come back to the room with food, but it'd been over an hour, and Elide was getting tired. So she sat there trying to keep her eyes open. Starla was searching for a show to watch while they waited. They could have eaten with the other novitiates in the great hall, but Elide was too tired from the day's events. Her anxiety had taken more energy out of her than she'd realized.

"You know, I can wake you up when the food gets here," Starla said, looking at Elide. "If worse comes to worst, I'll have Pepper shock you awake."

Elide shook her head. But she could feel her eyes getting heavier. In some ways, she hoped that if she slept, she would wake and find that it had all been a dream. Then tomorrow, she would laugh it off with Hansel. They'd laugh at the thought of anyone trying to kill her, and the possibility of her meeting Mother Superior, whose vulture-like disposition faded when the old woman spoke. And she'd know that she'd never felt the Apostate's hand holding her own. Perhaps she would wake up to Lilah making pancakes in her kitchen, and they would have a discussion about boundaries again, and Hansel would close it out by reminding them both that the three of them are a family. No matter how messed up things got.

Elide felt tears stinging her eyes. She wiped them away, knowing in her heart that somewhere in Baptiste, Hansel was thinking about her too. And if the Apostate's words were anything to go on, nothing would stop him from getting to her, and so she would do the same to get back to him.

# 10

Elide woke at dawn in her bedroom, though she couldn't remember climbing into bed the night before. She faintly remembered eating chicken and mashed potatoes and flicking peas across her dinner plate. Pepper hadn't spoken much last night; she ate a light snack and went to bed. She'd looked sad about something but didn't explain. Elide wasn't sure if she should ask her about it this morning, as she didn't want to overstep Pepper's boundaries. But if Elide didn't ask, she'd always wonder what would've happened if she had. But either way, she'd have to manage to get out of bed first.

This bed was much more comfortable than the one she had back home. It felt like she was sleeping on a cloud, and after years spent on a mattress that might as well have been a rock slab, she was grateful but also exhausted.

Above her, the ceiling was painted in pastel colors, a gorgeous mural of a periwinkle sky and the shadows of birds in flight. She imagined that the colors were bolder in the past and had faded with age. When she finally got out of bed, she showered and slipped on a new novitiate dress and the pointed boots. Then Elide stuck the Apostate's gift into her wardrobe beneath her old shoes. She shut the wardrobe, convincing herself that she could put the gift out of her mind by keeping it hidden. The gift box could spend the rest of its days underneath those shoes for all she cared.

Today, Starla had promised to show her around the academy. Elide wasn't sure if she was looking forward to it. She still felt afraid and unsure about what came next. She didn't know what time Starla would be arriving, but she could keep herself occupied, so she went into the common area.

Elide searched her bookshelf, though she had no idea what she was looking for since all she had were textbooks. Finally, she found one that interested her: *Ethical Enchantment* by Orestes Hackman.

It was for her Secular Evocation I course. The syllabus described it as a course meant to provide the foundational knowledge needed for entering someone's mind and navigating their memories *ethically*.

*I'm not sure how ethical that is,* Elide thought, flipping the textbook open to its first chapter. She had to read three chapters for her first class on Monday, and the last thing she wanted was to be the only student that hadn't read.

But she couldn't focus. Elide took a deep breath, shut the book, and set it down beside her. The schedule they'd given her had her attending five courses and an additional one-on-one course with a private instructor. She'd hardly managed five courses when she attended Miller, and now she had to attend six classes? *At least I have the weekends off*, she thought, but it didn't make her feel any better. Like all Mourners, as a Teller, she had certain pre-requisite courses: Remedial Demonic Taxonomy for Mirais, Ethical Psychic Mastery for Kedehs, Necromantic Philosophy for Raphas, Combat Training for Laskas, Rudimentary Bibliomancy for Letas, and Philosophy of Illusionary Engineering for Hamles. She could feel her anxiety getting worse by the second. The thought of attempting to use her power made her queasy.

"You all right, Elide?" asked Pepper, who was standing in her and Starla's bedroom doorway. "Not to be rude, but you look like something the cat dragged in."

Elide sighed and signed, "Yes, I'm fine. Are you all right? You looked upset last night."

"I'm fine," Pepper said as she walked into the kitchen and grabbed a cereal bowl. "Have you eaten anything yet? I'm sure Starla will have you walking around all day if you let her."

"I'm not hungry yet," Elide signed.

Pepper nodded and said, "Yeah, I understand. Heavy is the head, right?"

Elide looked at her. "Are you mad at me?" Elide signed.

Pepper poured cereal into the bowl and shrugged.

"I guess—I don't know, maybe I was hoping you'd be a Laska like me," she said, walking over to the table with her cereal bowl and milk. "I mean, Hamles call us cannon-fodder, Kedeh think we're weak, and—"

Pepper paused and shrugged.

"I'd heard them talking about Laskas but didn't understand why," Elide signed.

Pepper laughed.

"Well, we don't heal like Raphas do or cause our enemies pain without ever lifting a finger like Letas do. On the battlefield, we just die. I can electrocute someone at close range but no farther than a foot away. My power has limits like everyone else's," Pepper explained, mixing her cereal. "Mancios and Tellers may as well be gods compared to the rest of us."

"Mancios?" Elide signed.

Pepper laughed. "I keep forgetting you're new to all this. The Apostate is a Mancio."

"What does that mean?" Elide signed.

Pepper set down her spoon in her cereal bowl and got up from her chair. She walked over to her bookshelf and grabbed a textbook from it.

When Pepper offered it to Elide, she took it. It was larger than her first-year textbooks and bound in black leather.

"Page 105," Pepper said when she sat back at the table. "The Mancio is an order of males with telepathic abilities —that is, an order *if* there were more of them alive. The only known ones are from the Apostate's family, and last I heard, he was the only one left." Pepper crunched her cereal and hummed happily.

"Do you know why?" Elide signed.

Pepper shrugged. "No," she said. "Daegal might know

though! He had a theory about genetics. He's teaching all his wife's classes this year because she's pregnant."

"Men can teach here?" Elide signed.

"Well, someone has to do it, and he volunteered weeks ago," Pepper said. "I think they were having trouble conceiving before, and Mother Superior feels sorry for them."

Elide nodded silently. Pepper shook her head and continued eating her cereal.

"I wonder what Isadora is doing today—" began Pepper.

Then the front door slammed open, cutting her off. "Oh, my goodness! I'm so sorry! I know I'm late. It's crazy out there. I'll give you that tour now," Starla said.

"Isadora and I can take her—"

"The Apostate insisted that I do it," Starla said abruptly.

Pepper rolled her eyes, and Starla practically yanked Elide off the couch and out the door. Elide hoped Pepper had seen her wave goodbye but couldn't be sure. She didn't know why Starla was in such a rush, but Elide was ready for a tour of the academy.

"Sorry about Pepper. She's a bit rude in the mornings," Starla said.

Elide followed Starla downstairs and down a hallway. The paintings lining the walls looked different in daylight, as did the statues, some were headless, and others were posed in peculiar positions. Starla didn't pay them any mind. They stopped next to a pair of double doors with an elaborate design carved into them, surrounding a smaller carving of the academy itself.

"Well, we're in the main building, and as you already know, our dorm is that way," Starla said, pointing back the way they'd come. "If you go left and walk all the way down, you'll run straight into a portrait of Esther Kedeh, and right next to it, is the library. The doors are silver, you can't miss them," she said, pointing to the left. "If you get hungry, you go right, and the great hall is only a few doors down," she said, pointing right.

"And those doors," Elide signed, gesturing to the doors next to them.

Starla smiled wickedly. "I thought you'd never ask."

Elide followed Starla out the double doors and was immediately hit with the smell of roses. Hedges flanked both sides of the dirt walkway they stood on. Dewy pink roses were growing out of the hedges and in the sunlight. Starla led Elide on the path until they were clear of the hedges and beside a green lawn that was part of a larger quadrangle. Disciples and Mourners were socializing and, perhaps, even flirting with each other while the former was patrolling the lawns. There was a water fountain near two buildings with banners running down them. The first had a Mirai banner: a jackalope with two heads on green. The second had a Laska banner: a ram on yellow. Novitiates were sparring on the lawn next to the building, wearing burgundy pants and shirts, while a crowd of novitiates beside them waved green and yellow flags, cheering them on.

There were four other buildings with the flags of

different orders as well: a badger on purple for Letas, a griffin on silver for Kedeh, a bear on gold for Hamle, a stag on royal blue for Rapha. The Apostate's symbol was nowhere to be found on any of the buildings, but Elide assumed it could be at the academy for Disciples.

Large groups of novitiates stood in front of the buildings; others sat near planters and worked studiously, taking notes with their textbooks open. The cold didn't appear to bother any of them like it did Elide. She was trying to ignore it but couldn't help but shiver.

Elide turned back to the main building, trying to distract herself, and saw gargoyles protruding from the roofs. Elide smiled. The stone creatures weren't in the best shape. In fact, most of them didn't have teeth. And for creatures meant to ward off evil, she felt they should have teeth. They looked rather silly without them, and she couldn't imagine a demon being frightened by a gummy gargoyle.

"What is it?" Starla asked, hearing Elide giggle.

"Nothing," Elide signed.

Starla nodded silently and then looked at a small group passing them. "Everyone is pairing off already. They're making me feel like a late bloomer."

Elide glanced at the group and noticed that each novitiate was walking with their hand in the crook of a Disciple's arm. She glanced at Starla and noticed that her lips were pursed in a perfect pout. Elide understood her envy but sometimes had a hard time picturing herself in a long-term relationship. Baptiste men didn't marry mute women unless they wanted to control them, but she wasn't in Baptiste anymore, so maybe there was hope for her.

"It happens every year, I swear," Starla said the moment they sat down on a bench. "First years immediately go looking for husbands, and all the guys that want commitment end up taken."

"Why don't you have a boyfriend?" Elide signed.

Starla blushed and shrugged.

"Honestly, Disciples have always made me a little nervous. I guess I went into the wrong career. I mean, I knew I wasn't baroness material like my mother, and now I'll either marry or swear off men entirely to stay in Prana," Starla responded, looking around at the campus.

"There's not more to Prana?" Elide signed.

"No, of course not," Starla said. "Prana is solely for the Apostate's leading universities. Well, and the Prana communities for graduates and families. It was in the brochure," she said, and Elide stared blankly. "Most people spend their entire lives in one place, though I certainly don't blame them for doing that here. After all, Prana is *beautiful*. But it's outsiders like us that have to worry about finding someone. I hear most people in Prana are promised to someone by eighteen."

"It's the same in Baptiste. My best friend, Fiona, got engaged to her boyfriend when we were eighteen," Elide signed. Then Elide hesitated before she asked her next question. "How many elite academies are there?" Elide signed.

Starla thought a moment. "Three in total. The Disciples study at Thanatos Institute on the north campus.

Libertas University is for the Enochs—that's not far from Thanatos—and Prana Academy for Mourners, of course, and that's it. It's rare for anyone to marry an outsider, so take your pick while you can, I guess."

Elide lost track of time sitting in the quad with Starla. But eventually, she found herself following Starla to the Kedeh building, conscious of the stares following them as they passed other novitiates.

When they reached an archway carved with elaborate designs, they stopped. Through the archway, a ten-foot griffin statue stood on a platform, holding an olive branch in its beak. Its eyes were focused and seemed to follow her as she moved.

"And here?" Elide signed to Starla.

"The Apostate felt it was best for you to meet Calliope before the semester starts," Starla said. "You just pull the lever in the corner there, and it'll raise the staircase to her classroom," she instructed, pointing at three pipes that connected to the wall.

"Calliope?" Elide signed.

Starla nodded. "She's an instructor for the Kedeh. But Mother Superior chose her for your training, and Calliope's one of the best."

Again, Elide looked up at the fearsome stone creature before them. It was hard for her to imagine that the woman waiting for her was any less fierce.

"Mother Superior chose her?" Elide signed nervously.

"Well, you can't expect the Apostate to have a say in everything that happens. Mother Superior is still in charge here."

"You want me to go up there?" Elide signed. "Alone?"

Starla nodded. "Yes, I'm afraid you'll have to introduce yourself. There's no reason to worry, though. Calliope is quite nice when you get to know her."

Elide hesitated and then approached the pipes. "Which one?" Elide signed, looking back at Starla.

"The one in the center," Starla answered.

Elide pulled the center pipe and nearly fell backward. The ground shook as stone steps emerged from the wall behind the griffin one by one, kicking dust and dirt into the air. When the dust cleared, a spiral staircase wound around the creature's back.

Elide walked up the steps until she reached a door and knocked. She stood quietly, waiting for someone to answer, but no one came. And when she went to knock again, the door opened, revealing a Disciple. He had brown eyes, a neat beard and warm brown skin, and wore a black blazer —with the angry-looking golden raven of the Disciples embroidered on it—and men's dress pants. He was the most attractive man she'd ever seen.

"Pardon me, Elide," the man said, bowing to her as if she were royalty and then quickly going down the stairs.

Elide was taken aback by the action but had only a moment to process it before someone said, "Enter."

Elide stepped in nervously, noting how dark it was in the room. She could faintly see a shadow sitting behind a desk. As her eyes adjusted to the darkness, she could make out an armchair just as she was about to run into it. It was pulled up to a table covered in a white tablecloth, and another armchair sat on the other side of the table. The same seating arrangement was repeated throughout the room. And though it was difficult to see, Elide noted, she was certain mirrors covered the right wall.

When a pair of shutters slammed open, she jumped and fell into the chair. As she sat there, the shutters throughout the room sprung open as if they were alive.

"Sorry, I'd forgotten how dark it was," a soft voice said.

Elide stared at the woman. She had dark, pensive eyes, and pale skin, and wasn't wearing a Mourner's uniform. Her dress was emerald green—*not black*, Elide noted—and cinched at the waist. Her hair stopped at her hip framing her figure. She had a necklace on her neck with a bird's claw attached to it. And if her heart wasn't in her throat, Elide might've asked her why she was sitting in the dark in the first place. Especially considering the man who'd left.

Elide approached Calliope nervously, but her nerves took over, and she sat in a closer armchair. Calliope smiled.

"No need to be afraid of me," she said lowly. "We'll be seeing a lot of each other, Elide."

"I'm not afraid," Elide signed.

"We'll have to work on your lying as well then."

"I don't lie—I rarely do," Elide signed, correcting herself.

Calliope smirked as if she was holding back a laugh.

"We'll work on it," she said. Then she crossed the room to a trunk on a shelf. It was only when Elide noticed the jars and frames on the shelf that she shuddered.

*Taxidermy*, she noted apprehensively, restraining another shudder. Elide leaned closer to get a better look and immediately wished she hadn't. Calliope's collection was extensive: bones, bats, and dead creatures at various stages in their life cycle. There was also a human heart floating in a jar. It made her nervous about what would come out of the trunk.

"Now," Calliope said, "let's begin."

11

Elide felt like she was holding her skull together. When Calliope told her to call on her power, not only did Elide not understand what she meant, she couldn't. She was on the brink of giving up when Calliope placed a hand on her shoulder. Elide closed her eyes. Then when they opened again, she was standing in a forest. There were only trees around her, enormous trees with canopies that blocked out the sky, and dirt beneath her feet. She was still in her novitiate uniform but nowhere near Prana.

Behind her, Calliope said, "Interesting."

Elide turned to her and signed, "Where are we?"

"I was about to ask you that," she answered calmly.

Elide looked around then as she heard something moving in the trees. She looked up and saw a little boy hiding in the branches.

"What is this?" Elide signed to Calliope.

Calliope stared at her intently, and Elide noted, in the

midst of everything else happening, that Calliope's pupils had turned black. Elide stared back at her, hoping against hope that it wouldn't get any worse. But then, she heard running. She turned to where the sound was coming from and saw her younger self—she couldn't have been more than four. The little girl's clothing was made from patched-together rags, and the moment she saw Elide, her mouth opened and let out a petrifying scream as the child pointed at something behind her.

Elide turned to see what it was and saw seven cloaked figures surrounding a woman kneeling on the ground. Elide couldn't seem to make out who they were.

"Elide!" a young boy's voice called.

*Hansel,* Elide thought, but then she gasped for air. Her heart felt heavy in her chest. She was sitting back in the armchair with her nails biting into her palms. Calliope was standing in front of Elide, and her eyes were dark but not black. Elide checked her surroundings, worried she was still stuck in a dream.

"We'll meet again after lessons start," Calliope told her. "You should take some time to rest."

"What was that?" Elide signed. "Who were those people?"

"You need rest," Calliope stated.

"Who was that woman?" Elide signed as the answer dawned on her. "That was my mother, wasn't it?"

Calliope looked away from Elide and took a deep breath. Elide could see her eyes watering when she looked back at her.

"Do you know what happened to my mother?" Elide signed.

"Yes, your mother died after she left Prana."

"Did they kill her?"

"I think that's enough for the day."

"But Calliope—"

"Go. Rest now, child," Calliope said sharply. "There's no need to worry about this now. You're dismissed."

Elide nodded, realizing that she was being given an order, and left the classroom. She walked the hallways for the rest of the morning, navigating around novitiates and professors. Eventually, she found herself in the library, where she hid in one of the hundreds of narrow rows available. She found solace in the size of the place, as other novitiates prowled the aisles but didn't pay any attention to her.

The library was divided into ten sections marked with blue signs. Study tables in the aisles were pressed against bookcases, and novitiates sat at them, researching facts or exploring fiction. Elide had seen a younger novitiate having a fitful sleep with her head resting on a bookstack. There were thousands of shelves and thus thousands of books. Elide hoped to lose herself in one of them, at least for a few hours.

She managed to find her favorite collection of fairytales: *Sovereign of the Night* by Cornelius Delacroix. Her mother had bought it from a used bookshop one day when they were out. She read a story from it to her every night for three years. She said it was half-written in poetry, half-born of song. A song of her people—who Elide had the faintest memories of meeting but couldn't remember their names.

The story the book was titled after was more gruesome than Elide remembered. It spoke of the horrors of war and men with a penchant for violence. She preferred the romanticized version her mother had read her. The prince was the first man she swooned over; now she couldn't understand how she ever had.

"What are you reading?" a soft voice said.

Elide nearly jumped out of her skin at the sound of Isadora's voice.

"Sorry, I didn't mean to startle you," Isadora said. "I came to find you for combat training. Professor Grim wanted to hold an introduction period before the term starts. She hates wasting class time."

Elide groaned. She had hoped the day wouldn't get any worse. Or that she could have rested beforehand, but instead of saying any of that aloud, Elide nodded her head and followed Isadora.

"Lucky you," a novitiate said as they walked out the library doors.

Isadora smiled and glanced at Elide.

"Lucky, why?" Elide signed.

"Well, you and I are sparring partners this term."

Elide nodded.

"You would've been better off with a Kedeh," said Yvette as she bumped Isadora's shoulder and strode past them with three other girls in the hall. "Instead of a Hamle who got held back."

Isadora glared at Yvette's back.

"At least I've covered most of my general ed," Isadora snapped back.

*Held back?* Elide stared at Isadora. She thought they couldn't get held back a year in their studies after leaving Miller.

"It really isn't that bad," Isadora said, drawing her attention. "After my mother died in the war, I failed one term. I'd asked to sit out, but Mother Superior wouldn't let me. She thought it'd be a lesson in *perseverance.*"

"I'm sorry about your mother," Elide signed, and Isadora smiled.

They spent the rest of their walk talking about classes and Yvette's superiority complex being based on a foundation of nepotism. A second-generation Mourner was referred to as a legacy, they were the second in their family to be bid on in a career. Legacies usually were given special consideration when it came to Selection Day, their LAT scores could be lower or even nonexistent. Yvette was a brat who couldn't be bothered to study and should've pursued being a baroness in Prospero. There she could take a baron as a husband and spend her life as a kept woman. Isadora took her time in explaining that while she couldn't stand legacies, she was perfectly fine with people continuing in their family's line of work if it was done fairly. And Isadora could rant all day about nepotism if she wanted, but once they'd passed through a door labeled Classroom A4G and stepped into what Elide assumed was once an atrium, Isadora fell silent.

There were two floors above them, where novitiates were gathered on opposite sides in front of beige-painted walls. On their floor was a large black square that all the students could see, and standing at its center was a frail-looking woman in a black dress. Their instructor, Professor Olga Grim, had a scowl on her face. She was tall with tawny skin and gray eyes. Elide's first thought was that she was the last person anyone in their right mind would cross.

"I'll have no heckling here. You will learn maneuvers in this class that could very well be the difference between life and death outside Prana. Anyone with a particular interest in comedy will be removed from my class and repeat it next term. This is your only warning," Professor Grim said sternly.

Elide and Isadora exchanged a look. Isadora grabbed Elide's arm and began leading her up the stairs.

"And if you are late—" Professor Grim began, and they stopped in place. "Do not make your arrival into a spectacle. Is that clear, Ms. Aimes?"

Isadora faced Professor Grim and said, "Yes, Professor Grim. Elide and I just got a bit turned around."

"Don't let it happen again."

Isadora nodded, and Elide followed her quickly upstairs to the second floor, where the Hamles were gathered around one ledge. Elide noted the eyes on her as they stood there, but when Professor Grim cleared her throat, all eyes went back to her.

Professor Grim started with the sparring rounds, calling forward two Kedeh and two Leta, and Elide wasn't sure which power display was more shocking. The Leta that caused her opponent to shrivel to the ground in pain without moving a muscle or the Kedeh who shut her eyes and attacked the same Leta. The next two hours were a series of endless matches of skill, screams, kicks, and punches.

"Fight without!" Professor Grim demanded, clapping her hands. "Don't use your power! Use your hands and your head! Maybe you want to fail this class?"

Elide became more afraid with every match that passed. A novitiate's nose was broken, and someone else had to wipe up her blood while her partner took her to the academy infirmary. When Professor Grim called her and Isadora's names, she nearly fainted. Isadora held her up and walked her downstairs. By the time they reached the black square, Elide's heart was hammering in her chest.

The two Laska novitiates standing across from them were smirking, and Elide couldn't have felt less ready. Luckily, the girl Elide fought didn't have any more practice than herself, as a few jabs landed, but she didn't use her power on Elide.

Elide was more embarrassed that she didn't know how to use her own power. And when she punched the other girl in the face, she was surprised that it landed. The girl's lip started bleeding. Elide started to apologize . . . but then the world went dark.

## 12

When she woke again, her heart was hammering in her chest, and she was in a large room with different archangels painted on the ceiling. Archangel Michael was the most familiar to her. He healed the sick—or, in her case, wounded. How she was injured remained to be seen. Elide sat up slowly, surveying her surroundings. She was in a bed, and her legs were covered with a white sheet. There were multiple beds with similar bedding throughout the room, and three were blocked by privacy screens. She saw a novitiate having her nose taken care of by a nurse and from the state of her fellow students, she could safely assume that she'd been brought to the academy infirmary.

"Oh, thank God, you're all right," Isadora said, pulling up a chair beside Elide's bed.

"What happened?" Elide signed.

"Marie Fang happened," Isadora said, shaking her head.

"She got an earful from Professor Grim after. I doubt she'll be in our class for the rest of the term. Serves her right! She shouldn't have been using her power in the first place."

"What?" Elide signed.

"Fang was embarrassed," Isadora said, rolling her eyes. "I told you legacies were nothing but trouble. She shouldn't have shocked you. She clearly has no self-control."

Elide stared at her.

"Right—erm, you fainted, or were *knocked out*, so to speak, but no one blames you. Fang broke the rules," Isadora assured.

Elide flushed red. She'd been knocked out. And to think she had been worried about fainting. How's she supposed to live this down? Now Elide wanted to punch something.

"I'll see if Nurse Sharpe will clear you for release," Isadora said. "Marie hit you quite hard, but your face isn't as swollen anymore."

Isadora excused herself and walked to a door at the south end of the room.

Elide sighed and stared up at the ceiling. She didn't feel any pain, and when she looked in the mirror on the bedside table, her face did look swollen—Elide wondered how much more swollen it must've been. *How embarrassing*, she thought. She couldn't remember a time she wanted to disappear more.

By the time Isadora brought the nurse over to examine her, Elide felt a pang of sadness in her heart. She was supposed to be special, but she certainly didn't feel special at the moment.

Nurse Olivia Sharpe was kind and oozed grace like Elide had never seen. From her perfect ginger hair tucked under her white cornette to the way her white gown swept the floor as she walked. She wasn't a Mourner; she was a bridget who had helped deliver babies alongside midwives in her early twenties and was selected by the former Mother Superior to be the matron for the academy infirmary. She was only thirty-one now and had achieved so much in her career—Elide would feel lucky to have as many achievements when she reached thirty.

Nurse Sharpe discharged Elide close to dinner time. But instead of eating in the great hall, Elide returned to her room and bathed rather than brave the stares of her fellow students. The swelling in her face was nearly gone by the time she dressed in her pajamas and ordered room service with the dorm room phone.

Elide sank into the couch and searched the wide selection of movies and series available on the television. *Things are so different here,* she thought, biting her lip. She was overwhelmed by even the smallest decision.

"Want to talk about it?" Starla asked Elide as she sat down beside her on the couch.

Elide shook her head, and Starla frowned.

Starla leaned forward and said, "You know, it's hard for everyone when they first start out. I remember getting knocked flat on my back by Yvette in my first lesson with Professor Grim. But I eventually got her back, and maybe you'll get Marie back."

"How do you know what happened?" Elide signed.

Starla stammered. "Well—" she began nervously.

"The whole academy knows," Pepper said, cutting Starla off. "It's hardly a big deal, they'll probably feel less intimidated by you now."

"Pepper!" Starla snapped, and Pepper shrugged.

Elide groaned aloud.

"It isn't too bad," Pepper said softly. She was trying to be reassuring, but Elide didn't want her pity either.

Elide wanted to go to sleep and put today behind her. But only after she ate, so she could stop the hunger pangs in her stomach. She'd worked up quite the appetite.

An hour passed, but her food hadn't arrived. Elide could feel the pit in her stomach growing and drank a glass of water to hold herself over. Starla and Pepper had chosen a romantic movie for the three of them to watch about a woman caught in a love triangle between her best friend and a new man—it was one of Starla's favorites. And as much as she loved romantic movies, Elide planned on excusing herself after she got her food. She couldn't imagine staying up any later, even for a movie.

Then someone knocked on their dorm suite's door, and Elide's heart leapt in her chest, but it dropped again when she opened the door. A tall, brutish-looking Disciple stood in the doorway, towering over her like a shadow. His uniform was more informal but still black, and the golden badge he wore bore the Apostate's symbol.

"The Apostate has summoned you," the Disciple said.

Elide hesitated and turned to look back at Starla.

She looked amused. "Well, you're certainly not the food runner," Starla said, taunting the Disciple.

The Disciple glared at Starla, and she smirked.

Then he looked back at Elide. "You need to come with me."

"Don't you think it's a bit late?" Starla said as she approached the door and stood beside Elide. "I mean, we should really be going to bed soon. Shouldn't we?" she said, looking at Elide for a response.

Elide could see that the Disciple's patience was wearing thin, and she got the feeling Starla could sense it too. Although, her friend didn't seem to have any intention of leaving her side.

"All right, I'll come with you," Elide signed to the Disciple.

The Disciple's face contorted as though he were confused by her statement, but then his face returned to normal.

"Really? At this time of night—"

"Honestly, Starla, knock it off," Pepper groaned, interrupting Starla. "Just let the man do his job."

Starla scowled at the Disciple but remained silent.

"Come," the Disciple said to Elide.

Elide stepped out the door. Clearly, her night was going to get much worse. What could the Apostate want to speak to her about? Had Calliope told him that she couldn't call on her power? Of how quickly she'd failed?

Or perhaps her failure in Professor Grim's class had reached his ears.

The novitiates they passed as they left the dormitories were whispering about her. Elide didn't have to be a scholar to know that.

The Disciple didn't speak to Elide unless it was to give her an order as though she was a dog, and perhaps she was in his eyes. Elide followed him down a hallway with portraits of different families on the walls. They wore dark attire and held stern expressions. The older black-and-white portraits, she noted apprehensively, had men with missing limbs.

When they reached the end of the hall, the Disciple led Elide through a door with doorknobs embellished with the Apostate's symbol. Her fears nearly evaporated as they stepped into the room. She had only read about privy chambers in books she'd purchased from secondhand shops in Baptiste. A chandelier hung from the ceiling, illuminating the room from end to end. It was a much larger room than she was accustomed to. There were tapestries covering the walls and a stone fireplace with a roaring fire. The room itself was warmer than the hallway but not sweltering. Above the fireplace was a large map of Scopus, unlike any she'd ever seen. Elide stopped beside a tapestry of a woman, man, and child standing in a garden and stared up into the woman's emerald eyes and if she didn't know better, she would've sworn the woman was alive.

"Lysandra Norwood, wife of Rudolphus," a voice said from across the room.

Elide looked at the speaker and was nearly taken aback. He *almost* looked normal.

He'd traded his formal attire for a black turtleneck sweater with a velvet blazer and matching pants. But remained the most intimidating person in the room.

"She's one of my ancestors," the Apostate finished, as if they were the most important words he'd ever spoken in his life.

Then he took a seat at a table with three domed platters on it.

Elide looked back at the tapestry and noticed an equally intimidating man beside Lysandra. *Rudolphus, I take it,* she thought.

The Apostate laughed to himself. "Please, join me." He gestured to a chair across from him.

She looked to the Disciple, but he didn't look at her. Instead, he stared at their host as if acknowledging her presence would somehow insult his leader.

"That will be all, Altair," the Apostate said.

The Disciple bowed to him and walked out the door, shutting it behind him. And somehow, Elide felt more afraid after he left.

Her stomach growled and, betraying her better judgment, she walked over to the table and sat down. If this was her final meal, at least it would be better than what she'd ordered from room service.

"I heard you took some lessons today. How were they?"

Elide nodded. "They were all right," Elide signed.

"Hmmm," he said as he removed the cover from a platter. "It's normal to struggle when you first arrive."

She stared at the lamb on the platter, and the Apostate smiled slightly and put some on her plate. Elide blushed.

"Sorry," she signed.

"It's quite all right," he responded, dishing some onto his plate as well. "I'm sure you must be hungry after today. I understand, you know. It's more complicated when you've grown up elsewhere."

Elide nodded. She didn't want to admit how much she'd felt out of place in Prana, so instead she changed the subject. "Are you really a Mancio?" Elide signed.

She hoped changing the subject would make it easier to avoid talking about her day. Or at least give her time to convince him not to punish her.

"Yes, it's in my genes, I'm afraid," he answered. "My father was one, as was his father. It never matters whether the woman carries the gene, though I've heard the survival rate is higher. But I suppose that's why Outlanders don't try to have Mancios themselves." The Apostate turned to her then and smiled softly, as if he realized he hadn't said something. "My mother passed bringing me into this world while my father was in the war room making plans with his men. All the blessings in the good book couldn't save her. My great-great-grandfather proposed that the first of our title was a child of the devil himself. And God punishes the women with death and the men with war." He dished asparagus onto her plate and passed it to her. When Elide took it, he looked more serious. "It was a Teller that caused the stalemate of the Civil War, Elide. And a Teller will end this one."

Elide hesitated. "I'm sorry about your mother," she signed, and the Apostate smiled.

Elide grabbed her fork and started eating. She sighed when the meat hit her tongue, it was by far the best lamb she'd ever tasted. The Apostate didn't speak again until they both had finished their meal.

"Feeling better?" the Apostate asked.

Elide smiled and nodded.

"All right, follow me," he said.

She gulped, and a nagging feeling entered her stomach. But she followed him out of the room and down a different hallway with no windows, until he stopped in the center.

"Altair will take you back to the dormitories, and you'll be able to get a full night's rest for lessons tomorrow."

"You're not upset?" Elide signed. "You only had me brought down here to eat with you?"

A strange look came over the Apostate's face. "Yes, I invited you for a civil conversation over dinner. What would I be upset about?"

Elide took a deep breath and nodded slowly. "I had thought that you'd heard about my lessons and were—" she signed then hesitated, "going to have me expelled."

That was a lie. She'd thought he was going to have her killed or, if he was feeling generous, have her sent to a labor camp. She didn't need anyone to tell her that if she couldn't call on her power, she was useless.

He scoffed. "I have no intention of harming you, Elide. Your training is just starting. I don't expect perfection."

Elide stared at him.

"Are you reading my mind?" Elide signed.

"Not reading, *listening*. People are often louder when they're afraid."

"And why shouldn't I be?" Elide signed. "I was assaulted by someone I've known my entire life. Then I was taken from Baptiste, from my *home*, and tossed in the back of a carriage without any explanation. And then Outlanders tried to kill me—and you. *You* have every soldier in Prana at your disposal. All you have to do is snap your fingers, and I'm dead. I have every right to be afraid."

The Apostate stood silently, observing her, and Elide felt her heart skip a beat. She couldn't believe she'd told him that. How could she tell him that? But then he laughed, and a smile spread on his face. "Understandable."

Elide stared at him nervously.

"Altair, make sure she's returned safely to the dorms," the Apostate said, looking past her.

When Elide turned and saw a statue move, she nearly screamed. Altair stood a few feet behind her and bowed to the Apostate.

The Apostate gestured toward her escort and said, "Good night, Elide."

"Good night," Elide signed back.

She followed Altair through the hallway and only dared to look back once, but by then, the Apostate was gone.

# 13

When Monday morning came, Elide stared at the ceiling for ten minutes before forcing herself to get up and putting on her uniform again. Failing again. And aching and moaning the next day. Luckily, she only had combat training twice a week on Mondays and Wednesdays. Her other two classes were easier, and the professors were excited to introduce their subjects and the lighter coursework that came with them. That convinced Elide that someone somewhere was having mercy on her. She was good at keeping up with her assignments at Miller. She knew how to keep her work organized, but the problem was she couldn't imagine how she would manage Secular Evocation 1. There was nothing in the textbook that explained how to call on her power. At least in the first three chapters. She wasn't a mute student in Baptiste anymore, and who would she be if she couldn't become a Mourner, a martyr?

She could still hear the certainty in the Apostate's

voice on Sunday night. *It was a Teller that caused the stalemate of the Civil War. And a Teller will end this one.* Hansel was the only other man she'd ever heard sound that confident in his words. As a mart, it was his responsibility to sound sure as Baptiste's leader. He had to soothe frightened mothers sending their sons as Enochs or Seekers or their daughters as Scouts to war. He had to appease angry merchants and bawds when sickness or crime depleted their wealth. But the Apostate, he led the marts and the reverend elders. He was wise, and he believed Elide would end the war. And if she did, no mother, father, or child would have to fear the Outlanders striking again.

But as the minutes ticked down to the start of her Secular Evocation 1 class, Elide couldn't have thought of a more ridiculous claim.

The classroom wasn't particularly large. It had three rows and six desks per row, with each desk fitting two students at it. Elide hoped to see a familiar face among them and was relieved when Isadora sat down beside her. Elide saw Yvette take a seat on the other side of the room beside one of her cronies, and Elide nearly snorted. To think she'd been mocking Isadora about retaking beginner's courses.

"Not so high and mighty now, is she," Isadora whispered to Elide with a smile. "Maybe she got lost and needs directions."

Elide laughed.

Then the classroom door opened and slammed into the wall. A tall, brown-haired man in a gray blazer and matching trousers walked to the front of the room and wrote his name on the whiteboard. He had very sharp, angular features complemented by the beard on his face. He was handsome, and that nearly distracted Elide from the angry-looking golden raven embroidered on his blazer's breast pocket. Professor Daegal Murik was a Disciple. Just what she needed—a man who could immediately report her failure to the Apostate.

The other novitiates were practically drooling over him. Under different circumstances, she would have too, but at the moment, she was preoccupied with giving herself a pep talk. *We just have to make it through this class,* she thought, *and the thirteen other weeks in the semester.*

Elide took a deep breath.

"I am Daegal Murik, and I am substituting for my wife for the time being," he said, surveying the room. "Secular Evocation is a complicated task for any telepath, but one that I am well versed in as I am a Mancio myself."

Elide had to restrain a gasp. Though other novitiates suddenly had an array of questions. How old is he? Is he related to the Apostate? How do they know he isn't lying? Elide would've expected the questions to annoy their substitute professor. But, on the contrary, Professor Murik didn't mind. In fact, he seemed to revel in the attention he was receiving from the young women in the class and the questions that came with it.

"Yes, it is all very exciting," Daegal said, taking papers from a briefcase on the desk beside him. "We're going to start off with a quiz on your reading. No reason to panic unless you haven't read."

A few of the other novitiates groaned, but luckily Elide had woken up early and done the reading. She had originally hoped the Mourners' powers were simply mind games or parlor tricks. Unfortunately, when she considered her very real experience with Calliope inside her head and the basic definition of evocation, the only answer was telepathy.

Calliope hadn't drugged her. She used an advanced form of evocation that even highly trained telepaths struggle with, and she accessed a memory inside Elide that she hadn't known she had. Most Mourner weapons were intangible. Tangible weapons like daggers and poisons were reserved for those with a "tactile disadvantage." And chapter two named two orders that had one. Weapons training was marked as a *necessity* for Laska and Mirai, but Mirai were more respected among the Mourners. They were the first found among southern slaves, and it only got more complicated from there. Every battle won during the Civil War wasn't linked to luck but to the skill of Mirais, who could foretell the future and discovered the first Teller. *Ethical Enchantment* referenced the moment in time as "a slave master having reaped what he sowed in the land and received a gift from his property." That *property* was Eliza Cross, a woman with an affinity for creating an illusion of pain on those who were lying. Or, as expressed by a Confederate soldier's letter, *killing bluebellies*, Union soldiers.

They used her in torture sessions. The thought of torturing anyone made Elide feel sick to her stomach. The fact that she could somehow trick someone's mind into believing they were in pain or even cause death was terrifying. Historians described a Teller's power as *"simply marvelous."* Elide couldn't disagree more.

Some days she wondered what God thought of her; today, she knew. Elide sat on the grass in front of the Kedeh building, writing a letter to Hansel. She had failed another session with Calliope, and though her mentor didn't say it, Calliope had looked disappointed. Elide wasn't trying to fail, but she was overwhelmed and missed her brother.

"Perhaps you should write to him. A heavy heart can make any practice more difficult," Calliope told her. "And remember to practice those exercises before our next meeting."

Calliope had given her a few postage stamps and instructed Elide to hand the post to an Enoch trainee named Aidan, who was practicing his riding and running. She almost felt bad for him, but considering his combat training wouldn't begin until spring, she envied him.

He didn't have an instructor telling him to meditate or stand in poses that were supposed to help him find balance. Both literally and metaphorically. He could come and go from the academy as he pleased. Elide was blocked by two burly Disciples when she'd gotten *too* close to the academy's entrance. And what did they think she was going to do? Steal a carriage? Where would she go?

She was writing down all her complaints in the letter to her brother and asking him to visit her. Marts had some power, so he could at least put in a request. Elide didn't want Hansel to know that she was afraid. She'd been scared all her life. Though she didn't avoid *all* of her fears, she started small by telling him that she wasn't going to practice any poses on the lawns like the Mirai did but would be comfortable practicing them in her room. And then came the darker fears of what she was and who she might become. Or, in this case, who Eliza Cross became. And if God had planned for her to be a female soldier that tortured and murdered, why would he choose her to defy His law?

Elide sealed the envelope and ran to hand Aidan the letter. The moment he took it out of her hands, Elide found herself hoping that Hansel would have the answers.

# 14

Days passed, and time and time again, she would walk to Kedeh Tower to visit the mailroom. All incoming and outgoing mail went through there. The second years outside the tower didn't mind other novitiates coming and going, in fact, most of them would stop studying to speak with them and were even kind to those who weren't Kedeh. The reception room sported shades of silver and white. There were window seats with stuffed gray cushions and armchairs spaced throughout the room. Thick silver throws were tossed over novitiates' legs as they sat together, gossiping and giggling over the Enochs guarding the room. They were flush to the wall like statues, changing guard every few hours.

A Mourner named Glinda Briar managed the mailroom. She had a hooked nose, sallow skin, and a permanent scowl on her face that aged her by the day.

"No letters for you today, girl!" Glinda spat out as though Elide were interrupting her busy day. Then Glinda returned to reading the herbology book on her desk and occasionally glared at Elide as if she was overstaying her welcome.

But every afternoon when Elide arrived, the Kedeh were quick to invite her to join them. And she was running out of excuses not to. Elide often overheard them planning trips to Westerby, a little village in Prana that, according to Isadora, had the best sweet shop in Texas. And like her peers, she was ready for Adoann and the two-week break from the academy that came with it. It was her second favorite holiday after Christmas. She and Hansel always made wreaths for Adoann, and this would be the first time she would spend it without him. She was trying to adjust, but her brother never left her thoughts. Elide paid attention in classes and passed quizzes but kept failing in combat training, which bothered her most of all.

As she walked back to the great hall, Elide was beginning to think that all her training was in vain. And the only person she wanted to talk to about it wasn't writing her back.

As she stepped into the great hall, she crashed into another person.

"Watch it, half-breed," a harsh voice snapped.

Elide glared at the girl. Her hair was different, but her attitude hadn't changed.

Ayla had freed her black hair from the bun, and it was a mass of waves complemented by the fringe that stopped above her piercing gray eyes. She wore a long gray coat that cinched at her waist and had the Leta symbol embroidered on it. She was beautiful and pleased with Elide's reaction to her words.

"Heard you've been failing," she said with a smug smile.

Elide stiffened. Ayla's smile got bigger.

"I told them they shouldn't expect much," Ayla said with a shrug. "You need to watch where you're going. I'm sure I'll see you later." And with that, she waltzed by Elide and said her hellos to the Enoch, flirting with a few Disciples on the way.

Elide got to her feet and dusted herself off. And after she took a deep breath, she joined her friends in the great hall. Isadora looked at her as she sat down.

"What happened?" Isadora asked.

"Ayla," Elide signed.

Starla rolled her eyes. "Ugh, I can't stand her. She never stops talking about herself. 'The Apostate is having me do this. *Oh* the Apostate sent for me, and that's why I'm late.' *Honestly*, it's so annoying. She never shuts up about him," Starla said.

"Well, you can hardly blame her. Have you looked at him?" Isadora said, drinking from her cup.

Starla smiled and shrugged. "When you're right, you're right." Starla laughed. She looked over at the professor's table at the head of the great hall. "Do you think it's a Mancio thing?"

Elide looked up and had to stifle a laugh as she saw Daegal whispering something to a Disciple who'd come up to him.

"Genetically predisposed hotness," Isadora whispered, a smile playing on her lips. "I'll have to look it up."

Starla tossed a french fry at her, and the three laughed. They ducked their heads when the Laska table looked over at them, quieting down as best they could.

"Okay, but seriously, Elide. If Ayla is messing with you, you can always tell someone. I mean, it's not as though they'd ignore it. The last thing they'd want is to upset the only Teller," Starla whispered, glancing at the Leta table as if she was worried they'd hear.

"No," Elide signed. "I don't want any special treatment."

"Well, what happened exactly?" Isadora asked, leaning in.

Elide looked between her friends.

"She called me a half-breed," Elide signed.

Isadora scoffed. "*Fucking* legacies—"

"*Isadora,*" Starla warned, looking around the room again. "You know better than to use that language here. You'll get kicked out." Isadora rolled her eyes. Then Starla turned to Elide. "Ayla can get in trouble for saying that too. It's racist, and she clearly needs to learn to be civilized."

"She wouldn't be kicked out?" Elide signed.

Her friends exchanged a look.

Starla hesitated. "Well, *no,*" muttered Starla. "She's in the Apostate's service. At most, she would get a warning, or be sent to be retaught for a few weeks. But he wouldn't send her away permanently."

"They were hand-picked for a reason. He only wants the best, and Ayla is arguably the brightest Leta of our generation, so she gets special treatment along with the rest, like Daegal over there," added Isadora.

Elide looked back up at Daegal. He was looking around the great hall, paying particularly close attention to the Laska table with a grimace on his face. And as if he knew she was staring, Daegal turned and looked at her, his eyes cold and distant.

After they finished eating, they roamed the halls, passing painting after painting, each with a story that Isadora knew by heart because she had taken an elective course about the academy's history and artifacts. She'd received a high mark in it and was taking an elective on genetics this year.

When they were out of the academy and onto the quadrangle's lawns, Elide overheard Ayla speaking to a group of novitiates all about her missions. How her heart went out to the border towns that they'd brought rations and medical attention to, the Outlanders they'd had to interrogate, and the harlots they'd delivered to bawds. She glanced at Elide when she mentioned "the harlots" and began whispering feverishly about a woman named "Juliette." Elide's heart lurched at the thought of Juliette. *Great, she's talking about Hansel,* Elide thought.

Elide did everything in her power to ignore Ayla. Elide was trying to focus on what her friends were talking about, but it seemed like Ayla got louder as if she wanted Elide to hear.

"I swear, it's like she has nothing better to do," Isadora said, gesturing toward Ayla.

"Just ignore them, she'll get bored eventually," Starla stated. "Anyway, back to my Disciple crisis. Do you think Calvin or Abel would suit me more? Calvin has always been rather sweet, and I quite like men with broad shoulders, but Abel just has this way about him, you know?"

"You mean that he's more brawn than brain?" Isadora said, and Starla scoffed. "Calvin has always been smarter, and he's strong too—if that's what you're looking for. Maybe you can dance with him at the festival?"

Starla sighed. "I would, but I'm not sure if he has a shift that night. You know, they've got more guards now because—" Starla stopped and smiled at Elide nervously. "*Sorry.*"

"It's all right," Elide signed.

"What Starla means to say is that you're important, and we can't risk you missing out on Pretty Pixie's Sweets and Treats, and that's why there's extra security," Isadora said.

"Because the Outlanders might try to kill me," Elide signed.

"But we won't let that happen," Isadora said.

A high laugh broke through their conversation. Ayla stood near them on the lawn with two copper-haired novitiates with pursed lips and freckled faces flanking her sides. Elide faintly remembered them from her combat training class. And some Laska and Leta seemed to have stopped their own conversations and began watching them.

"You can't seriously think that either of you could handle an Outlander," Ayla said with a smile.

"How hard can it be? You fight them," Isadora said.

Elide looked between the two of them. She wasn't sure what Ayla's problem with her was, but her blood was boiling.

Elide got to her feet and her friends did the same.

Ayla laughed in Elide's face. "Are you threatening me, little girl?"

The twins flanking her sides seemed like they were waiting for Ayla's permission to strike.

When Ayla's first jab hit Elide's stomach, they knew they had it. Elide stumbled backward and was surprised she kept her footing. She breathed as deeply as she could manage before Ayla struck again. This time aiming for her jaw, but Elide dodged it, and it passed through the air.

Ayla took a moment to recover, and Elide used that to her advantage and swung at Ayla. But she was faster and moved out of the way in the nick of time.

She heard a novitiate cheer from somewhere but only saw her friends fighting the twins out of the corner of her eye. Isadora was rolling around fighting with one twin in the grass. Starla was farther away, punching the other.

Looking away from her opponent proved fatal. A fist struck Elide's jaw, and she went down. But it wasn't over. Ayla kicked her in the stomach when she tried to get up, and Elide coughed. Ayla backed off for a moment and smiled smugly. Elide got back up and shook it off.

The moment she was up, her opponent didn't hesitate to press forward and attack again. But Elide blocked it.

Then she grabbed Ayla's other arm and felt as though fire was rushing through her veins, spreading through her fingertips, and suddenly Ayla cried out and collapsed to the ground.

The spectators paused, and there was a moment filled with horrifying silence. But slowly, Ayla recovered and sat up, holding her arm in her other hand. The other novitiates cheered and whooped as Elide stared at her hand and then at Ayla, shocked at what she'd done. But before she could process it, Ayla held out her hand in a claw-like shape. And Elide felt her heart lurch in her chest as her body became colder, and she collapsed onto the wet grass. Her heart began beating slower, and soon she was gasping for air as the blades of grass poked her cheek.

"Ayla!" a male voice shouted at a distance.

"Help," Elide tried to mouth.

She could hear someone calling her name. But before Elide could register whose voice it was, darkness closed in on her.

Elide heard someone sigh as she woke. Starla sat at her bedside, grinning from ear to ear. Isadora was in the hospital bed next to her, sitting up with a sling on her left arm.

"Thank God you're all right!" Starla exclaimed. "I was so worried that you were going to go into a coma or something. Do you remember what happened?"

Elide lifted her hands, and though she felt sore, she

signed, "I remember fighting, and then everything went dark."

"Ayla tried to kill you," Isadora said, adjusting herself on the hospital bed.

Starla nodded and added, "Yeah, like three Disciples had to restrain her. Pepper told me that Altair took her to see the Apostate and Mother Superior, and neither of them were happy to see her. You could hear her sobbing on her way back to her room after."

"Serves her right," Isadora said plainly. "It's about time she got in trouble for something."

Elide nodded. She felt as though she was trying to catch her breath, but she couldn't.

"How did she—" Elide started to sign but stopped, realizing it was a stupid question. Letas could learn to control blood if *bloodwork* was their specialization. It helped them heal others, but she'd never thought about how it could kill someone. Elide shuddered.

"At least we only got detention," Isadora said with a yawn. "Three weeks of detention and then break. Not a bad deal."

"Speak for yourself," Starla said, pouting. "I finally get to tell Calvin that I choose him, and now we won't even get to start planning our commitment ceremony until after break."

Isadora laughed and shook her head. "Come on, you know it was worth it. Ayla's finally been knocked off her high horse and brought back down here with the rest of us," Isadora said.

"What do you mean?" Elide signed.

"Well, she's always been the favorite, but you're a Teller. She's just another ambitious Leta. Ayla might've had the limelight for a little while, but now she's *barely above average*. And, of course, *ridiculously* jealous of you," Starla said with a giggle.

Elide stared at her.

"Jealous of what?" Elide signed.

"You have the Apostate's favor," Isadora answered, flexing her shoulders and trying to relax in the bed. "And she can't beat you in a fight. She's *beneath* you."

Elide considered her words. The thought of anyone being beneath her had never once crossed her mind. Not even when she wanted to be a baroness or a lina. And if Ayla was envious, who's to say that there weren't other novitiates that felt the same? Her friends had fought alongside her, but she hardly wanted to get into any more fights with her peers.

"Can we talk about something else?" Elide signed.

Starla's eyes lit up. "We can talk about my Hera appointment at Heaven's Door!" squealed Starla.

A Leta nurse shushed her from the other side of the room, and the moment the woman turned her back, Starla stuck her tongue out at her. They laughed, and in time Starla was talking about her appointment. Hera appointments were named after the goddess of marriage in Greek mythology. Women made them for commitment ceremonies and selected dresses at the store. Starla went on and on about Heaven's Door—located in Westerby in

Prana—being high-end and extremely selective of who they allowed in. There were several dresses she wanted to try, in different styles, that she hoped would be easy for Calvin to remove before taking her virginity. Starla wanted to get the "messy part" out of the way before their wedding ceremony at the end of the school year. She was also worried about pregnancy and planned on finding contraceptives in Westerby.

After an hour of discussing the appointment, the nurse shooed her away and demanded that Elide and Isadora get some rest.

Elide tossed and turned for a while but couldn't manage to get any sleep. She stopped trying after her seventh time flipping over her pillow.

By that time, Isadora was fast asleep, and all Elide could do was stare up at the ceiling. She sat that way, practicing deep breathing as she did in Calliope's lessons, hoping it would help her relax. But all Elide could think about was the fight. She should have lost. Of what she had retained from her training sessions, she shouldn't have beaten Ayla. Ayla had to have a few more years of experience than her, and Elide had never beaten anyone in a fight before. What was different about today?

Elide looked at her hand. How had she called on her power? Why did it choose that moment to help her? And why couldn't she use it now?

On the opposite side of the room, an owl landed on the window. And perhaps Elide imagined it, but she swore it was staring at her, looking directly into her soul, and at the same time, she felt something inside her humming. The feeling was small, but it was there. Elide wanted to belong in this academy, and if she could find a way to harness her power, to make it obey her, maybe she would.

# 15

Elide spent the rest of the weekend in the infirmary. On Monday, she attended classes as usual and showered at the end of a long day. But instead of staying in and talking about Westerby with her friends, she went to the library. She hoped that studying would ease her mind in some way. But reading old theory books wasn't doing her any good. Every morning she checked with Aiden for her mail, and every day she was met with disappointment.

She had thought about writing a letter to Fiona, but her stomach tied in knots every time she'd started writing it. *Would she respond,* Elide wondered. She found Fiona's wedding announcement in a newspaper someone abandoned on a carrel desk. The paragraph itself was in a corner column dedicated to Baptiste. Elide's heart panged with sadness. Fiona had moved on, and Elide could only guess about the new friendships and obligations in her life as a baroness. But she was happy for Fiona, thankful she wasn't working under a bawd, paying off some undisclosed amount of debt with her body in Whitehill or some other city in Texas. *It's nice to see a friendly face, even if that face is in black-and-white,* Elide thought silently.

She tossed the newspaper to the side and stared at the book underneath it. Whoever had been there before her had been researching family trees, and if she had to guess from the notes beside it, they'd been tracing their bloodline. And whoever Morgan Rathmore was, she was a third-generation Mourner.

Elide laughed and shook her head. *Probably a legacy thing,* she thought.

But when she saw a familiar surname in the tree, her heart dropped, and she turned to another family. The Shelley family had names listed in the margins with portraits but without birthdates for descendants born in the last few decades, which stopped at four children: Jorah, Erik, Abram, and Marianne—her mother. Her mother was much younger in the portrait, but it was her. Her hair was straightened and past her shoulders, and she had a smile on her slender brown face. Elide had never met any of her uncles as they had all emigrated to the Outlands, but according to the book, they were Mancio. Someone had amended Erik and Abram to note that they were deceased and childless; Jorah, however, was alive and had several children. *But never bothered to contact his niece or nephew,* Elide thought. Elide nearly slammed the book shut until she noticed that underneath her mother's name was the word *Kedeh*. Her heart lurched in her chest.

*I'm a legacy,* Elide thought. How could she be a

legacy? Hansel had never mentioned their mother being a Mourner.

But there it was written in cursive, and she bookmarked the page and took the book with her. When Elide reached the hall, she began walking faster, taking large strides, and only nodded at a few novitiates who greeted her as she passed them. And before she knew it, she had broken into a run.

Her hands were shaking. Elide lay on her bed, head hanging off the edge, staring at the open book on her desk. She hoped against hope that the words would somehow evaporate from the page, and for a few moments, she'd even hoped she'd misread it.

Her mother couldn't have been a Mourner. She couldn't be second-generation. Not if she wanted to believe that her brother had told her everything about their mother, not if Hansel were telling the truth.

Could that be it? Marianne had died when they were children. Elide's memories of her were fragments. It was never clear how young she was or where they were. Hansel had shared all the warm memories he had of Marianne with her, as if he were trying to keep her alive. And maybe Hansel hadn't thought it was important. *Or maybe he didn't even know, and you're assuming the worst of him,* Elide chided herself.

A knock came from her bedroom door, though it was open, and she wanted to be left alone tonight.

"Don't ignore me, Elide!" Starla demanded. "It's rude."

Elide glanced at her but didn't respond.

"Pepper said you came in upset, and you barely looked at her," Starla said, stepping into the room. "Not that the two of you interact much."

Starla looked herself over in the bedroom mirror and grimaced.

"This nightgown makes me look ghastly," Starla said, shaking her head at her reflection.

Elide sighed.

"I'm not leaving until you tell me what's wrong," Starla said, crossing her arms.

Elide looked at her and tried to think of a lie but decided against it.

"My mother, Marianne, was a Kedeh," Elide signed, gesturing toward the book on her desk.

Starla gaped and walked over to the desk. For a few moments, she was silent as she inspected the Shelley family tree.

Then Starla snorted.

"Of course, they can choose a woman's suitor, but they can't be bothered to write down her children's names . . . or their father. That's strange," Starla said, shook her head at the book, and then looked at Elide sympathetically. "Why didn't you tell me?" she said softly. "I mean, I understand Isadora—she has problems with just about every legacy she meets, but it's literally in your blood. It's a part of you, and you're my friend."

Elide sat up and signed, "I didn't know. Hansel might not have even known. He only ever talked about how she was smart and caring and beautiful. We were kids when she died."

"Well, I suppose his memory might be spotty then," Starla said. "What about your father? Didn't he tell you anything?"

*He was too busy drinking,* Elide thought but didn't say. *Whatever memories he had were drowned by whiskey and malice.* Elide shook her head.

"That's rather strange, isn't it?" Starla said, sighing and rolling her eyes. "And, of course, you find out now. Right when you're meant to be enjoying your new life. I swear I can't stand it. I don't know why things like this happen, but they do. But I'm sure there's some reason for it. You know, *God's plan* and all."

Elide laid her head down on her pillow. She hated when people wrote things off like that. It was the same excuse the doctor had used when they realized she wouldn't speak again. *How could this be His plan for me?* Elide thought as she stared up at the ceiling.

"If you need anything, you know where I am," Starla said softly.

After Starla left, Elide found herself wishing that she would never leave her room again. The day had gone from bad to worse in a matter of minutes. She couldn't sleep. Tomorrow she would meet with Calliope and hope her power would come when she called it.

She had enough to deal with now that she was well enough to sit in detention. But the reason for her getting detention felt worse now than it had before. Elide had never pictured herself as a troublemaker. And she was sure the Apostate hadn't reacted positively to the news that she was fighting. She was the only Teller, after all. She's supposed to be the solution to Scopus's problems, not create more of them.

If that didn't make Calliope lecture her, Elide wasn't sure what would. And maybe she needed a good old-fashioned lecture. Someone had to be the voice of reason.

The next morning, Elide felt surprisingly well rested. Pepper was sitting in the living room when she entered. She glanced at Elide as her eyes scanned a letter in her hand while her breakfast heated on the stove. Elide reached the kitchen and was pouring herself some cereal when Starla cleared her throat. She turned and noticed Starla gesturing toward her while looking at Pepper.

Pepper sighed.

"Your brother is in Carden," Pepper told Elide. "Starla thought you should know."

Elide's heart sank.

"How do you know that?" Elide signed.

"My cousin's regiment is stationed there, and the marts came to talk about recruiting more troops and raising taxes for the war effort," Pepper said matter-of-factly. "You don't need to worry though. They're far from the action."

Elide winced and wanted to run from the room. How could he not write back?

"I'm sure he wants to write," Starla said quickly. "He's probably just distracted. This war has everyone in a fritz nowadays, but Scopus has something the North doesn't —*us*. Well, not us, I suppose—we're still in training, but the Mourners. They're the best of the best and nearly won it last time."

"Ugh . . . I've heard enough about the Civil War, Starla," Pepper groaned. "I have a test on Wednesday and don't want to think about history any more than I have to."

Starla and Pepper continued to argue, and Elide ate her breakfast in silence.

After getting through her classes while overhearing gossip about herself, she was almost relieved to be going to see Calliope. Though, the walk to her mentor's classroom felt longer this evening. And perhaps that had to do with her wanting to disappear. Apart from a few hellos and congratulations from the other novitiates she passed, she almost felt unwelcome. Ayla's cronies—the twins—were on a warpath now that their leader had been asked to temporarily vacate the academy due to a certain Teller.

Elide noticed the first snow of the season gathering on a windowsill as she walked up the stairs to the classroom. There were Enochs having a snowball fight with a few novitiates outside, and she almost wished she could join them. But she knew what her duties were. As she reached the door, she heard raised voices. Elide thought about turning around and coming back later. But going against her better instincts, she knocked, and the voices stopped. Elide grabbed the doorknob and entered the room. The Apostate was surveying the jarred specimen on Calliope's shelves and smiled at Elide when she entered.

"You look well, Elide," the Apostate said. He picked up a book from a chair and opened it.

"Thank you," Elide signed.

"Had you expected her to have taken ill?" Calliope said harshly. "You'll have to leave. She and I will be quite busy this afternoon."

The Apostate laughed and said, "*Relax*, I'm only checking in after Friday's events."

Calliope scoffed. "There's no need for you to. She erred, and it won't happen again."

The Apostate looked at Elide and ran a hand over his beard. His eyes were soft, and she had an inkling there was something he wasn't saying, and then he looked back at Calliope.

"I'm sure your mentor is training you to the best of her ability," he said lowly.

"Don't speak as though I'm not in the room!" Calliope snapped. Her eyes grew darker, filling with an inky black. "I have lived and taught for *centuries*. These things take time. And I've managed to teach the unteachable time and time again."

"And even at your age, you can err," he said sharply, with a tone of warning.

Calliope's eyes narrowed. But they returned to normal. Elide gulped as she stared at the two. She began wondering if her mentor thought she was unteachable, that she wouldn't become the Teller they desperately needed. She even thought about excusing herself from the classroom to eat with her friends in the great hall. Surely, they would want to finish this conversation in private.

"Our *noble leader* believes that I should use alchemy to accelerate your training," Calliope said. "How does that sound to you, Elide?"

Elide bit her lip as though it were possible to hold back her expression. She had barely begun drinking alcohol and couldn't imagine what type of potion Calliope might whip up. But if it could help, she would be able to save thousands, possibly millions. And suddenly Elide felt hopeful. This was their chance! She would take anything. Why was Calliope so opposed? A Teller hadn't been found in years, and Elide was struggling to call on her power on her own. She had probably drank worse medicines growing up in Baptiste, so why should something as small as drinking a potion stand in her way? Never mind what it might taste like.

"Honestly, I wouldn't mind," Elide signed.

Calliope snorted.

The Apostate ignored her and turned his attention to Elide. "Have you ever heard of marrowroot?"

"I've already told you that it's too dangerous. Amplifying any telepaths given power can do more harm than good," Calliope snapped. "If she can't manage without it then she can't manage at all."

"She can manage. Don't be so narrow-minded," the Apostate said, glaring at Calliope, and then he returned to his usual demeanor. "Come, let us leave your mentor to figure out her priorities," he said as he took a book from a nearby bookshelf. He gestured for Elide to follow him.

She followed him out of the classroom and nearly

tripped down the stairs, but the Apostate caught her by her waist and steadied her.

"Careful," he said lowly with a soft smile on his lips, and Elide felt herself blush.

She steadied herself and mouthed an apology.

"No harm done," the Apostate said, though his hands lingered for a moment before releasing her.

He gestured for her to follow him, and they made their way through the halls, eventually reaching an enclosed bridge. It was her first time on this side of the academy. They crossed the first half of the bridge in silence, Elide looking out the wide windows to see the carriages traveling on the same interstate trail they'd arrived on and the Apostate flipping through the herbology book in his hands. There were no other novitiates present on the bridge, but there were Disciples heading in the opposite direction.

"Marrowroot can be a difficult herb to find," the Apostate suddenly said. He showed her the book. "I would assume one of your professors may have mentioned it."

Elide looked into the book at the drawing of the bulb-shaped plant, faintly remembering it from one of Daegal's lessons. "They look like peony buds, but they never bloom. Professor Murik called them a Rapha's best friend—extremely tricky to find and lethal to your enemies if used correctly," Elide signed.

"Lethal, if used for *dark arts*," he corrected. "But when used to save our allies on the battlefield, there is nothing that creates more hope as something so powerful."

"Is there somewhere we're going right now?"

"I'm afraid not. Apostates before me felt it was necessary to remove the herb from our storeroom lest some misguided student or professor use it for deadly purposes."

Elide felt a chill snake down her spine. Knowing how Daegal had described its effects—victims thrashing, convulsing, and eventually turning a surreal shade of blue—she wondered what would possess someone to poison another person with it. She would hardly think a bad grade would drive someone to murder.

"Where are we going?" Elide signed.

"Thanatos Institute," he answered. "Possibly the safest place in Scopus."

Elide nodded. Then she had to restrain a shudder as she saw the large black doors ahead of them, carved with elaborate spirals and swirls, with a large raven in the center.

He opened the door for her, and while it was gentlemanly, she was almost too frightened to step through. But she did. And once on the other side, Elide gasped. The Thanatos Institute was just as intimidating inside as Prana Academy. The corridor they walked down was lit by chandeliers, and she did her best to avert her eyes from those around her. Most were too busy playing games to notice her while others saluted the Apostate when he passed. The older boys, who looked to be in their twenties, were drinking and chatting about their day.

The younger men were dressed in casual clothes, with their Enoch and Disciple novice coats draped over chairs—the uniforms shared a similar navy-blue hue with an altered version of the Apostate's symbol on a patch. And to her surprise, Elide noted, the raven looked much more at ease sitting on a perch.

Elide saw Aidan among the boys, and he smiled and waved to her. She waved back at him, and two boys with him teased him.

"My great-great-grandfather, Vigo, designed this long gallery. He felt it was best for the men to have an area indoors to unwind, and he was right. It boosted morale. Daegal and I would wander in here when our fathers were trying to change the world," the Apostate said, nodding at Altair, who stopped his conversation with a fellow Disciple to do whatever was being bid of him.

"You and Professor Murik grew up here?" Elide signed.

The Apostate laughed, a deep, warm sound that echoed throughout the cold room.

"Don't look so shocked," the Apostate said with a smirk. "Did you not think I was capable of making friends?"

Elide blushed, but before she could sign an apology, he waved it away. He was teasing her.

"Marrowroot?" she signed nervously, trying to change the subject.

"When it is found, its pollen can be used in a tea to amplify your power." He tilted her chin up, and Elide met his gaze—and for a brief moment, she felt a warm energy ripple through her lower jaw. "You don't need to be afraid of me, Elide."

He pulled his hand away, and her skin became cold.

"I'm not afraid," Elide signed, trying to understand what came over her, sensing it was his power.

He smiled. "Good, because what comes next will be harder. Marrowroot is not known for being pleasant, no matter what the alchemist's intention may be."

Elide gaped. "And you want me to drink it?"

He nodded.

"What about something lighter that might do it? Like ground sinea nut or cherdill? There are plenty of theories about spices and plants," Elide signed.

His gaze became hard and focused. "I'm afraid neither of those herbs would work. If we intend to make you the Teller that ends the war, the Teller you are meant to be, it has to be marrowroot."

"What's so special about marrowroot?" Elide signed.

He cocked a brow. "You haven't been reading your herbology book?"

"I'm not taking herbology this semester," Elide signed. "I've just been doing some light reading on it."

He almost looked amused. "I'm surprised Calliope didn't take it upon herself to have that changed, but I suppose that'd interfere with her bibliomancy class. That's rather disappointing."

"I'm sure she finds me rather disappointing," Elide signed.

"What makes you say that?"

Elide looked away from him, and for a moment, she looked at a portrait on the wall a few feet away from them. Lysandra Norwood stared back at her, emerald eyes looking lifeless, perhaps even withdrawn. The Apostate moved to stand beside her.

"I can't call on my power," Elide signed at him. She shook her head at herself. "And when I did call on it, it was by accident. I never meant to attack Ayla."

"Good things come to those who wait, Elide."

"You aren't worried?"

"No, I'm confident you'll find your way. Besides, the Seekers are already searching for marrowroot. Even if they have to scour the Outlands for it, they'll bring it back."

Elide looked at him. The thought of the Outlands made her heart lurch in her chest. She'd only come in contact with them once, and she felt lucky to be alive. The amount of danger those men were facing, for her, made her feel guilty. She felt even the smallest substitute was better than having his men risk life and limb for an ancient plant. There were other ways they could fix it. Fix *her*.

"Or you could call them off rather than risk your men's lives. Why not simply substitute for some other ancient herb?" Elide signed.

"Marrowroot is the key. I know it. Other herbs won't put you at your most powerful. Most, if not all, other options would likely end in your death, Elide." He told her softly as he lifted her chin to meet his gaze. "You're too valuable to risk losing." His dark gaze was soft and steady, and somehow, she felt warmer and more sure of herself as she stared at him. He couldn't have looked more handsome and confident, and perhaps, his confidence was contagious.

"You aren't alone in this, Elide," he said lowly. "You just have to trust me."

Elide felt flustered. But she nodded.

He smiled down at her, and she blushed.

Then he led her back to the bridge, and they walked silently on their way back. When he spoke again, they were back in Prana Academy.

"The world is changing, Elide," he said as they stopped near the great hall. "The Outlanders are pushing their way through our borders, convinced that they are freeing us from our sanctuary." For a moment, he looked sad. "Reverend elders and apostates have waited a long time for a new Teller. One that would not only save our people but Outlanders as well." He smiled at her. "I searched for you, Elide. And now, we're going to bring in a new era."

Elide smiled nervously. She didn't know what to say to him. Of course, she could be patient with herself, but while the idea of bringing in a new era was both wonderful and exciting, it was also overwhelming.

"I hope I'll be able to help you," Elide signed.

He smiled. "I don't doubt you will," the Apostate told her. He was standing close to her now, and she could feel her heart in her throat. She searched his eyes but couldn't tell what he was thinking. He moved away from her, and his expression shifted as if he'd been taken aback by something.

"Have a good night, Elide," he said, turning on his heel and heading back to his quarters.

Leaving Elide alone in the hallway, to herself and her racing thoughts.

# 16

Elide hoped to prove the Apostate wrong, so she'd gone to the library and—after a long lecture from the librarian about the improper removal of a certain genealogy book and a heartfelt apology later—Elide checked out several volumes of herbology books from the library. Herbology theories were numerous, but she'd had no such luck in finding anything contrary to what the Apostate had told her. She did learn about Elijah Norwood, the man who discovered marrowroot, who was a distant relative to Lysandra and a Mancio. He had believed that his telepathic gifts had made finding the plant easier. Another philosopher disproved this theory in the early twentieth century.

But the two men agreed that marrowroot rivaled all other herbs. There was no doubt that it wasn't only the rarest species of plant—which was notably *lethal*—it was also the safest to ingest. Elijah Norwood went into greater detail in his journal entries, recalling the strength of his abilities before and after. Before, he believed he was weaker. After, he could break bones with the snap of his fingers and control the minds of thousands within a twenty-mile radius.

The power couldn't be taken away after it was given, but it could be balanced by a Teller, yet the world wasn't rife with those: *Tellers can unlock the mind from within and shift the telepathic powers of those around them, weakening or amplifying their allies. It is a power like none we have known. Only with the plant can we rival them. Marrowroot can be used to bring about great change in any telepath. A change with such permanence it can pass through genetics, as I've seen with my own kin. There will be generations like us, and we will not be extinguished.*

Later journal entries sounded like the ramblings of a mad man, but perhaps he was in the end. As recorded by one historian, *he chose the gallows after committing heinous crimes for blasphemous means against the Outlands.* But the historian was scant on the details, perhaps on assumption that it'd be found elsewhere. Their other statements detailed the joining of another state with Scopus: *Though some have chosen to assimilate with us, let it be known hereafter, that Baron Elijah Perseus Norwood's actions were not committed in the name of our Father who art in heaven.*

The words sent a chill down her spine. Elide didn't want to imagine what he had done. All she knew was that it was redacted. If the historian's words were anything to go on, there was nothing to be done about him—he was irredeemable. For the conviction to be execution, he had to be.

Was that the power of marrowroot? Or had his hunger for power driven him to it? For whatever reason, she had the strangest feeling that he had lost himself in it, and perhaps that came without having a reason for taking it. Her reason was simple, her power was living within her and would save the world, if she could wield it. She had the purest of intentions for seeking the marrowroot while Elijah wanted to experiment, he wanted to play God. That was what happened to those who strayed. But if she could heal Scopus, *save* their great nation, she would do it. No matter the cost.

The days in Prana blurred together. Soon the winter sun shone brighter, and the snow-riddled walkways of the academy grounds sparkled and crunched underfoot. The novitiates slowed to a calmer pace as the purity of the heaven-sent snow foretold days filled with merriment and laughter, as Adoann would soon arrive, bringing the first school holiday with it.

Adoann was meant to commemorate the Great Revelation, when the first Apostate came to power and the apolites were welcomed into the light. They'd helped reshape the South into a better land for all—and forgave the past indiscretions of the southern leaders of their time. But Elide remembered most Adoanns in Baptiste being more about gift giving than forgiveness—and wreath-making. She loved wreath-making when the time came for it.

Elide stood at the entry gate watching another group of novitiates squeeze into a carriage for their ride to Westerby. She had been given "normal" clothing at the academy's tailor shop. Normal meaning a pair of fleece bottoms and a knitted turtleneck sweater. They also gave her a muted brown coat—*to look normal,* the academy's tailor had said. Although, Elide had never seen such an elaborate design in her life, and the sweater itself was cashmere. Each sweater had a Mourner's order's animal on it—Elide had selected Hamle. She didn't feel the symbolic meaning of a bear fit her as much as she hoped but wasn't eager to try anything else. She'd received mixed responses for choosing it. Some orders were entirely indifferent, others were slightly bitter, but most were more annoyed that the Hamles were bragging about it.

Another carriage arrived shortly after, with two decoy carriages accompanying it—*for your protection,* Mother Superior had told her. Elide tried to not make a fuss about it, but somedays she wished it wasn't necessary. Prana was far from where any harm could come to her, but on the off chance that an Outlander snuck through, she was to be guarded. They gave her rules and armored guard to protect her. Unfortunately, those rules included a nine o'clock curfew. But lucky for Starla, that extra guard meant Calvin could be close by, though he'd be working.

As Elide thought of them, she heard two raised voices slowly approaching from behind her. Elide turned on her heel and smiled at them. Starla had a sour expression on her face. Isadora simply looked annoyed.

"What happened?" Elide signed.

Isadora rolled her eyes. "Calvin has been ordered to stay at the academy while we're off to Westerby," Isadora answered swiftly.

But before Elide could respond she was cut off.

"It's not fair!" Starla exclaimed. "Why is it when I finally find someone that he can't even be nearby? I swear Mother Superior constantly thinks I'm going to do something wrong. I'm so tired of that old woman."

"Shhh," Isadora shushed. "Do you really want someone to overhear you talking about Mother Superior that way?"

"Perhaps she's concerned about you staying pure," Elide signed.

Starla scoffed. "If she's so concerned then why the hell would she approve of my engagement to Calvin!" Starla said matter-of-factly.

"Perhaps it'd be better if we moved this conversation into the carriage," Isadora said, looking around.

Elide nodded. A surprising number of Enoch were mounting their horses and eyeing them as they spoke as if they were curious about what was being said. Starla pouted but climbed into the carriage and settled into the carriage seat. Elide took a seat across from her friends.

"I'm sorry that Calvin couldn't come," Elide signed as an Enoch shut the carriage door.

"It's all right, it isn't your fault," Starla said grumpily. "He's quite good is all, likely the best among them. He can't help being in demand as he is, and I wouldn't have him any other way."

Starla smiled at the thought of him and sighed.

"All clear," a male voice said outside the carriage.

Then the carriage jolted forward as it began to move. Elide watched out the window as the academy disappeared from view, and before long, she was staring into the forest. The forest looked devoid of life aside from a shadow here and there. After a while, the men began to hum a tune as they traveled. Their journey passed uneventfully over a pleasantly calm ride of thirty-odd miles in a relatively comfortable carriage through a dirt road with a blanket wrapped around Elide's body as she breathed in cold air and exhaled fog, her friends sleeping across from her. Elide was thankful they hadn't encountered Outlanders or bandits brandishing weapons and that a blizzard hadn't passed through.

By the time she saw their destination, they were riding down a hill. A bevy of men dressed in farmwear were slowly descending the hill on horseback. They tipped their hats respectfully at their escorts, peering at the carriages, clearly curious about who they were transporting.

The snow shower hadn't broken, but it was lighter here, light enough that Elide could see them crossing a wooden bridge that was a kilometer away.

The town itself was shaped like a rose. Each boulevard arched in organic swirls, unfurling from the center where the marketplace was held. The balconies bore twinkling Christmas lights and wreaths made of evergreen and red witch hazel for Adoann. The buildings were each even at five stories high, and all except the eateries were closed. If they'd left earlier, they would've arrived before eight o'clock, but now they would have to go to their hotel thanks to her curfew. She hoped they'd have something good to eat there.

Elide was more than a little hungry. She was sure she'd get crabby in a few minutes. She tried to distract herself by admiring the buildings through the window, particularly the building decorated like a Christmas calendar. *Heaven's Door*, Elide thought to herself. There were two lit trees outside whose light reflected off the glass display windows where mannequins stood proudly posing in wedding gowns and commitment ceremony dresses. Today's deal was FREE VENUS VEILS FOR BARONESS BUYERS, and she wondered if the baronesses ever traveled this far out. But, as if to answer her question, a small horde of women stepped out of the store, white dress boxes in their arms, each with legs like Aphrodite and effortlessly beautiful.

And as if they knew she was staring, they looked at her carriage as they passed, pointing and gaping at it. Unsurprisingly, when they turned the corner, the townspeople didn't miss their chance to gawk and crane their heads at them. It wasn't long until the Enoch moved to flank the sides of the carriage, protecting them from outsiders. Luckily, they were only a quarter mile away, and when they made it there, Elide was barely keeping her eyes open.

"Finally," Isadora said, sighing. "I guess nothing ever happens here."

"Nonsense, people are just nosey," Starla interjected. "It reminds me of home. And besides, we should be enjoying ourselves, no coursework, no classes—"

"No Yvette," Isadora said, interrupting Starla.

"Yes, well, we hardly need to worry about her. I heard she's failing Professor Murik's class and stayed back at the academy to study while we'll be staying at the *Centre Royale*, the best in hospitality since 1919, drinking champagne and eating the finest cuisine in Texas," Starla said, fake swooning afterward.

Elide giggled. Although she wasn't accustomed to the luxuries that Starla was born into, she didn't mind being exposed to them. Starla's parents deposited money into her bank account every month in case she needed it, and she was adamant about sharing that wealth with her friends. Elide's funds were limited, as most of what she had in her accounts went toward her home back in Baptiste and was normally deposited into her account by Hansel from his mart's salary. *If it's still my home*, Elide thought to herself.

"Aye, no sad faces on this trip," Starla said, patting Elide's knee. "We're going to have the best time, you'll see."

# 17

When they'd first arrived at the Centre Royale, it was particularly bland looking in light of her expectations. The lobby had a wide waiting area with couches and tables evenly spaced throughout the room. Above them, chandeliers lit every inch of the lobby and reflected off the tinted windows, which kept their affluent guests' stays private. Those guests, at the time, were staring at them, likely puzzled by their common attire.

The male receptionist shared a similar cold demeanor, unimpressed by the Disciples and Enochs guarding them, but he warmed the moment Starla flashed her smile and credit card. And perhaps ignoring the overwhelming number of stares they were receiving was starting to get to Elide—but this morning was different. After she'd brushed her teeth and dressed, she'd walked into their suite's living room to find a Seeker waiting among the pack of Disciples, all chatting and joking with each other.

The Seeker, Cyrus Coin, was nearly as handsome as the Apostate. A skilled tracker burdened with honors and awards and notably polite, with a smile that could send any woman swooning over him and a father who was a well-liked reverend elder. His little brother Aiden more closely resembled their father, but he didn't share Cyrus's confidence. Aiden was an Enoch trainee that was shy, soft-spoken, and never had mail for Elide.

"Good morning, Elide," Cyrus greeted with a smile. "I'm afraid your previous escort ate some bad fish last night and won't be able to accompany you. So I'll be escorting you in his stead."

Elide nodded. She looked at him from head to toe. He wore the same formal brown coat he'd been wearing when they'd first met, but this time there was a raven pin on his lapel. *Someone got a promotion*, Elide thought to herself, staring at the bird. Was the Apostate spying on her? Or had Cyrus been sent to protect her?

Elide shook off the thought. It wasn't as if Cyrus would learn anything interesting from Starla's commitment ceremony shopping or whatever Adoann festivities Isadora had planned for them. And at the moment, Elide was hoping they would bore him enough to leave.

"Thank you for accompanying me," Elide signed.

Cyrus smiled and said, "Shall we?"

He opened the front door, and Elide stepped out into the hallway. Unfortunately, when Cyrus followed her, two brutish-looking Disciples followed close behind them, walking in a matching stride that made Elide particularly uneasy. She wondered if they always looked angry to intimidate onlookers or if it was their natural disposition. Either way, people wouldn't enter elevators with them, and curious spectators moved out of their way when they reached the lobby.

The lobby looked particularly festive this morning. String lights were being hung around the reception desk, and hotel workers were decorating large and undoubtedly expensive, strategically placed Christmas trees along the walls. A fireplace in the corner of the room was decorated with holly and a nativity scene.

The other guests looked happier this morning. And Elide was happy to see her friends walking into the hotel with breakfast in takeout boxes.

Starla was the first to hug her.

"Here's a croissant! We'll be having champagne at Heaven's Door—" Starla paused, noting the two brawny Disciples standing behind Elide and then Cyrus. "I wasn't aware we'd have *guests* at my appointment," she said more to Cyrus than Elide.

"I'm afraid we'll have to be in attendance as Elide's safety is of the utmost importance," Cyrus explained, then leaned in closer to Starla. "A protection detail is important for the Teller. We can't have anything happening to her now, can we?"

Starla wrinkled her nose. "If you're implying that I don't care about her safety, then you'd be mistaken, and you can go back to the Apostate and tell him I said so. I'm planning a very important day, and I only get one commitment ceremony in my lifetime, and *you* and your burly cronies won't mess things up for me," Starla said harshly.

"That isn't our intention, but we will be in attendance," he said again, rather pleasantly, given Starla's tone. "And I'm afraid you'll be enduring us for the duration of your trip."

Starla went to retort, but Isadora grabbed her arm.

"We'll endure you," Isadora said suddenly. She looked him up and down. "And I believe what she's trying to say is that she doesn't want any Disciples, particularly *newly* minted officers or their soldiers, to ruin her appointment by exposing any of the details to her fiancé, Calvin."

Cyrus laughed. "Of course," he said pleasantly. "I would never do anything to jeopardize a fellow officer's ceremony." He paused and bowed slightly to Starla before standing and saying, "*Congratulations.*"

Elide was sure he didn't believe Isadora. But was more so willing to play along to appease an angry Starla. Elide was still hoping they'd choose not to attend or be barred from entering Heaven's Door. Unfortunately, neither of those things came to pass when they arrived for the appointment.

Elide took a champagne flute from a tray offered to her by a well-dressed woman standing at the entry door, noting that neither Disciple took one but Cyrus did. Starla was gushing about her ideas for the ceremony to a bridal consultant. Elide was glad that her friend's earlier frustration had disappeared. And as Elide raised the glass to her lips and took a sip, she couldn't help but admire the bridal store.

Heaven's Door had mannequins displaying dresses throughout the store and plenty of clothing racks with dresses. The white marble floors reflected the skylights above, and Elide could faintly see her reflection in the floor. A few brides-to-be were wandering around with their mothers, giddy with excitement, as their mothers inspected dresses for them to try on. Each mother shook their head dismissively at dresses that simply wouldn't do. There were a few extremely satisfied brides standing at the checkout counter, tapping their cheeks as they discussed veils and other accessories with their cashiers. It was exactly how Starla had described it, right down to the cherub statues evenly distributed throughout the store.

"All right!" Starla said excitedly, pulling Elide along to the fitting area.

It wasn't private. It was in the center of two others. On the right, a woman was pensively looking herself over in her gown on the fitting platforms before nodding to herself and facing her bridal party for outside opinions. The left one was vacant.

Elide took a seat on the couch beside Isadora. There was another couch and an armchair near the fitting plat-form by the mirror. And when Elide saw herself in the mirror, she grimaced. The dark circles under her eyes were getting worse.

"So you'll all sit here—*including* the men—and my mother will arrive shortly, and then we'll have her opinion on my gowns as well," Starla told them.

The latter detail would've been more of a shock if Elide wasn't already curious about Starla's mother. Mostly she wondered what type of woman it took to birth and raise someone like Starla, and while Elide knew that Starla's mother was a baroness, she still wasn't clear on what that meant. She had never thought to ask. She and Fiona had only known that the career would allow them to live by their own rules.

Starla was called away by her bridal consultant, who was eager to show her the gowns they'd selected for her—emphasizing the word *gowns* as if "dress" was too common for the current venue. They disappeared through a door behind the mirror.

Cyrus looked amused and knelt beside Elide.

"All this fuss over a man that's half her caliber," he whispered lowly to Elide.

"What do you mean?" Elide signed.

"Honestly, have you ever met Calvin Timber?" Cyrus answered.

Elide stared at him. "Timber? As in Amos Timber's older son?" she signed.

But before he could answer, someone cleared their throat, and he quickly rose to his feet. He turned to a woman a foot shorter than himself, with her just a few inches above five feet tall.

"It's hardly appropriate for a Disciple to be so close to the Teller, wouldn't you say, boy?" she stated. She looked over at Elide and what she was wearing before nodding her head in approval.

Cyrus took the woman's hand, brought it to his lips, and said, "I beg your pardon, miss—"

She snatched her hand from him and said, "*Missus* Octavia Howler, Starla's mother," Octavia said pleasantly, fanning herself with the silk fan she'd brought with her.

Her cheekbones sharpened with the look of disdain she directed at Cyrus.

"My sincerest apologies, *Mrs.* Howler," Cyrus responded sincerely.

Octavia *humphed* at him and continued to fan herself. The resemblance between mother and daughter was almost uncanny; their only dissimilarities were her mother's reddish-brown eyes and straight nose. But her skin, like Starla's, was brown and smooth. A colored baroness wasn't uncommon in this day and age, but she was the first Elide had ever seen. And the way she'd spoken to Cyrus, Elide had never heard a Disciple apologize and hadn't been sure they knew how until now. But even Cyrus's followers looked ashamed when she'd scorned their commanding officer.

"Do you plan on standing there all day or making your men useful? Ms. Hester is running out of refreshment, and I've yet to receive any," Octavia said.

Cyrus laughed dryly. "I'm sure the consultant will be more than pleased to serve you," Cyrus said bitterly. Then he turned and went to speak to his men.

Elide was stunned. Cyrus didn't appear to order either Disciple to fetch Octavia champagne, but one did grab his cell phone and call someone.

"You just have to know how to talk to them," Octavia said suddenly, and Elide jumped.

Elide turned to her.

"You can't let them push you around, especially if you're going to lead us one day," Octavia said.

Elide stared at her blankly.

"What do you mean?" Elide signed.

"Darling, you're the Teller. Who exactly do you presume that you'll marry?" Octavia asked apathetically. She waited a moment, but Elide didn't answer.

When she thought of marriage nowadays, she assumed she'd marry a Disciple, like her friends would. Otherwise, she would die a lonely old spinster, or perhaps a *happy* one.

Octavia sighed and rolled her eyes. "The Apostate, dear," Octavia said lowly.

Elide's heart leapt at the thought of him.

She could feel herself blushing as Octavia signaled a server with a tray of champagne flutes. Elide's thoughts were racing. Had the Apostate thought of her that way? *No.* Elide doubted the thought had ever crossed his mind. His focus was on protecting Scopus and ending the war. She was just one of the many players in that plan. And marrowroot was the next step toward their common goal if she was indeed *unteachable.*

"I'm sure the Apostate has more pressing concerns than marriage," Elide signed to her.

Octavia scoffed. "He'll need an heir eventually, dear, and you're one of a kind—the first Teller in centuries. I doubt he'd be willing to miss that opportunity if he's as wise as others say," she said matter-of-factly. Then Octavia shook her head, and when she looked forward, Starla's bridal consultant was calling her over.

But before Octavia stood, she turned back to Elide.

"If that's truly what you believe, my dear, you would not have done well as a baroness," Octavia told her candidly. And unfortunately, the pleasantly spoken insult stung more than Elide would have expected from a woman she'd just met. "To be a baroness, you would have to understand powerful men." Elide was confused by her implications. "And *perhaps* you're still too naive to know this, or the absence of your mother was more detrimental than I could have predicted. So I'll leave you with the same piece of advice my mother gave me: know thy enemy—*always*."

Octavia patted Elide on the leg, and her expression softened as she approached the bridal consultant, leaving Elide to her thoughts. And she thought over Octavia's words for a long time, no matter how much she wished she wouldn't.

She knew who her enemies were, and as long as the Outlanders weren't within their borders, Elide was safe. As for Octavia's other proposal, she did her best to force it out of her mind. But instead, Elide found she was so distracted by her thoughts that they robbed most of the appointment from her. The many, many gowns Starla tried on were a blur of white, periwinkle, and lavender hues in various styles and lengths, and no compliment or comment they gave was enough to make her friend satisfied with any of them. Elide watched as Starla strode out in her final dress. It was *simpler*, satin, without beading or tulle, and had a halter neck, which Starla loved. Starla looked beautiful, and she danced happily the moment she chose it.

"What's on your mind?" Isadora whispered into Elide's ear.

Elide shook herself and looked at Isadora.

"It's like you're not even here—are the Disciples bothering you?" Isadora asked lowly, gesturing toward them.

Elide looked over at them. They had multiplied from three to fifteen over the course of the appointment. Unsurprisingly, other women in the bridal store took note of them as well, mostly swooning over the well-built men, and they knew it too. Disciples were an intimidating but physically attractive brood. They were devoted to their service, faith, families, countrymen, and the Apostate himself. If they weren't so fearsome looking and callous, Elide could see herself dating one of them. But they were here to guard her and from the number of them present, she doubted they had received good news in the last few hours.

Elide turned back to Isadora and signed, "I'm fine."

"Are you sure?" Isadora asked softly.

Elide hesitated.

"I'll tell you later," she signed.

Elide turned to look back at Starla, as someone stopped behind her and bent down beside the couch she sat on.

"We need to move you, *now*," Cyrus whispered in a stern voice that sounded deeper than earlier this morning.

Elide could sense the urgency in his voice and looked at him, trying to read his expression. There were perhaps several emotions on his face, with anger being the most obvious. Directed more so at the mother of the bride-to-be, Elide noted silently, though she was choosing not to call Starla a bride-to-be in front of her mother again. Octavia was insistent on calling Starla "betrothed" at the moment. Elide shamelessly felt otherwise because attributing either title to age as Octavia had was ridiculous.

But to Starla's dismay, Elide conceded to Cyrus's insistence of returning to the hotel, where she'd be better guarded.

In the hotel suite, food was readily available. The men had taken it upon themselves to order their dinner, including wine, various kinds of cheese, chicken, lamb, and steak.

But Elide didn't feel hungry, so instead, she went to sit on the small couch on the balcony. She looked down at Westerby, watching people filing out of shops and climbing into carriages. The sun was sinking into the mist that was rolling over the hills, beckoning in the darkness.

"There's a storm coming."

Elide jumped at the sound of his voice.

She turned and saw Cyrus leaning against the doorway.

"May I?" he asked, gesturing toward the couch, and she nodded.

Cyrus sat beside her, leaving just enough space for another person.

"You didn't want to watch a movie with your friends?" Cyrus asked.

Elide shook her head. She couldn't help but feel that she disappointed Starla. This was the second time her presence had ruined something involving her friend's pending nuptials.

"Heavy is the head, I'm sure," Cyrus said.

"Why does everyone keep saying that?" Elide signed,

narrowing her eyes as her movements became more pronounced.

Cyrus laughed. But he stopped when he noticed Elide's irate expression.

"*Sorry*, I'd meant it empathetically," Cyrus told her. He stared out at the sunset. "I can't imagine bearing all that weight at your age. I could barely manage what little I did have. And you're holding the fates of two worlds." He paused and smiled at her playfully. "No pressure, right?"

Elide laughed. "Yeah, none at all," Elide signed, shaking her head.

"You'll be fine though," Cyrus said with a nod as if he were reassuring a friend. "Besides, you don't have to think about it now. Adoann is in a few days, so you should enjoy it. That's why the Apostate sent us."

Elide stared at him blankly.

"He thinks that you're stressed, and it's making things more difficult for you. So we're here to make sure you're guarded but can also enjoy your vacation safely with your friends." Cyrus said, pausing to clear his throat. He looked her directly in the eyes. "If you don't take a break every once in a while, stress will eat you alive. Why do you think I got myself reassigned?"

"Reassigned?" Elide signed.

"Yeah, *reassigned*," he repeated. "I asked my superior officer if there was something more I could be doing than seeking out criminals. I'd tried search and rescue, but it wasn't for me. Too many dead. And bounty hunting takes its toll after a while. So they sent my inquiry to the Apostate. He saw all my honors and suggested discipleship."

"And that's easier than being a Seeker?" Elide signed.

Cyrus shrugged. "In a way, *yes*," Cyrus said, trailing off. He took a moment to consider his next words. "As an officer, I kill less and sleep more. Seekers are trained longer in the field. They need more study than most of the Apostate's elite. I could tell you things about both worlds that'd make your hair stand on end."

"Worse than murdering someone?" Elide signed.

Cyrus sighed and said, "Far worse than you can imagine."

Adoann couldn't have come soon enough. In time, the Disciples following Elide were like shadows, and she barely noticed them aside from the moments when she needed a champagne bottle opened or when strangers stared at them, which had become fewer as the Centre Royale filled for the holiday. On the first weekend, attendants filed out of the hotel to stable horses, taking their reins from their masters and tucking carriages out of sight. On Monday, the caterers came from near and far, arriving two by two, bearing fifty crates of champagne and wine and more decorations to fill the hallways. And soon, the tables at the end of every floor had oversized ornament bulbs, and matching red and gold tinsel hanging off them.

By nightfall, an orchestra arrived, carrying clarinets and oboes, drums and trumpets, and flutes that twinkled nearly as brightly as the xylophone that bore a sign declaring THE PROSPERO PHILHARMONIC

ORCHESTRA. The most affluent guests were excited about the music and followed them out the back door into the gardens. Luckily, this meant that Elide and her friends could shamelessly attend the wreath-making party without too many annoyed looks from elders. Most in attendance were middle-aged and coupled up, so the girls went to a table in the back, and the Disciples stood at attention against the walls like toy soldiers in their darkest uniforms—though they managed to be festive by wearing black velvet blazers and pants.

"I swear, you'd think they believe you were planning to make a run for it," Starla said, making sure that her glare passed over every Disciple in the room.

"They're just like that," Isadora said dismissively as she set pine cones on top of her wreath. "No use paying them any mind. Any more pressing news for us, Elide? Aside from Starla's mother's ideas about your possible impending nuptials."

Starla scoffed. "Yes, that was rather far even for mother," Starla said lowly. "She couldn't seriously think that the Apostate—not that you aren't beautiful, Elide," she hastily corrected. "But it's just that he doesn't seem preoccupied with finding a wife, or at least not *visibly* so."

Though the three were in agreement, somehow, Elide still felt insulted. The Apostate was controlling the military and keeping Scopus safe, and he didn't seem to be looking for a wife. But she still felt a pang of sadness at Starla's statement.

"The suggestion is completely baseless. He's too busy looking out for the good of the country," Isadora said, gluing her first pine cone onto the wreath. "You know, back home we would use tree sap, but it was much messier."

Elide sighed and shook off the feeling. She tried to preoccupy her mind with the image of Isadora trying to get tree sap off her hands in between applying bulbs to her wreath. She giggled aloud.

"See, that's the spirit," Isadora said, smiling at Elide. "*Now*, changing subjects. Since we can't attend the festival tomorrow due to a certain Disciple's pessimistic view of crowds, what should we do?"

Elide thought for a moment. She hoped Starla would pitch a new idea, but she said nothing. Instead, Starla continued sprinkling white powder onto her wreath to make fake snow.

"Hopefully, Calvin gets his suit in time. That'd be embarrassing for me to be the only one formally dressed," Starla said suddenly. Her lip protruded as she stared down at her wreath. "I've never been any good at these. Mother once told me that she thought mine might summon a witch."

Isadora took a deep breath.

"Well, I think we've established that your mother is an absolute *delight*," Isadora said sarcastically.

Elide had to restrain a smile.

"She isn't that bad," Starla said, looking between the two of them. "She so rarely comes to visit that I think she forgets what it's like to be around other people."

"You mean *common* people. God, I'm glad you didn't become a baroness," Isadora said with a shudder.

A few strangers looked toward them.

"Yes, I said *God*," Isadora repeated loudly to a group of women. "As in our Father who art in heaven. It's only blasphemous if you state his name in vain, not in thanks."

The women ducked their heads and returned to their wreath-making.

"You speak about my mother as if she's some terrible shrew," Starla said as she tied a bow onto her wreath. "She always means well and was simply trying to help Elide."

"Help?" Elide signed.

"Yes, help! You're clearly too frightened to stand up for yourself in social situations and don't seem to know what's good for you," Starla exclaimed harshly.

"What about Ayla?" Elide signed.

"What about Ayla?" Starla repeated. "You're kidding? Would you really have done anything if we weren't there to back you up?"

Isadora glared at Starla.

"Fine, your mother isn't a shrew. She's a *damn* cow," Isadora said lowly.

Starla narrowed her eyes. She looked between Elide and Isadora.

"Elide's a second-generation Mourner," Starla said harshly.

Isadora blinked. She looked at Elide, bewildered by Starla's statement.

"Is she telling the truth?" Isadora asked weakly.

Elide felt a pang of guilt.

"I found out a few weeks ago," Elide signed hesitantly. "I didn't know how to tell you."

Isadora was silent for a moment.

"I think I'm going to go back to the room," Isadora said, getting up from the table and abandoning her half-decorated wreath.

Starla rolled her eyes, and Elide shook her head at her.

"What's your problem?" Elide signed.

Starla scoffed. "Did you hear the way she was talking about my mother?"

"I did, but you didn't have a right to tell her that. You promised me," Elide signed, poking Starla in the chest.

"Okay, *sorry*. I've just been a bit angry lately because we have Disciples watching our every move while I have an entire ceremony to plan *without* my fiancé. And not to mention the fact that they interrupted what is supposed to be the third happiest appointment in my life! I am *so* sorry, Elide," Starla stated.

While Elide understood her friend's frustration, sarcastic apology aside, she felt betrayed. Elide got up from the table, deciding that wreath-making may not be worth it this Adoann, and returned to her room followed by the Disciples.

Their return to Prana wasn't met with any fanfare. They were met with the same melancholy greetings as the other novitiates as classes started again. Neither Isadora nor Starla had spoken to her since their arrival, or more accurately, Isadora hadn't, and Elide had chosen not to speak to Starla.

The only thing of note was that Mother Superior had

smiled at Elide when they'd arrived last week. Other than flopping back onto her pillows in her bed, Elide hadn't found a more pressing matter than mending things with Isadora. If there was hope that the two could still be friends now. She didn't know what caused Isadora's hatred of legacies but had a hunch it had something to do with Yvette and her equally snobby friends.

Elide had written to Hansel about their trip, including her questions about marrowroot and her friend's betrothal and the news about their mother. But there was a little voice inside her telling her that she was wasting her time writing him. He'd been with the other marts to decide how to recruit more military trainees, dividing the necessary numbers and efforts among the forty-seven other marts. That meant he had to have received mail about the meeting, which meant he'd received her previous letters. And the longer she lay there, thinking over how much she missed her brother and needed his advice, she couldn't help but think that her letters were sitting on his kitchen counter collecting dust.

Elide flipped herself over and screamed into her pillow. Perhaps he didn't miss her. Maybe he was glad that she was gone.

She looked back at the letter in her hand and tore it into pieces. Her mind was racing, and her heart ached. She couldn't keep doing this to herself. And the worst part was that she couldn't bring herself to cry. Instead, she sat up and decided to face her training session with Calliope.

Elide rushed out of the dorm suite and walked quickly down the halls. She also shoved Yvette when she'd gotten in her way, and after she climbed the staircase to Calliope's office, she opened the door.

Elide wiped the sweat from her brow with her dress sleeve. It wasn't ladylike, but Elide didn't care.

Calliope glanced up just as Elide sat down in one of the many armchairs in the classroom.

"Well, you're quite the sight. What's wrong, dear, getting impatient with our *noble* leader's plan for you?" Calliope mocked.

Elide took a deep breath but didn't answer.

"All right, spit it out."

Elide shook her head defiantly. She wanted to hold back all her thoughts. The memories of Hansel and her playing on Baptiste's dirt roads, running through puddles in the rain. The day he'd taught her to read. *Everything.*

Her nails bit into the arms of the armchair.

"What?" Calliope demanded impatiently.

Elide huffed out air. "I'm tired of being under all this pressure," Elide signed. "I'm tired of hearing that I'm going to change the world. I'm tired of people staring at me for being a Teller. I fucking hate wearing this uniform. I want to wake up to people shouting in the street over horse manure in the road. I want to listen to Frank Sinatra until five in the morning. I want to go back to Baptiste. I'm done listening to you and Professor Grim telling me who I'm supposed to be and how I'm supposed to be it."

Calliope focused her gaze on Elide. But to her surprise, her mentor's eyes didn't darken or turn black as she had thought they would. Instead, Calliope shook her head, went to her shelves, and retrieved a jar with a heart in it.

"You would rather be told by the Apostate?" she questioned, examining the heart inside the jar.

Elide wondered what animal it belonged to more than the implications of her mentor's statement.

"No," Elide signed, narrowing her eyes. "I don't want that either. I just want to—"

"Abandon your people? Tell me then. How do you think they'll react? All they've worked so hard to achieve, thrown away because the Teller wanted to return to the slums of Baptiste."

"That's not it. I'm just so tired—"

"Tired? You think you're the only one who's tired?" Calliope said, pausing suddenly. Then she scoffed. "Or perhaps it's jealousy—your friend Starla is betrothed is she not? Perhaps you want our dread king to extend the same favor to you?"

Elide had heard enough. She stood from her seat and headed for the door.

"If it's not that, then what is it? And how long do you intend on running toward it? Because here we don't run. We *fight*."

Elide's hand shook on the doorknob. She had already opened the door, she could leave. She could walk out and never come back. Maybe she could get away from Prana. Maybe she'd only make it as far as the forest before she was dragged back to her studies. Maybe some small part of her was still hoping that Hansel was coming to get her. And that part was eating her alive.

"That's what's wrong with Baptiste, everyone that comes out of there has always amounted to nothing."

Elide's heart lurched at her words.

"Your mother tainted your entire lineage by breeding with your father. It's made you weaker, more vulnerable and *incapable*."

Elide felt tears welling up in her eyes.

"Go on, out!" Calliope spat harshly. "I have no time for the weak."

When the insult reached her ears, Elide turned back around and signed, "I am not weak!"

She slashed an arm through the air to emphasize her point and watched as armchairs flew backward into bookshelves and the classroom windows burst, spewing glass in all directions. For a moment, Elide was shocked. She could feel the energy pulsing through her body. It was calling to her. Her heart was hammering in her chest, but she'd never felt better. She could feel her power coursing through every vein in her body. Elide looked around at the remains of the classroom: the knocked-over tables, the destroyed jars on the floor, and the dangling fragments of the mullioned windows. She expected her mentor to be furious, but Calliope was surveying the same damage and smiling.

"*Finally,*" Calliope said, staring at Elide. "I knew you had it in you."

# 18

After Elide left the training session that night, she felt proud of herself and wanted to celebrate. So, she walked to Kedeh Tower, where the Kedeh novitiates sat discussing their studies. A few welcomed her and invited her to spar with them in the dueling club, held in Classroom A4G on Tuesdays. Professor Grim supervised the club while reading a book. And Elide was able to hold her own with her sparring partner, managing to take them down twice.

The rest of her classes that week came easier. She didn't feel afraid when she woke up or anxious when she walked around the quad spending time with the other novitiates. She discovered that the Rapha enjoyed playing practical jokes on one another and studying how to bring flowers back to life. And the Leta—despite the rumors about Mourners that stemmed from their mind control abilities—were a relatively peaceful group that loved psychology and teaching. Though few wanted to enter the *re-education* sector, many had dreams of working with hospice patients or troubled youth. But they couldn't choose their assignments. *Choice is an illusion*, one had told her.

Elide thought the girl had sounded rather pessimistic. But didn't let the idea bother her too much. She was finally fitting in. It was the first time she truly felt she did. At Miller, she had Fiona and, by extension, Gabriel—and Ryder—but she hadn't made many friends there. Most people couldn't use sign language, and perhaps it was good that the Mourners had bid on her, seeing as they worked with so many cities, they had to know more than one language.

Since she wasn't an outcast here, she never had to worry about being alone. Elide didn't talk about her trouble using her power with anyone, but the other novitiates were excited to see what she could do. She had no problem knocking a Hamle off their feet on the quad's lawns and accidentally injuring her. But a Rapha quickly healed the other girl, and immediately the Hamle began excitedly questioning how she'd done it. However, the feeling wasn't something Elide could explain, it wasn't tangible, but she couldn't even tell them that.

When she returned to her dorm suite, she was surprised to see Isadora and Starla sitting on the couch together. Both stared at three oddly decorated wreaths with mismatched tinsel set on the coffee table. One had pine cones dangling off the bottom like legs.

For a moment, they stared at each other in silence.

Then Elide signed, "Isadora, I'm—"

"Don't be sorry," Isadora said, cutting her off.

Isadora sighed. "You don't have to be sorry for something you can't control. I just wish you would've told me."

"I know. I hadn't really finished processing it myself," Elide signed. "Starla found out by accident. I hadn't closed my door, and she walked in."

"Humph, well I'm glad your stories match up," Isadora said, looking at Starla.

Elide looked at Starla.

Starla's eyes were soft. "I made this for you," she said, holding up a wreath with dangling tinsel.

Elide immediately recognized it—or half of it. She hadn't finished decorating hers and could see the pine cones poking out of the tinsel. Elide stifled a laugh.

"Don't laugh," Starla said, clearly horrified. "I told you two I was bad at making them."

Isadora laughed. "Yeah, you're god-awful at making them."

Starla rolled her eyes and smiled.

"Okay, so they won't win any beauty contests," Starla said. "I just wanted you two to know that I'm sorry for being a total bridezilla over the break. I don't know what came over me."

"It's all right," Elide signed.

"Well, hopefully, I'll be able to make it up to you two," Starla said.

"You can start by ordering us something to eat, I'm starving," Isadora said playfully.

Starla went to the phone to order, and Elide joined Isadora on the couch. Isadora started talking about her genealogy lessons and how she was feeling suffocated by the idea of spending all day in the library researching for her final paper. It was due in a few weeks, but it felt like it was closing in on her.

Elide didn't mind listening. In fact, she didn't mind much of anything lately. She rarely saw the Apostate. If she was awake at five in the morning and looked down at the quad from her bedroom window, she would see him walking with his personal guard, usually chatting with Daegal or Cyrus. In the evenings, she saw him returning to his tower. But he never seemed to see her. She assumed that since their shared obstacle had been overcome, he had no reason to speak to her. And she didn't know why that bothered her, only that it did.

There were some days it distracted her in combat drills, and Professor Grim would shake her head at her critically before calling the next pair of students forward. Isadora would help Elide off the sparring arena and to her next class. After that class was over, Elide would enjoy lunch with her friends. And every once in a while, and perhaps she imagined it, she swore she noticed Daegal staring at her in the great hall.

One Tuesday afternoon, Daegal called her aside after a lesson on using their abilities to help people process traumatic memories.

"Is everything all right, Elide?" Daegal asked her.

"Yes, why?" Elide signed.

"It's been brought to my attention that you're rather distracted," he said calmly, erasing the whiteboard as he spoke.

Daegal turned and looked at her.

"No," Elide signed. "I'm perfectly fine."

He smirked.

"You're lying," Daegal said, leaning against his desk. "Do you know how I know?" he asked as if he wanted her to guess, but Elide could only shrug. "Your mother had similar tells when she was alive."

Elide's heart sank in her chest. "You knew my mother?" Elide signed.

Daegal chuckled lowly. "I watched her grow up," Daegal explained. "She was no Teller, but she was quite bright, as you are."

"Watched her grow up?" Elide signed, confused by his statement.

"Yes, *watched*," he repeated calmly. "I'm much older than I look, Elide. It's a gift shared among the orders that few manage to master."

"So, you're what? Immortal?"

Daegal shook his head. "If you study properly and master your abilities, your body ages slower, and in turn, you live much longer."

Elide stared at him blankly. She would've laughed if his expression wasn't so serious.

"The problem is most telepaths won't ever master their skills. They're blind to their weaknesses. But once you realize that you're standing in your own way and relinquish the illusion of control, you can achieve great things," Daegal said, packing books into his briefcase. "Mother Superior is 234 years old, and while I may be younger in years than her, I have much more time left. She's dying, and everyone senses it. But perhaps you'll end the war before then."

It took Elide a moment to process what he'd said. *234 years old*, Elide thought, remembering how fragile the elderly woman looked, even with her cane in hand. What happened to them when she was dead? Who would take over? Perhaps there was more than one reason that the Apostate was in Prana. He had to choose her replacement before she died.

"What happens when she dies?" Elide signed, daring to ask her question.

Daegal cocked his head at the question and looked almost amused by that statement.

"Funny, isn't it, how it's the little details that no one thinks about that worry us the most," Daegal said, shutting his briefcase.

"What about Calliope?"

"No longer in the running," he said softly.

Elide was surprised. The Apostate had trusted her with Elide's training—but she remembered Calliope's reaction after he'd suggested marrowroot. A man in his position wouldn't want to risk butting heads with her in front of an audience while presiding over the country. Marts had lost their positions when their authority was questioned. How would he maintain control of the country if he had an adversary to worry about among his administration?

"He wouldn't be thinking that I would take over," Elide signed.

"So rash," Daegal responded softly. "But *no*, not you. You will play an important part in Scopus's new era. The people hear about you, and they have hope. We can't have you locked away in Prana. Overseeing the next generation of Mourners is honorable—but not for someone with your potential."

"My potential?" Elide signed.

Daegal smirked. "Have a good evening, Elide."

And with that, he walked out of the classroom.

The conversation frightened her. Why would Daegal tell her that? Though she didn't know Mother Superior well, the thought of her dying gave Elide chills. She assumed the next Mother Superior would also be a Kedeh, seeing as they were the order that could sense abilities.

But if it wasn't her mentor, who would take over? While the academy did have Kedeh faculty, most were adjunct professors that preferred fieldwork in the form of traveling city to city to conduct testing or research. None seemed eager to be bound to the academy.

That same evening, Elide slowly made her way to Calliope's classroom, hoping today she would learn to better control her power. Calliope was standing at her desk, looking through a stack of papers, and glanced at her when Elide entered the room.

"You're late!" Calliope shouted.

"I'm sorry, I was distracted," Elide signed.

"That seems to be a common theme from your teacher's reports," she said, slamming the papers down on the desk as her eyes narrowed at Elide. Elide bowed her head in shame and set her schoolbag down in an armchair.

"We don't have time for this—show me what you've been practicing," Calliope demanded.

Elide called her power, cupping her hands together, drawing the air around them into a sphere. The air spun faster and faster, trying to escape her hands, but the expression on Calliope's face disheartened Elide, and the air escaped her hands, spreading out in all directions, shattering the windows again. Elide dropped her hands to her sides.

"Again!" Calliope shouted.

"What's this supposed to teach me?" Elide signed, stomping her foot. "We've been doing this for days—"

"*Focus*," Calliope said, abruptly cutting her off. "Something that you've been lacking as of late. If your grades suffer because of it, you'll fail the term like that friend of yours."

"Isadora had—"

"Again!" Calliope shouted.

Elide called on her power again. The air came in through the windows and caught between her hands, shaping the ball once more. But as she looked at her mentor, Elide's anger got the better of her, and the ball burst. She watched in horror as an armchair soared through the air and crashed into the wall behind Calliope. Elide went to apologize, but a strange feeling came over her.

"I take it lessons aren't going well." Her heart leapt to her throat at the sound of his voice. The Apostate stood at the classroom door.

"I'm afraid not," Calliope said impatiently. "She can't control her power yet. Her mind is too distracted. But I take it that's not why you're here. I'm assuming you've come to tell us about your men's marrowroot *excursion*."

The insult was so subtle that Elide nearly missed it. The Apostate had caught it, and he was glaring at Calliope. She doubted her mentor would be promoted to Mother Superior if she continued calling the expedition an *excursion*.

"It's going well. But I'm sure our situation would improve if you refrained from speaking to the Teller as though she is a child," the Apostate said.

Calliope let out a bark of laughter. "I will when she stops acting like one."

"I'm tiring of your callous behavior in the academy. Mother Superior feels the same."

"And I'm sure that you had nothing to do with that, your *grace*."

Elide was beginning to feel uneasy.

"I'll manage," Elide signed, drawing their attention away from each other. "I just need to practice more. I have been going to dueling club with the Kedeh, and I'm slowly getting better." Her statements didn't even receive a nod. The Apostate and Calliope just stared at her blankly. "Not *slowly*. I am. I need more training, that's all."

The Apostate spoke first. "Elide, you have improved. But there is more to it than that."

"I know there's more to it. It's about all of Scopus and the Outlands. I just need more—"

"Time is not on our side right now. The sooner my men have the marrowroot for you, the better. Nurse

Sharpe has already agreed to brew the tea we so desperately need," he said, interrupting Elide.

Elide nodded and bowed her head.

"Come," the Apostate said to Elide.

"We aren't finished," Calliope said.

The Apostate turned to Calliope. "I believe you are."

Calliope scowled at him, but she said nothing. Then she picked up the papers and started looking through them again.

Elide followed the Apostate out of the classroom.

As soon as they reached the bottom of the stairs, the Apostate looked at her and smiled.

"What?" Elide signed as he started walking down the hallway.

She caught up to him as he stopped by a large tapestry of previous apostates spanning the hall's length. It looked nearly like the one in Baptiste's church, only this one's colors were richer. They'd called it the Saint's Tapestry, though none of them considered themselves saints. The marts always put them up after Adoann; they were meant to mark how far they'd come. In the moonlight, the men looked more gallant, even though not all of their actions were. Jacques was the most memorable from her history class—he'd taken five wives against his advisors' wishes. Those five wives had been collected from the Outland states that they'd conquered. It was a two-fold act that caused his leadership to be questioned, and after his death, the next Apostate had to deal with the fallout. She wondered what the man beside her thought of that.

"You look nice," the Apostate said suddenly turning to her.

Elide felt herself blush.

"Thank you," Elide signed, looking away. She hoped he hadn't seen her blush, that would only add to her embarrassment.

"I'm sorry you've had to be present during Calliope and I's squabbles. We don't always see eye to eye," he said.

Elide nodded. For a moment, she stood there, looking at the tapestry on the wall. She noticed that the Apostate's gaze was focused on Rudolphus, and she was beginning to wonder what it was about him that he admired so much. Was it his achievements? Was it his unyielding bloodthirst throughout his rule—he killed far more than he saved? Perhaps he was a reminder of what not to be. *A tyrant,* Elide thought, staring at Rudolphus.

Then she felt the need to broach the subject. "It can be good to be challenged every once in a while, don't you think?" Elide signed.

"I presume you're speaking of your mentor."

"She is a good mentor," Elide signed hesitantly. "Though she can be a bit callous at times."

He stared at her for a moment. "She can be, but she is not a *leader.*"

He had caught what she'd implied, but that didn't stop her disappointment. She considered what he meant by it. *Not a leader.* She could only think of so many qualities that made a leader.

"Calliope is quick to anger. I can't have someone who reacts before they think leading the Mourners."

"Maybe it would take some time—" Elide stopped, remembering what he'd said earlier.

There wasn't time. That's why Calliope wasn't *in the running*. If Mother Superior died tomorrow, Calliope couldn't be the one to take over.

"I don't think you lack control, Elide," the Apostate said suddenly.

Elide looked up at him.

"That is why I want to give you the marrowroot. A lesser telepath would use its power for conquest and throw Scopus into darkness."

"I'm not the conquesting type," Elide signed. "I prefer to be in bed by midnight."

The Apostate chuckled.

"Who knows, you might surprise me," he said sarcastically. He smirked at her, and she felt the blush creep back onto her cheeks.

Elide shook off the feeling and signed, "Have they had any luck finding the marrowroot?"

"I'm afraid not. It appears your mentor may have gotten the better of me at the moment."

Elide's heart sank in her chest. What was she going to do?

"Everything will be okay, Elide," the Apostate said reassuringly. "I'm sorry that I failed you."

"You haven't failed me," Elide signed.

He looked down at her. Suddenly her skin felt warmer as she looked up into his eyes. She knew she wasn't blushing but felt as though her power was dancing inside her chest.

He smiled at her again and said, "I'm glad you feel that way, but—"

And then she kissed him.

She didn't know what came over her. Perhaps it was something in his eyes. For once in her life, she had done something uncharacteristically bold, and in that same moment, she felt his lips against hers. Her hands were cupping his face and her breath caught in her chest. By the time she found reason, her heart was hammering in her chest, and she stepped back. His expression was unreadable.

Elide went to apologize, but he pulled her back into him. He tilted her head back with one hand and kissed her deeply. Her hand found his chest and smoothed over the embroidery on his coat.

"Your grace," a familiar male voice called.

The Apostate pulled away, letting her go and turning as Cyrus approached them. He bowed to the Apostate and looked at Elide suspiciously. Suddenly, she realized her fingers were touching her lips, and she dropped her hand to her side.

"Daegal has found the deserter," Cyrus said, still looking at Elide. "And the men are awaiting your orders."

"Then it's best we get back to Thanatos before we have a riot on our hands," the Apostate responded calmly.

The Apostate nodded toward Elide. Then he turned his back on her and went with Cyrus, leaving her standing in an empty hallway.

She touched her lips. For a moment, she wondered what had driven her to kiss him. But each moment that passed created more questions than answers. Elide stared at the tapestry as though the answers were somewhere on it. But aside from the piercing eyes of Rudolphus, she found nothing there. No new wisdom. No answers. Just a group of old men woven into a wall hanging.

Elide took her time walking back to her dorm, half-expecting the answer to dawn on her along the way. *Why did I do that?* She ran a hand through her hair. *Why would he do that?* The Apostate had kissed her. She could feel the passion in his kiss, the *yearning*, as if he'd been waiting for it.

Elide could feel herself blushing again, but she couldn't stop it. She wanted to talk to someone about it. But Starla would likely want her to explain everything, Isadora would be stunned by the news and possibly even want to alert Mother Superior, and Calliope, dear God, she couldn't tell her. After a few more minutes of deliberation, she decided to go to her bedroom and stay there until morning.

But when she made it back to the dorm suite, she found Starla, Isadora, and Pepper waiting for her.

Apparently, Starla had spent the day in Westerby at Heaven's Door for her commitment ceremony dress fitting.

Elide sat on the couch and listened to her talk all about her trip. Starla had ridden in this morning and arrived on a sample sale day. Starla had found the event fun. Though this form of fun involved her fighting another woman over a one-of-a-kind wedding shawl and winning. But Elide was having trouble focusing on their conversation.

"You all right, Elide?" Pepper asked suddenly. "You look ill."

Elide hesitated.

"I'm fine. I just need some rest," Elide signed.

Starla gasped. "Well, don't let me hold you up. Go on, off to bed!" Starla said, putting her hands on her hips. "And I'm not taking no for an answer. Go on!"

Starla smiled at her.

Elide hugged Starla and went to her room. Elide was almost sad to leave, but she couldn't focus. She hoped a shower would change that but found that it didn't. By the time she shut her bedroom door, Isadora was leaving their dorm suite.

Elide towel dried her hair and scrunched the remaining water out of her curls. She dried herself and pulled on a pair of pajamas. But the moment she went to stick her dress in her hamper, she blushed when she saw the black dress box in the wardrobe. Everything was reminding her of the Apostate tonight. She dropped her clothes in the hamper and climbed into bed.

Her pillows were softer tonight, and her heart was warmer. Perhaps the kiss had flustered her, and she wouldn't be able to sleep tonight. But somehow that didn't matter. The memory of the Apostate's lips on hers made her nervous, and yet the thought of it made her heart skip a beat.

And she wondered if it would ever happen again.

# 19

S oon clouds rolled into the sky, obscuring the sunlight, and whispers around the academy turned to conversations about the Festival of Saints in Prospero. The elite were expected to attend a "grand masquerade ball," as Starla referred to it. The holiday came every year, but Elide usually sat in front of the television with her sister-in-law, watching the proceedings. Every year there was a different theme, and this year it was Divine Violence.

"Such a marvelous way to describe it, don't you think?" Starla said. "To think I hadn't thought we'd be attending with all the breaches in security. I can't imagine Mother Superior is pleased though. She's always hated balls."

Elide imagined that after attending them for over a century, she would hate them too. And having never partaken in more than a birthday party when she was six, she wasn't sure what to make of it. But the other novitiates seemed thrilled. When Elide first stepped out of their dorm suite this morning, she'd been surprised to see how many Hamles were sitting on the carpet sewing their dresses by the fireplace. Several looked up to wave at Elide as she left, though some were too frustrated with their sewing to stop for even a moment.

At breakfast with Isadora, they noticed the Leta unpacking their dress orders, and they seemed to have jointly decided on wearing purple dresses made from tulle. And from the look of things, they intended to accessorize with beaded jewelry and belts with badger buckles.

Starla joined them after breakfast. And Isadora, hoping to escape thoughts of the festival, went out into the quad with Elide.

"I'm already getting tired of all this myself," Isadora said as they made their way onto the lawns. "I mean, do you see them?"

Elide looked in the direction Isadora was pointing. Mirai were sitting in the grass, attaching fake antlers to headpieces and giggling at their work. Beside them, Laska were pretending to ram each other with horns.

Starla rolled her eyes. "Oh, don't be such a spoilsport! It's all in good fun! Back home, we would spend months planning out our ball gowns—and what better theme could there be for us?" Starla said, beaming. "We're divinely blessed with power, which we use in battle! Or *elsewhere*, depending on assignment."

"Divine violence," Isadora repeated. "It sounds a bit much to me. Like we're in the Dark Ages." She shuddered. "And the last thing I want to see is groups of liberty men walking around with swords or something."

"Ugh, don't be so dramatic," Starla groaned. Then she turned to Elide. "What do you think, Elide?"

Both her friends stopped and stared at her.

"I don't know what I'm supposed to wear," Elide signed.

"Well, we'll just have to fix that, won't we!" Starla said gleefully. "I'll make an appointment with the seamstress!"

Elide nodded. Although she wasn't nearly as disturbed at the prospect of a masquerade ball as Isadora, she certainly wasn't as enthused as Starla. In fact, she hoped against hope that Starla would take it upon herself to decide what Elide's dress would look like. But despite her best efforts, she found herself being pulled down to the seamstress's wing on the second floor of the academy. The seamstress, Madam Aurelia "Pomp" Cummings, was a native of Prospero, and a relatively short woman in stature. Her snow-white skin contrasted with bright pink hair, which bounced as she nodded her head while taking dress orders. The woman was noticeably excitable and had a love for sweet-smelling candles. Today it was a cinnamon candle and an apple candle, creating a blend that surprisingly didn't overwhelm the senses. Though the way Madam Cummings flitted around the room certainly could. Elide assumed that her being asked to make a dress that wasn't red with a fabric other than cotton was what had made her so excited.

The small woman climbed her rolling ladder to the fabric shelves and selected each roll carefully before getting back down. Then zipping by before another novitiate could say a word to her.

"Are you paying attention," the raven black-haired novitiate asked.

Starla shook herself. "Yes, I was, Cherie. You were talking about your dress."

"Your eyes looked a bit glazed over, so I couldn't be sure," Cherie said, twirling her hair around her finger. "But anyway, none of us are going to look the same," she said, rolling her eyes as if the thought were insulting. "There's really no reason for all of us Kedeh to dress alike. I mean, we're individuals—*and* we spend all year in uniform. Why dress the same at the biggest event of the year?"

They had been sitting here for half an hour, but Cherie had managed to make it feel like half a century. It was as if she worried that somehow her individuality would be ripped away by her identity as a Kedeh.

"Well, I plan on wearing a gold dress," Starla said, interrupting Cherie's rant. Then she paused, perhaps for dramatic effect. "With wings of some sort."

"But Hamles are bears," Cherie spat out, suddenly defensive. "Bears don't have wings."

Starla scoffed. "Why on earth would I go as some hairy, burly bear? What about that screams divine violence to you?"

Cherie's eyes narrowed. "Better that than to walk around dressed as an angel!" Cherie exclaimed, rising to her feet.

"I am not going to dress like an angel!" Starla shouted back, standing up in protest.

Other novitiates had stopped looking at the fabric on the walls to stare at the two.

"I'd hope not, that'd be *blasphemy*," Cherie stressed.

Starla gaped. "Don't you dare accuse me of blasphemy Cherie Rathmore!" Starla said. "You're the one who got pregnant out of wedlock last year."

"Travis and I were married before the baby came," Cherie said weakly. Her green eyes were filling with tears. She grabbed her bag from her seat and ran out of the room.

Starla sat back down, and the other novitiates returned to their conversations. Five Kedeh stared at the walls, examining the fabrics. Elide, however, couldn't help but stare at the vacant seat that Cherie left behind.

"I have no idea what came over her. Cherie is rarely that rude, but that's Kedeh for you, they're always prone to dramatics. Doesn't matter, that's one less number to wait behind."

Starla looked down at the number ticket in her hand, and Elide felt her stomach seize. She wondered how her friend could expose something so private in front of an audience, but she sensed it was the same reason Starla had done it to her. Was it because she felt threatened? Perhaps a skill Starla learned while living in Prospero? The thought made Elide wary of the upcoming festival, so frivolous an event now felt like a warning.

Selecting a dress had taken most of the afternoon. Elide had chosen a ballgown from Madam Pomp's dress portfolio and told her that she trusted her expertise. Then she returned to her room to rest.

Her nap only lasted a few hours, but it had felt longer. Elide woke from a pleasant dream. Though less of it was familiar, outside of her kissing the Apostate. She was attending the masquerade ball, and the room was decorated in silver, but it was hazier than her other dreams. He found her in the crowd, and they'd danced to the awe of those around them. It surprised her that no one made any comments about his choice of partner. But she knew the dream wasn't real. Time was nonlinear, and moments skipped from one to the next. All those unimportant moments, walking from place to place, making her way to the balcony, and then kissing the Apostate again.

She almost felt robbed of it, staring up at the painting on her ceiling. *Stop thinking about him,* she told herself, shoving her face into her pillow. *It was one kiss. He's hundreds of years old, he's probably kissed plenty of women in his time.* Perhaps women who'd become Mourners themselves. Elide desperately wanted to tell her friends but couldn't imagine their reaction. Somehow the moment felt sacred. She couldn't share it with someone else. If there was something between them, she didn't want it to be disturbed by outsiders.

As the week came to a close, the carriages rolled in, and the gowns were delivered. And Elide found herself opening her wardrobe and taking out the black dress box. When she stared at the gray coat this time, she didn't feel overwhelmed. She ran her fingers over it and hoped it would go well with her dress.

Elide held the raven pin in the palm of her hand, staring at the bird that didn't look nearly as fearsome now as it once had. She checked the time on the clock on her desk. *Time to get ready,* she thought to herself. Elide styled her curls, letting them fall to her waist before taking her ballgown out of its box. She set the underskirt to the side and pulled on the white gown. Madam Cummings had chosen a sweetheart neckline for the gown with draped sleeves. The delicate boning of the corset-style bodice made it appear more modern, while floral appliques dispersed over the skirt created a dreamlike effect.

When she finally fastened the last clasp, Elide stepped into the underskirt, pulled it up, and watched the gown take shape. It was beautiful.

A gasp came from her doorway, pulling Elide from her thoughts. Starla stood gaping in the doorway in a sparkly, gold-colored gown beside Isadora, who'd chosen to wear scarlet and gold.

"You look absolutely marvelous," Starla said. "No man in his right mind will be able to ignore you."

"Except for the married ones," Isadora added.

Starla scoffed. "*Especially* the married ones."

Elide shook her head at her friends.

"Ready?" Elide signed.

Isadora sighed. "As I'll ever be."

And with that, Elide put on her coat, placing the raven pin in her pocket. The three left the dorm suite and walked out of the dormitories, filing out Prana Academy's doors with the other novitiates.

~

Elide had just stepped out of the carriage and onto the brick road when Cyrus appeared with a much smaller Aiden.

"I'd heard you didn't have a mask," Cyrus said, taking a white masquerade mask from Aidan.

She nodded and turned, allowing Cyrus to tie the mask around her eyes.

"Be careful tonight," he whispered suddenly as he fastened the masquerade mask against her face.

She looked back at him.

"Is the mask too tight?" Cyrus questioned, and Elide shook her head. "Good."

He looked at Isadora and said, "The Apostate has instructed me to escort Ms. Hester to the ballroom."

"That's fine," Isadora said, looking between the two of them. "I'll go."

Isadora quickly hugged Elide, promising they would meet the moment she was free of the stiff, and then went to join Starla, Pepper, and the Laska.

"Come, *quickly*," Cyrus said lowly, though Elide could hear the urgency in his voice.

She had to walk faster to keep up with his long strides, but once they were inside the entry tunnel, his pace slowed.

Elide tapped his shoulder, and he looked at her.

"What did you mean by be careful?" she signed.

Cyrus hesitated.

"Exactly as I've said, *be careful*," he repeated.

"Are you saying I need to watch my back?" Elide signed.

Cyrus took a deep breath. "I'm saying you weren't given a clear understanding of what you're walking into. But you're the Teller, so you should always be exercising precaution and not pulling any silly stunts like your fight with Ayla."

Elide shook her head.

"It was a one-time thing," Elide signed glaring at him.

"Good, it can't happen again," Cyrus repeated. He suddenly became more serious. "There are a lot of powerful players here tonight, and there's no way of knowing if an assassin will be here."

Elide felt her heart lurch. "An assassin?" Elide signed.

"If the reports are anything to go on, then yes," Cyrus responded lowly. "The Apostate wanted a large audience for the moment he confirms your existence. With that audience comes risk."

"Couldn't the Mourners just check what everyone's thinking?" Elide signed.

Cyrus laughed and shook his head.

"That was my suggestion," Cyrus said with a smirk. "However, Mother Superior informed me that even the best Hamle can't read every mind that enters the room. And only a Teller can establish what's the truth."

"Hamles can read minds?" Elide signed.

Starla had neglected to mention that to her.

"Yes, but they can also project visions and ideas into others' minds," Cyrus told her. "They're quite good in battle."

"Ideas like what?" Elide signed.

Cyrus shrugged. "I've only experienced the positive

visions and feelings that came with them when I was being stitched up in the field," he said, thinking for a moment. He nodded to himself silently. "From what I do remember, she was very kind, her voice sounded like honey, and I dreamt of having a family—wife, kids—but when I woke up, I found out they weren't real."

Elide stared at him. He looked sad, clutching his side as though there was still phantom pain there.

Cyrus cleared his throat.

"As for the assassins, you have no reason to worry," Cyrus said calmly. "My men and I are more than capable of handling any threat that could come our way."

As they stepped into the room, Cyrus put on a mask, guiding Elide through the entry doors. And soon, they were accompanied by Altair and four other Disciples. She almost felt safer.

Elide crossed her arms protectively over her chest, brushing away the goosebumps on them and stopping when her escort did. Cyrus went to speak to a mart who wore a silver badge proclaiming his status.

The ballroom was enormous and buzzing with life. The noble elite were talking to each other, drinking wine from wine glasses, and dressed in eccentric outfits. She saw one woman with peacock feathers in her hair that matched her gray ballgown. Elide wasn't sure how that fit the theme, but the woman's laugh seemed to bounce off the walls. On her left, an orchestra was playing music, and Elide noticed a few lina scanning the enclosed bookcases at the south end of the room. Most people were dancing in the center of the room in what appeared to be a waltz. She didn't know what dance they were doing but did notice that Starla was among them, moving gracefully over the marble floors and dancing with her fiancé. And Elide had to admit, Calvin was quite handsome, even with the black mask on his face. His jawline was sharp, and his curly brown hair moved with every twist and turn.

The Mourners and novitiates were mingling with the nobles; their colors appearing brighter and more distinct among the masses. Elide was almost beginning to feel left out until Cyrus told her to follow him.

They passed noble men and women alike, and Elide noticed them bowing as they did, and then she realized they were bowing to her—like she was the Apostate. She had to stop herself from blushing.

Clearly, they knew who she was, even if she didn't know them. She understood that rumors spread quickly, but she wasn't sure whether it unnerved her that they'd so easily spotted her. But then she remembered that she was surrounded by Disciples, and if nothing else, she found herself glad that she was. A few times, she instinctively looked around, though uncertain of what or who she was searching for. But when they finally stopped at an indoor bench where she could rest her feet for a moment, she was surprised when she saw a certain reverend elder enter the room.

"Looking well, Elide," Reverend Coin said, complimenting her. He wore a gray uniform; his jacket bore military medals and service ribbons on the left breast. His wife stood beside him in a matching gray gown. She was younger, looked about fifty, with fine black hair that shined almost as brightly as the diamond necklace she wore around her neck.

"So are you, Reverend Coin," Elide signed. He paused as his wife whispered into his ear, and he smiled.

"Thank you. I've been getting more sun lately thanks to our great leader's orders," he said.

He laughed, and Elide laughed politely with him.

"Have you seen your brother around?" Reverend Coin said, scanning the attendees. "I've been meaning to discuss something with him."

Elide felt her heart lurch painfully in her chest at the thought of Hansel, and she found herself looking for him too. She wanted to see him. He was considered a noble, and she wanted him to see her. But even more than that, she wanted to confront him and demand he tell her why he hadn't been responding to her letters.

"Ah, Dad, Mom, good to see you," Cyrus said, hugging his mother.

Elide smiled. Something about hearing a high-ranking officer refer to his parents that way made her want to giggle. It was sweet. Especially when his mother cradled his face as though he were a young boy.

"The Apostate's presentation will begin soon," Cyrus told Elide as he cupped his mother's hands in his own. "I need to take you to him."

Elide nodded.

Cyrus turned back to his mother and kissed her on the cheek.

"We'll be standing up front," his mother said, as though she were talking about an elementary school performance.

Her escort smiled at his mother and hugged his father before leading Elide away from them.

Cyrus led her far away from the other guests and stopped in a room with a piano and walls covered in green wallpaper with ornate white leaves on it. He walked up to the wall, took his raven pin off his lapel, and slid it flat against a portion of the wall. For a moment, she heard something banging inside the wall until one panel of the wall came out. *A secret door*, Elide thought, staring at it as Cyrus opened it. "Through here," he said lowly. Elide nodded, stepping past him and into the narrow, dimly lit passage.

The walls shared similar wallpaper, but the branches connected to depict a greater family tree. The tapestry reminded her of those in the academy, ancient and intimidating. But here there were portraits of men and women's sullen faces on them, dating back to the Mayflower. She wanted to ask Cyrus about it, but as she turned to him, Cyrus shut the door. Elide stared at the emotionless faces on the walls, feeling suddenly nervous. She tried searching for a knob to get out the same way she came in, but there was none. The wall was flat on this side.

She set her head against the wall for a moment, staring down at her gown, and sighed. *What the hell, Cyrus,* she thought bitterly. She backed away from the wall and could faintly see the locking mechanism peeking out from a hole in the wall.

Elide thought for a moment and reached into her pocket. *This better work,* she thought, grabbing the pin and placing it against the wall. She tried moving it against the wall, but it didn't budge. No matter what pattern she moved it in, it wouldn't move.

She sighed in frustration and turned her attention down the dim passageway. And Elide began walking forward. If she died, it would be Cyrus's fault, not hers.

But as Elide pressed on through the darkness, passing the last portrait on the wall, she saw a crack of light. She gathered up her dress into her hands and ran toward it, pushing the door open and nearly falling flat on her face.

"I was wondering how long it would take you to get here," the Apostate said.

He was staring down at a map on a table. There were miniature ships and small markers on them. *Marching orders,* Elide thought to herself. *During a party?* She stared at the Apostate blankly. He was wearing a black-clad uniform, but this one was more formal. His coat was black with golden swirls embroidered onto it that twisted and turned; on his collar were two ravens.

"The announcement went well, by the way," he said suddenly.

Elide looked back at the secret passage. She was sure that she hadn't been in there for more than a few minutes.

"How long have I been gone?" Elide signed.

"You should relax," he said calmly as he scribbled something onto a piece of paper. "There's some warm tea on the desk over there."

"How long have I been gone?" Elide signed again, staying rooted to the spot.

The Apostate stared at her but didn't speak.

"Answer me!" Elide signed, narrowing her eyes at him.

His gaze didn't waver for even a moment.

"A few hours," he answered. "The mind can distort time in darkness. It seems yours made your time in there shorter." The Apostate walked toward her and squeezed her hand. "Mourner novitiates react differently to fear. In time you'll learn to master yours." He let go of her hand and let it drop to the side.

She went to protest, but before she could respond, he cut her off, kissing her passionately, and her heart leapt in her chest. Clearly, he wasn't repulsed by her or put off by the thought of kissing her. He pulled her flush against his body, and she melted into his embrace. She pressed her fingers against the embroidery on his coat, exploring the broad planes of his chest and then exploring higher until her hands rested on his cheekbones. He pulled her closer to him, though she hadn't thought it was possible. One hand cradled her head, and the other was on the small of her back, holding her to him. Suddenly, she felt warmth spreading over her skin. It was like she was standing at the center of a bonfire. The embers seeping into her skin, permeating through every vein in her body, saturating every nerve but never burning her. Every muscle of his body pressed against her from chest to knee. Suddenly, she could feel everything he felt—his lust for her, his pain over the war his people were enduring, his *rage*.

Elide wrenched herself away from him, gasping for air. She felt dizzy suddenly and had to force herself to shake off the feeling. The Apostate steadied her.

"Did you feel that?" Elide signed.

She looked up at him, staring into his dark eyes. They

were focused on her, and somehow in this brightly lit room, his handsome features were rendered cruel.

"I'm afraid I lost control," he responded calmly, but she could hear the uncertainty in his voice.

"Of your desires?" Elide signed, faintly recalling a memory inside his head of the two of them.

He stared at her and stepped toward her, cupping her face with one hand. "Of my lust," he said lowly.

When their lips met again, his kiss was slow, deep, and possessive. His arms snaked around her waist, pulling her back into him.

He broke the kiss but didn't move away from her. His lips grazed her cheek before finding her neck.

Elide resisted the urge to let him continue and signed, "Your grace."

"Ares," he said, looking her in the eyes. "Call me Ares," he repeated softly, his lips a few inches from hers.

She blushed with some faint comprehension of a question she wanted to ask. "Ares, what's changed?"

"Daegal has alerted me that they've found a marrow-root plantation just beyond our borders. The farmer there is a loyalist of the Apolitian people. I'm meant to be drawing up a statement for a speech about providing asylum to loyalists stuck on the wrong side of the border who wish to convert to our faith. I should be planning a contract of settlement to induct an entire town into Scopus. And yet, I'm here," he said, kissing her again.

Elide gave into the kiss. She wrapped her arms around his neck as he lifted her onto the desk. She felt his hand sliding up her leg, lifting the skirt of her gown around her hips. She could feel her heart beating faster. He broke the kiss to meet her gaze.

"You and I are not so different," he whispered, staring down at her. "There are not many of us," he said and nipped her neck, "and there is only one you." He finished as he slipped his hand down between them.

He kissed her passionately, sliding his fingers between her legs. She gasped at the contact, shuddering in pleasure and anticipation. His mouth went back to her throat, and a moan escaped her lips. His fingers moved unhurriedly over her clitoris, and soon two fingers slid inside her. Elide had touched herself before, but his skillful and unfamiliar fingers seemed to add to her arousal.

"Do you want me to stop?" He asked softly, but she couldn't think.

She'd wanted to see him for weeks. He had avoided her all that time, confusing her and making her feel almost unworthy. But at the moment, she was lost in the sensation of his fingers sliding in and out of her. Her thoughts were muddled by the memory of Cyrus warning her to be careful. Had he meant the Apostate? But the Apostate had done all he said he'd do. He believed she could change the world. She wanted to believe that herself.

He pulled his fingers from her body and looked down at Elide, waiting for an answer.

"No," Elide signed, shaking her head.

His gaze was steady and filled with desire. "Are you sure?"

"Yes," Elide signed, nodding.

And with that, he removed her underwear before

unfastening his belt and letting his pants fall to the floor. He positioned his erection between her legs and thrust himself into her body.

As he entered her, she felt a sharp pain between her legs. Elide gasped, and her grip tightened on the desk. He leaned down and whispered in her ear, "It'll only hurt for a moment. Tell me if it becomes too much, and we'll stop."

Elide nodded as he began to move inside her. Her arms bent at the elbows, holding her up against the desk, his hands gripping her hips, her body moving with every thrust he made into her. The pain was faint but present in her nether regions, it was like he was passing over a small wound inside her. But her pleasure managed to overpower it, and she pulled him closer to her. The room filled with their moans of pleasure. The Apostate seemed to move deeper inside her with every thrust. The connection between them spread through her body once again, and she felt his desire—the sensation was overwhelming, and it felt as though it was beckoning her as his lips came back down onto hers. His movements never slowed, and she felt the feeling grow more and more. Her orgasm ripped through her, and she shuddered in his embrace. He continued to move within her, changing the tempo of his thrusts to move slower. She could hear his ragged breathing as he thrust more firmly inside her until she heard him gasp. Then he pulled away from her.

Elide was still trying to catch her breath as he redressed in his clothes. He ran a hand through his disheveled hair before turning and checking his reflection in the looking glass on the wall. She pulled up her underwear and tidied her gown, still reeling from the realization of what they'd done.

"I have to go," he said, looking at her in the mirror. "Daegal and the Disciples will be waiting for me in the war room."

Elide nodded, trying to reconvene her thoughts. He straightened his coat and took a deep breath. The Apostate walked to the wooden double doors on the other side of the room and opened the door a crack.

"You should wait at least ten minutes before leaving," he said. All earlier passion gone from his voice. "I'll send Cyrus to find you. Be somewhere in the ballroom."

Elide nodded again. She felt her heart lurch in her chest. A few moments ago she had given herself to a near stranger. She could hear her tutor's lectures about propriety and how a woman should act and carry herself with dignity. That a woman should remain chaste until marriage and be ashamed if she did not. But Elide didn't feel ashamed of herself.

"I'll send for you when we return to the academy," the Apostate said, stopping in the doorway.

Elide smiled and nodded. And then the Apostate stepped out the door, shutting it behind him. She waited at least thirty minutes, watching the owl cuckoo clock on the wall, trying to put her thoughts together.

Was it so wrong for her to have given herself to him? What did it mean that she had? It couldn't have all been driven by lust. *Fate then,* she thought to herself and felt herself flush with embarrassment. She shook her head at herself and left the room behind.

Elide managed to leave without being noticed by too many people. She said a few hellos to drunken classmates and greeted a few smiling Enoch. But as soon as she reached the ballroom, she decided she would find Reverend Coin and talk to him. If she stood around talking to him and his wife, surely Cyrus would have an easy time finding her.

Although, as Elide moved through the masses of people in the ballroom, scanning the room for Reverend Coin, she couldn't find him. But then she saw his wife speaking to other noble women by the door. Elide greeted her and would've continued talking to her, but she saw Reverend Coin chatting outside with a certain violet-clad mart.

*Hansel,* she thought.

# 20

lide's heart was hammering in her chest. *He came*, she thought, staring at him with the elder man. Hansel was a few inches taller than him, but at six feet, Hansel was taller than most people. *Well, of course, he came, he's a mart, they have to come,* she scorned herself. But no matter how mad she was, she was glad to see him. He looked healthy and relatively normal, though his knuckles were bruised.

She hesitated for a moment, then approached the two men, and Reverend Coin stopped speaking. For a moment, she thought she might faint at the sight of a familiar face. But Hansel didn't look nearly as happy to see her.

"Hansel?" Elide signed, staring at him.

Hansel looked down at the ground. And soon, she realized he was looking her gown over. She blushed nervously. She supposed it looked rather outlandish compared to what Baptiste women would wear, but she was too giddy to care.

"Well, I'll leave you two to catch up," Reverend Coin said to them. "Good to see you, Elide. Hansel."

The reverend elder said his name as if he were warning Hansel to mind his tongue, but before long, he joined his wife inside, leaving them alone.

Though feeling rather nervous and wanting to tell him all that had happened since she'd last seen him, she decided to start with the small talk first.

"How was your trip?" Elide signed.

"Fine," Hansel said sternly with a hard expression. "Our noble leader was so kind to extend me an invitation to this *soiree* as a gesture of good faith."

"Good faith?" she signed. Her mind was scattered for a few moments, and then it dawned on her. "Right, I had heard you'd met with the other marts in Carden."

Hansel stared at her, holding the same unreadable expression. He glanced over her shoulder and said, "I'll have to leave soon. I need to get back to Baptiste as soon as possible. Glad you're doing well."

Elide's heart sank. How could he be treating her like this? He was her brother, for Christ's sake. What happened to always being there for her? She could feel her blood boiling.

"I'm so sorry to hold you up," Elide signed, shoving him. "But I suppose I can't expect much since you never bothered to respond to a single one of my letters! I'm sure you have more pressing matters to get back to in Baptiste. Well, go ahead then! Rush back to your perfect life in that stupid little house on Mansfield Street."

Hansel looked stunned. "What letters?"

"Like you haven't seen them," Elide signed, rolling her eyes.

Hansel stared at her blankly.

She stared back at him, uncrossing her arms. She felt a pang of guilt. The longer she looked at him, the less he looked like himself. There was a small scar on his cheek, and his brown skin had tanned slightly, likely from being in a rougher climate. Underneath his violet coat, his shoulder was bandaged, and she would guess so was the rest of his arm. And his knuckles were bruised—but who had he been fighting?

"What happened to you?" Elide signed.

He laughed dryly, adjusting his coat.

"Some Enochs in Carden got the jump on me," he explained. "They didn't like the way I'd spoken to their beloved master. And I was roughed up a little, but I'm fine."

Elide was taken aback by his answer. "You have to tell someone. If the Apostate knew—"

"If the Apostate knew?" he repeated before letting out another dry laugh. "He certainly didn't care about Lilah when the Mourners attacked her the day they took you from Baptiste."

Elide hesitated. "What are you talking about?" she signed. "I don't remember—but Lilah let them in."

"They'd told her they wouldn't use any unnecessary force," Hansel told Elide. "When one of them attacked you, she tried to stop her, and the other *accidentally* lashed out. But I'm not sure how they can claim that was an accident."

Elide was too stunned to respond. She didn't remember that, though a flash of her dream pressed back into her mind: Lilah gripping her stomach, her fingers covered in blood, blood trickling down her lips.

"When I found Lilah, she was covered in blood," Hansel explained. "Reverend Warner called for a doctor, but by the time they reached the house, there wasn't anything they could do for her. They *killed* her for getting in their way, Elide. I'm not sure how you manage to trust them."

"Did Reverend Coin have anything to say about her death?" Elide signed. "Or about the men who attacked you?"

Hansel laughed. "Now that's rich," he said, shaking his head. "Reverend Coin and his wife offered their condolences at her funeral. As for those Enochs, Carden might be under his jurisdiction, but even he's still too scared to stand up for peace. And Reverend Warner has some sort of pride attached to the war effort. So as always, I'm on my own."

"You aren't on your own," Elide signed, then took his hand.

He looked her in the eyes. For a moment, she saw his eyes soften, but then he snatched his hand away, and his eyes turned cold.

"Of course, I am," he snapped. "You're the Apostate's prize now, bending over backward to please him like everyone else."

"No, I'm not," Elide signed. "Perhaps if we just go and speak to him. Maybe then—"

"There's no speaking to him, Elide. He won't stop until he's taken the Outlands," Hansel hissed, cutting her off.

His words shocked her.

"He's just trying to bring peace to Scopus—"

"And the Outlands," Hansel finished angrily. "*Yes, I've* heard the sales pitch, time and time again. And I'm sure it sounds all well and good to you. I'd expect it to, seeing as you've been around his lapdogs in Prana."

"They aren't lapdogs. There are actually those that oppose him," Elide signed, thinking of Calliope.

"Do you oppose him?"

Elide hesitated. She hadn't thought about it before and didn't know where to begin answering it.

"He give you one of those pins?" Hansel asked, studying her outfit, from her undone coat to checking the neckline of her dress. "Surprised you're not wearing it."

"It's not my symbol, it's his."

Hansel let out a bark of laughter. "Well, that makes a world of difference then, doesn't it?"

He was being sarcastic, and she winced at the insult.

"I wouldn't want it if he gave it to me," Elide signed.

"Well, he must've given you some token of his affection. Or is that not why he sent Baptiste men to search for marrowroot? But I'm sure you've heard that by now. He certainly wasn't in the war room when he was meant to be."

Her heart lurched at what he was suggesting. Elide

took a deep breath and tried to blink away the tears forming in her eyes.

"If you just take the time to speak with him," Elide signed, but she couldn't finish her thought. She felt a mixture of emotions—shame, guilt, despair, but mostly *loss*. It was like Hansel could see it in her face. He was being cruel to her, but maybe he was right to be. But at the same time, she wanted to scoff. Why did it matter that she had sex with the Apostate? Who was he to go around casting judgment? He had an affair with Juliette—how was that any different? If anything, it was worse.

"Your precious master longs for battle and the spoils of war," Hansel said suddenly. "And I'm sure he's enjoying himself while doing so."

"I am allowed to do as I please," Elide signed. "The same way you do."

He scoffed. "I'm sure there are many unimaginable things you do with your time in that place," he said sharply. "But as far as lapdogs go, clearly, you're being treated well. Pampered like a proper queen for her dread king."

"What does that make you then?" Elide signed angrily. "If I'm a dog, then are you a flea?"

Hansel winced at the statement.

"A flea," Hansel repeated, laughing dryly. "Enjoy your night, Your Majesty."

He bowed to her. Then turned and walked back into the building.

Elide stood there, breathing raggedly, trying to keep herself from crying. She went back inside the building, pushing her way through the elite, their colors blurring together as tears welled up in her eyes. When Elide made it to the room with the piano, she slid down to the floor and began to cry into her hands, wishing the night would simply end.

# 21

She was sobbing so hard that she hardly heard someone walk up to her. Elide wiped the tears out of her eyes, expecting it to be Cyrus or the Apostate. But when she looked up, she saw Calliope Vexx.

"Calliope?" she signed, sniffling.

Elide wiped her nose with her sheer sleeve, immediately regretting it afterward.

"Get up, Elide," Calliope said softly, helping her up and holding her at arm's length.

She wasn't expecting a hug from Calliope but hardly understood her mentor examining her.

"Good, you haven't taken it yet," she said.

"Taken what?" Elide signed, but then it hit her. "No, I haven't taken the marrowroot. Calliope, is everything all right?"

"There's no time for questions," she said, pulling Elide by the arm out of the room and down a hall.

She was moving so quickly that Elide nearly tripped

over her feet as they walked. Elide couldn't tell what had come over her mentor, but one thing was clear, Calliope was afraid.

They stopped when they reached a hallway, and Calliope held an arm out, forcing Elide against the wall. She peered around it, and they waited until three Disciples passed them, chatting drunkenly.

The moment the hall was clear, she began dragging Elide through the halls again until they were in a small parlor.

"Calliope, what's going on?" Elide signed to her mentor.

"No time for questions," Calliope said, pulling away the rug on the floor and opening a trapdoor. "After you."

Elide nodded. She stared down into the dark hole and gulped before stepping onto the ladder and making her way down the rungs. She didn't know how long she climbed down but was grateful when she reached the bottom.

The ground wasn't paved, it was dirt, but she could barely see in front of her face, much less trust herself to walk forward. Calliope snorted when she reached the bottom and shook her head at Elide. Her mentor snapped her fingers and opened her palm to reveal an orb of light.

Elide blinked at Calliope, looking between her and the orb.

"No time," Calliope repeated as she released the orb, and it floated up above their heads.

They walked through the tunnel in silence for a few minutes. A scraping sound echoed off the stone walls, sending a shiver down Elide's spine. It looked as though they were under a large stone bridge, with pipes running through it and broken lightbulbs overhead.

"Where are we?" Elide signed.

"Underground," Calliope said harshly. "This is one of the routes slaves took to escape to the North before Minister Samuel Davis, the first Apostate, and his followers took over." Calliope hesitated and corrected, "The *Outlands*. But before the Great Revelation, it was just the North, or the *Union*, and the Confederacy in the South."

Elide saw a mouse run across the floor and shuddered.

"General Lee wanted to win the war—and so he did. Now we're all paying the price for it."

"I don't need a history lesson! What's going on, Calliope?" Elide signed.

"Think, girl! Think!" Calliope hissed. "The Apostate is about to have an entire plantation of marrowroot in his grasp. You don't truly believe that he'll stop with you?"

"So you think the marrowroot will work?" Elide asked, staring at her.

"I have no doubt that it will work. I saw it firsthand when I was a little girl. But that doesn't make it something to meddle with. A Mancio shouldn't be going around playing God."

"Playing God?' Elide signed.

"He's going to take the Outlands."

"I know, he's told me," Elide signed. "He wants to bring peace and faith to both of our nations."

"Peace?" Calliope said, stopping in place. "That's what he told you?"

Elide's heart sank in her chest. Calliope shook her head. Her mentor hardly looked like herself; she was disheveled and wild-looking. And Elide was starting to think that perhaps Calliope was paranoid about her position at the academy.

"Do not think such things about me, little girl. I'm trying to save your life," Calliope snapped.

Elide recoiled, bowing her head and looking to the ground.

"There will be a bag up ahead with clothes in it. You need to change. You can't go out into the night wearing that—you're not a runaway princess," she said, pulling Elide farther down the tunnel.

They arrived in a dimly lit cellar made of brick and filled with bottles of wine. At the center there was a wooden table with a black sack on it. Calliope grabbed it and handed it to Elide.

Elide rolled her eyes and began to change into the outfit. She hadn't thought they sold jeans in Prospero but was grateful they did when she pulled them on. They were snug, and the turtleneck was too. A brown trench coat was folded in the bottom of the bag. She pulled the coat out and put that on too.

"The military has increased tenfold since your entry into Prana. They're not simply training them anymore. He's going to have every novitiate in the academy drink the marrowroot tea and use those that survive for war. He intends to send the First Class into the Outlands nearest neutral territories and take them. Scopus's armies will ravage those towns, and all those who do not kneel before him will be executed as he's done before, and he'll continue to do. Until he is stopped or there is nowhere to run."

Elide sighed. She was sure there was good reason for the armies expanding. But Calliope's other suggestions seemed presumptuous in nature, and clearly, the woman must've had too much to drink at the ball.

"Perhaps we should return to the party upstairs," Elide signed cautiously. She looked Calliope over. *No weapons. Except for her power.* "He's not going to poison the entire student population of Prana Academy. I'm sure you just need some rest. It's been a long day. I know I need some."

Calliope took a deep breath. She grabbed Elide's arm, her nails biting into her skin.

"I'm not some child speaking idle tales. He is not my father," Calliope said warningly. "Not the Almighty. Or my earthly father, Orion. My father was the previous Apostate, and he tried to set meetings for a new peace treaty with the Outlands, but the Outlanders' leader, their *president*, was a fool then and wanted to keep the war going. Tens of thousands of men, women, and children have died. And thousands more will if my brother isn't stopped."

Elide stared at her blankly. By some instinct, call it intuition, she knew Calliope wasn't lying.

"The Apostate is your brother," Elide signed.

Calliope nodded. "Yes," she responded weakly. "He saw how the Outlands' president and his followers laughed at our father's proposal. They considered it weakness. But my father was not a weak man, even in sickness he was powerful."

Elide was trying to clear her head, trying to understand what her mentor was saying.

Elide shook her head.

"My father drank the marrowroot to keep up his strength and used his abilities to take out a regiment of the Outlands' military before asking for peace a second time. But he had overlooked the small town that lay between them. He hadn't thought of the innocents that lived there. He toppled their houses, made fire rain down on them—he murdered them. My father burned men, women, and children alive to end a war. He committed genocide to keep what he called the Natural Order. To protect *his* people."

"Why didn't anyone stop him?" Elide signed.

"There were rebels, but most of them were caught and executed. Those that weren't are still in hiding, but between the Scouts and Mourners searching for them—I doubt it'll be long before they find the rest," Calliope said softly. Elide shook her head, trying to clear her thoughts. "My brother needs you, Elide, because you're the only one that can pull it out of the rebel they've caught."

"Me?" Elide signed. "I've just gotten better at fighting and can barely wield a knife. Getting into someone's mind would be—"

"Damn near impossible without the marrowroot," Calliope finished, cutting her off. "Which is why he's getting it. No one else can do what you can. Not even I could pry open that rebel's mind without killing myself."

Elide gulped. "Why can't you? You're much more powerful than me."

"The rebel has been trained to withstand Mourner powers," Calliope said. "At least those that she can easily be exposed to. But Tellers are extremely rare, and when your ability is to extract the truth from others, there's no resisting you."

Elide could hardly reconcile the man Calliope was telling her about and the one she thought she knew. The Apostate cared for her and the Apolitian people. He wanted to unite them with the Outlands. How could that be wrong? Clearly, Calliope had to have gotten it all wrong.

"I'm sure you're just misunderstanding—"

"Listen to me, little girl," Calliope hissed, and her eyes turned black. "He has spent lifetimes learning how to manipulate and deceive people to gain their confidence. He is not some dark prince sprung from a fairytale." She took a deep breath, and her eyes returned to their normal state. "He is a *dictator*. He has no plans of creating a safe haven for all. Why do you think he kept you out of his little announcement? He wanted you out of the way. The Apostate wants control. He craves power and will do anything to get it. Tell me, does he make you feel warm when he touches you? Do you know what that is? A *ruse*. He can manipulate feelings better than any Hamle, and there is no greater weakness than love."

The insult felt like a slap to the face.

"I wouldn't cooperate with him if I stayed," Elide signed. "I would fight back."

"You can't fight him," Calliope said sternly. "You would struggle against Daegal, and he's well versed but lacks control. The Apostate is your only equal. He could control your mind with ease—you've already let him in. I can see it all over your face. You're powerless against him."

Elide felt as though her heart was twisting in her chest.

He had been lying to her all this time. He didn't want to help her. *A Teller will end this one*, he'd told her. But not in the way she hoped. There wouldn't be peace. She should've known that Hansel wouldn't lie to her. *He won't stop until he's taken the Outlands*. And the Apostate wanted her power to help him. How could she have been so wrong?

She winced at her memories. Her stomach heaved. She could still feel him moving inside her, whispering to her. *There are not many of us, and there is only one you*. And perhaps that was the only disadvantage that he faced. Elide could see it when she looked into her mentor's eyes. She could feel her power rising within her. It was hers, and she'd be damned if she let the Apostate use it.

"Good," Calliope said, nodding toward her. "Now take this."

# 22

Elide tossed the pack over her shoulder and stared at her mentor, who now noticeably resembled the Apostate. Her hair shared the same luster, and her eyes were just as dark. "Don't think badly of me," she said suddenly. "This is the first time I fear he's eluded even me."

"Why betray him now?" Elide signed. "What's changed?"

"Everything has changed," she said softly. "Ares was a better man once. He was generous and kind. He wanted nothing more than to serve our people. But now, he intends to commit murder in the name of the divine." Calliope shut her eyes as though she were envisioning it. "I tried to persuade him otherwise," she said. "But I couldn't. And I couldn't kill him, even if I wanted to, he's too strong."

Calliope looked down the tunnel to the left of them. "This tunnel leads back to the surface. No one outside of the elite will know what you look like, so take one of the civilian carriages west to Kirekwall. I have an ally there that will help you."

"What is their name?" Elide signed.

"Dorran Bracken," Calliope said. "He owns brothels in Kirekwall. Ask for the King of Kirekwall at the door of any of them. Then tell him Calliope sent you."

Elide nodded and signed, "That'll work?"

"It should," Calliope said. "I'll cover for you back at the ball. I'll say you were feeling ill and are being treated in a back room."

Elide's head was spinning. She still had so many questions that she wanted answers to. Still so many things she didn't know. Calliope stared at her hard.

"What is it?" Calliope said suddenly. "Go on, out with it."

"I'm sorry, it's just—my mother," Elide signed and stopped as Calliope sighed. "You know what happened to her. Please, I need to know what happened to her."

Calliope shook her head. She looked down the tunnel again and then back at Elide.

"She took some tunnels from the olden days and was meant to get a ride from a fisherman who promised to smuggle her—and *her children*—from Louisiana to New York," Calliope said, gesturing toward Elide. "But life as a fugitive isn't easy, and someone gave her up."

"A fugitive?"

"Mother Superior had arranged for your mother to marry Daegal Murik, but instead, she wed your father in secret. When the Apostate learned of their marriage, and her *betrayal*, he saw it as an insult and demanded her capture." Calliope explained, shaking her head.

"My mother was on the run with Hansel and me?" Elide signed.

She could hardly picture it. Her mother, a fugitive with two children—where was her father?

"But what about—"

"Your father was expunged of any guilt by the same law that expunged your brother of his," Calliope said, interrupting Elide. "So, when they found her in Louisiana, she fought to protect you both." Calliope stopped suddenly as wind whistled through the cave. "That dream you have about the river—it's a quarter mile from where she died. She was on her knees begging for the two of you to be spared—"

"And they killed her?" Elide signed.

"*Executed,* I believe Ares called it," Calliope stated. "They would've done the same to the two of you if Reverend Coin hadn't interfered."

"Reverend Coin," Elide signed, puzzled by the thought. "But how—"

"Enough! You need to leave now," Calliope said sharply.

Elide bowed her head in shame and then signed, "The Apostate is meant to call on me tonight."

Calliope was silent for a moment.

"Such a child," she said lowly. Then Calliope sighed and shook her head. "I'll handle it."

Elide nodded, staring down the tunnel. She could feel

a lump in the back of her throat. And somehow, she found herself hugging Calliope.

Calliope patted her back. "Go now."

Elide released her and ran into the tunnel.

She didn't look back over her shoulder, even as the lights overhead became more sparse and the aboveground noise grew louder. Calliope sent three small light wisps to surround Elide, providing ample light to run as she reached the end of the tunnel. Her mind raced, tears streaming down her face as she stepped out into the cold air.

Civilian carriages always looked more rugged than the elites' carriages, some had chipped paint, and others had bright curtains. She saw more of the latter. There was a driver leaning against a carriage with turquoise curtains, which drew far too much attention. Another carriage with black-and-white doors. Most, if not all, of the carriages' color choices were peculiar, but then she spotted a crimson one with dark curtains. *Those will keep out the light,* Elide thought, feeling her eyes get heavier. *Nearly dawn.*

She yawned and approached its driver.

He cocked a brow. "You want a ride?"

"Yes, to Kirekwall," Elide signed.

He stared at her blankly. Elide flushed with embarrassment. But instead of mocking her as she half expected, he rummaged through a pack in his front seat, took out a notepad and pen, and handed them to her.

She smiled at him and spelled out Kirekwall. She wasn't sure if she'd spelled it right but handed it back to him.

He looked down at the notepad and nodded. "All right, get in Kirekwall."

The driver opened the carriage door, and Elide climbed in.

When they left, the carriage roared like thunder, scattering rocks as it rode out of Prospero. But Elide didn't dare look out the window. Every time she saw someone wearing green, she felt it was safer to assume that it was an Enoch than a civilian. The last thing she wanted was to be caught in the back of the carriage and dragged back to the ball. But, for the moment, she found every bump in the road and jostle comforting as they pressed farther from the council building.

For hours, she kept the curtains closed, dozing off when she was calm enough and waking again frightened and alone. Mostly she counted the money in her pack, which was far more than she had ever held in all her life. When she'd returned it safely to her pack after counting it again and rubbed her eyes, the carriage suddenly jerked to a stop.

Outside Elide heard shouting and was about to look out the curtains when the carriage door opened, revealing a large man with a scraggly beard and mousy eyes holding a knife. But before he could advance on her, Elide moved her hands in a cutting motion, and the man was sent backward through the air and into a tree. She threw her pack over her shoulder and climbed out of the carriage, narrowly dodging an axe wielded by a round man that was missing most of his teeth.

Elide punched him to his surprise, and he gripped his

nose. He was taken aback by the hit, but before he could return the blow, a gunshot rang out. And the man fell to the ground. Then another, and then four men scrambled into the forest. Elide stepped around the carriage, checking the driver, and her stomach seized. His neck was slashed open, and blood was still gushing from the wound, soaking his shirt. Elide vomited beside the carriage. She wiped her mouth and coughed, trying not to vomit again. Then she heard footsteps crunching on leaves behind her.

She turned, ready to deliver another blow but stopped and lowered her hands. Elide saw the gun in his hands, but she knew he didn't have any intention of using it on her.

*Hansel.*

"There's a lot of people looking for you," he said, putting the gun back into the holster on his belt. "You're a fugitive."

"I thought you'd left," Elide signed.

But he didn't say anything else. He looked up at the sky and gestured to it. The clouds were getting darker. He took her hand and pulled her into the woods.

Elide's mind raced as he did so. She tried to draw his attention twice, but he continued to pull her along. They made it deep into the forest before Elide pulled her hand from his grasp.

"How the hell did you find me?" Elide signed.

"I was a Seeker before you were born," he said, reloading his gun. "Honestly, I've tracked rabbits that were harder to find than you."

She glared at him. "Were you followed?"

"Of course not," Hansel said grimly. "I paid a carriage

driver to head back to Baptiste and got out when we were a few miles outside Prospero."

"How did you know to look for me?"

"I overheard two Enochs saying that you were missing while I was at a tavern," Hansel said, looking her over. "I have to say, I'm impressed. You made it two towns out." He paused and knit his brows together in confusion. "Why are you headed west?"

She hesitated. She could think of a few lies she could tell him, but she didn't want to lie. "I'm trying to stop the war," Elide signed.

"I thought that was the Apostate's plan. I thought you said he wanted peace?"

"I thought he did," Elide signed, closing her eyes. She felt like such a fool. "But it's worse Hansel, it's so much worse."

Hansel stared at her, masking his expression. Then he heaved a heavy sigh, stood up, and said, "All right. Let's find somewhere safe to stay before it gets dark. You look like you could use some rest."

He stepped closer to her and helped support her weight as she grew more drowsy. Elide wasn't sure how long they walked, but by the time they reached a cave, it had begun to rain, and when she lay down on the cool cave floor, it felt hard but familiar.

"Get some rest, Elide," Hansel told her, taking a coat from his pack and throwing it over her.

The brown coat was fur lined and warmer than any blanket she'd ever had—it had a small gold regiment number on the shoulder, customary for Seeker uniforms.

Clearly, he hadn't abandoned everything from his past life. She tossed a pebble, sending it skittering over the cave floor and bumping into Hansel's shoe. He looked at her.

"Thanks for not leaving me behind, Hansel," Elide signed.

He turned to her, and with a small sad smile on his face, he said, "Wouldn't dream of it."

## 23

Elide woke the next morning with a headache and her stomach rumbling. Hansel passed her some cooked rabbit from the fire he was roasting it on. She wondered what else her brother could do that he hadn't told her.

But the first thing that came to mind was perhaps not the most important at the moment. "Did you know about mom?" Elide signed.

"Know what about her?"

"She was a Mourner."

Hansel stared at her blankly. "No, I uh—didn't know that."

Elide stared at him intently but felt nothing. So he wasn't lying. But his expression reminded her that they had bigger problems.

"So, the Apostate."

She hung her head in shame and signed, "He's going to

use marrowroot to amplify the powers of the Mourners and use them to take over the Outlands."

Hansel scoffed. "I wish I could say that I was surprised." He shook his head as though having some faint recognition of something. "It's never that simple. Why would he need you then? If all he needs are the Mourners?"

"He needs the locations of rebel hideouts, and I can extract the truth from their prisoner," Elide signed.

"No one else can?"

"They were trained to withstand Mourner powers, except mine," Elide signed.

Hansel sighed.

"My mentor, Calliope, told me to go to Kirekwall and find a man named Dorran Bracken," Elide signed, hesitating for a moment. "She said he'd help."

"Kirekwall? They're up to their eyeballs in brothels," Hansel said abruptly. "You want to go there? I mean, it'd be safe for me, but certainly not for you."

Elide narrowed her eyes and threw the coat around her shoulders at him, and he caught it, looking shocked by her reaction.

She stood up and signed, "I can fight."

"Yeah, I noticed that little display in the forest," Hansel said, standing up. "But the men that visit Kirekwall are built like houses and twice as nasty as the highwaymen you encountered on the road. And with the number of Disciples that wander around that city, you'd be captured before you reached this Bracken character—why the hell would she send you there?"

Elide scoffed. "I can protect myself."

He shoved the other coat into his pack and fixed his coat. Then gestured for Elide to follow him, but she didn't budge.

"I'm your brother. I'm always going to be honest with you—forget what Calliope said. Kirekwall is by far the worst place you could go. What happens if you're caught? What happens if you aren't? But I'd guess the Apostate wouldn't let his pet be owned by anyone else. Would he?"

Elide didn't answer. Instead, she took a deep breath and joined him in walking down the hill.

He was right. Calliope may have meant well, but it wasn't the best plan. She had no idea what she was doing. Only that she wanted to get as far away from the Apostate as possible. He planned to use her. He planned to poison the entire academy to meet his own ends. There were no limits to his greed.

"We'll go east then."

Elide stared at him, then suddenly she felt a sinking feeling in her chest. "The marrowroot?"

"Yeah, we're going to go and get it. The Ainsley twins are stationed in Colchester, and I know a few other Seekers there as well."

"How do you know the Seekers won't betray you?" Elide signed, trying to keep up with his long strides.

"I don't," he said softly as he led them through the forest. "That's why I won't be mentioning you. I'll say that the orders came from the Apostate. That always seems to get things done."

"How can you be so sure this plan of yours will work?" Elide signed.

"If you take the marrowroot and it works, then maybe we'll stand a chance of getting out of Texas," Hansel said.

"You want me to leave Texas?" Elide signed. "What about everyone else? If he gives it to the Mourners—"

"I'll burn the rest," Hansel said, grabbing her hands and interrupting her. "We only need one bud. There's bound to be at least one mining town headed in that direction." He let go of her hands and said, "I'll buy some flint and use it to set them on fire."

Hansel turned away from her and kept walking.

Elide could feel her heart hammering in her chest. But she kept up with her brother, remembering how the Disciples saluted the Apostate in the halls. How his men obeyed commands without question, and even worse, their menacing ability to hide in the shadows. That thought in particular raised goosebumps on her skin. After walking most of the day, they stopped to set up camp. She had no idea where they were, but she was confident they were heading in the right direction. The sun set in the west, and as she watched it disappear behind the hill, she lay down on the ground beside her brother.

Days passed with Hansel pointing out towns and hunting for food as they made their way to Colchester, and Elide felt particularly useless. She could put out fires well enough and keep the wind from hitting them, but not much else. She wouldn't have survived out here on her own.

That evening, they decided to head into a small town near Colchester to bathe at an inn and get real food.

The moment the bathwater touched her skin, Elide submerged herself in it, scrubbing the dirt out of her curly hair and resurfacing when she felt clean. When she got out, she grimaced at the brown bathwater and dried herself with a towel. She pulled on freshly washed and dried clothes. After she'd drained the tub, Hansel went into the bathroom, leaving behind a plate delivered by room service.

She ate a chicken leg first and couldn't believe how good it tasted. It wasn't comparable to the academy's food, but it was good. And as Elide stared out the window, she almost forgot why they were there.

The forest around the town was dense, and on the main street was a farmers' market. The farmers' market in Baptiste came twice a month on Sundays when the weather was clear and bright out. Reverend Warner slotted it to commence after church hours. As soon as the congregation was free, they'd file out into the market and purchase homemade candies, fruits, and pastries. When they were younger, their father would purchase a mint chocolate bar for them to split, every time until his death.

"Do you want to go down to the market?" Elide asked.

Hansel patted his hair with the towel and fixed his shirt. Then he looked out the window, leaning both elbows on the sill.

"Okay, but only for a little while."

The moment they'd finished their meal, Elide dragged her brother down to the farmers' market. They maneuvered carefully around fellow shoppers, perusing the market for anything that was to their fancy. Hansel stopped at a stall to buy a rifle and other supplies.

When she spotted a chocolate stall further down, she slipped back into the crowd without her brother noticing and went straight for it. When she reached it, she was practically salivating. There were pretzels, marshmallows, and various fruits prepped for dipping into melted chocolate, as well as premade chocolate bars.

"First ones free," a small woman told her, tossing her a chocolate bar.

It was a chocolate truffle bar with raspberry filling, and Elide mouthed "thank you" to the woman and practically skipped back to her brother.

When she got back to him, his expression was unreadable. Then he dragged her back to the inn's lobby and shook his head at her. "What were you thinking?" Hansel spat out harshly.

Elide sighed. "I'm fine. You're getting worked up for no reason. No one here knows who I am."

"You don't know that."

"Hansel, we're fine."

"Just get back upstairs. I have to finish gathering supplies."

Elide wanted to groan aloud but instead nodded. Hansel smiled, and she watched him leave out the front door.

The attendant at the front desk cocked a brow at her,

clearly having roused his suspicion. She gave him a sweet smile, and he returned to typing. Elide plopped down on the lobby couch and took a bite of her chocolate bar. The chocolate was rich, and the tart raspberry filling made it taste even better. She wanted to savor every bite and perhaps even drown out the ringing phones in the lobby.

As she was enjoying her snack, a door creaked open, and the manager stepped out into the lobby with two heavyset men. The taller of the two had blond hair, but the other stood beside the man and she couldn't see more than his feet.

"As I've already told you, I think I would've noticed if a man of that description had walked into my establishment," the manager said pointedly. His accent thickened by his contention.

"He would've been traveling with a girl," the tall man stated. "Brown skin, curly hair—"

The manager laughed, holding his belly. "Ha! You've just described half the women in Leester! Including me mother-in-law, and you're more than welcome to take her."

"He's wasting our time, Demitri," a familiar voice said. "The Mirai girl saw her here, so she's here. We'll just have to look for her ourselves."

Elide's breath caught in her throat. She turned and finally got a glimpse of the speaker.

*Altair.*

In broad daylight, he looked more fearsome. The two Disciples were dressed in their usual black uniforms, and from the bulk of them, she'd guess they were armed to the teeth.

"Fine, you want to check my lobby?" the manager snapped. "Check then! I am a patriot, and I have nothing to hide. See if your Teller is here!"

Elide gulped. She suddenly became increasingly aware of how far she was from the front door and wondered whether she could make it unnoticed. Her head told her a million things, but as she turned to see how far the men had progressed, they were already looking at her. Altair's gaze focused on her, and she watched in horror as recognition spread across his face. Elide looked back at the door.

"Don't!" Altair shouted.

Elide ran out the front door and into the crowded main road, heart hammering in her chest. She didn't dare look back as she pushed past people, making it pretty far before she crashed into a woman and fell onto the ground with her.

Hansel grabbed her by the arms and helped her up. "What's gotten into you?"

Elide pointed back at the Disciples. He looked at them and suddenly grabbed her hand, pulling her through the crowd, darting around moving carts and running through alleyways until they were cut off by a wall.

Hansel boosted her up, and she climbed over it and onto the other side, landing near the forest. Hansel's pack came flying over first, but Hansel didn't follow. A few moments passed in silence, and then a gunshot rang out. Elide heard someone groan followed by screams and was about to climb back over the wall when Hansel hopped over.

She looked him over. He wasn't injured.

"What happened?" Elide signed quickly.

"Run!" he demanded, pulling her into the forest.

They stopped when they were deep in the forest, with Leester nowhere in sight. When Hansel was tired of running, they walked until the sun began to set. He lay down on the ground, passing her a new blanket from the pack. Elide lay down beside him. She wanted nothing more than to know what happened but knew there was no use getting the information tonight. They were both too tired.

Hansel fell asleep easily. But Elide found herself staring up at the moon. The Apostate's men were hunting her. She wasn't surprised. She wished she were better prepared. What would they report back to him? What would the Apostate think when he learned that she ran?

*He'll know*, she thought. *Like he seemed to know everything else.* But for now, they weren't caught. She was still free. She could still take the marrowroot and fight back. Tomorrow that could all change. But today, her brother lay beside her, and they were family once more. Today, she was somewhere completely foreign to her, and yet she couldn't have felt safer.

# 24

Hansel searched the sky for any sign of rain as Elide sat on the grass the next day, scanning a book on her lap.

"Did you find it yet?" he asked. She looked back at him and shook her head.

"There's nine species total," Elide signed, counting the illustrations of the plant again. "At least four of them are extinct." She hesitated for a moment. "Did you see any other plants growing around the farm when you went this morning? Maybe some weeds or something?"

Hansel thought for a moment.

"Now that you mention it, yeah," he said, scratching the back of his neck. "There were a few red-colored bushes around—I thought they were quite oddly placed—but I couldn't get too close to them with the farmhands walking around. I'd rather not get shot today."

Elide nodded and flipped the page. *Hamamelis*—witch hazel. She'd been seeing it more frequently the closer they got to Colchester. And, according to botanists, it grew near marrowroot throughout the year. And from the full-color illustration of a marrowroot flower, she didn't doubt that Hansel had found the correct farm. And at the moment, it didn't matter that the Apostate was planning to invade the Outlands as much as her and Hansel being caught in them. It had taken days for the thought to settle in, but now that it had, she couldn't shake it. Or the memory of the barbaric Outlanders that had attacked her on her way to Prana Academy.

"Our odds could be better," Hansel said aloud, looking through a pair of binoculars. "From the look of the patrol, I'd say they're worried about fugitives, and I wouldn't bet my life on the Ainsley twins not knowing I'm one of them."

He sighed and shook his head. "Well, there goes that plan."

Hansel set down the binoculars and was silent for a few moments. Then he nodded slowly.

"I imagine it'll be easiest when they change shift," Hansel said, turning to look at Elide. "The next one won't be until dark."

He shrugged and shook his head.

"I'm going with you," Elide signed.

"I would argue, but I know you wouldn't listen," Hansel said.

Elide smiled.

"You're a brat," Hansel said with a hint of a smile.

For a while they left the conversation at that, Hansel passing the time by taking a short nap while Elide learned the recipe for marrowroot tea. When she did find it, she was relieved to learn that the tea came from the flower's pollen and, depending on the species, it could have a medicinal quality. Although the species she'd be working with would be much more delicate, so she was afraid of what could happen if she made it wrong. Colchester was hardly the place she wanted to die. But what if she didn't die? What would the tea do to her? Would it be painful? Would she be able to beat the Apostate? She felt that the answer to her last question was a no.

He was powerful. Elide could still remember how his power felt coursing through her. How safe she'd felt in his arms. She'd been so intoxicated by it and all she could feel within him. But she'd been so naive.

Elide had played right into his hands. Part of her wanted to tell Hansel what he was capable of, but a larger part of her felt he already knew.

Hansel rubbed his eyes and rolled over.

"Has the sun gone down yet?" he asked groggily.

Elide shook her head.

Hansel groaned and sat up.

"I'm getting tired of this," Hansel said, leaning back against a boulder. "Of course, we're dealing with the only farm in the Outlands with an Enoch patrol. Our soldiers helping them—what a world we're living in. But that's politics, isn't it? The Apostate needs something they have, and he makes a trade," he said. Then he glared down the hill. "Thousands of our soldiers have been massacred, but he's more worried about protecting a plant."

Elide stared at the ground. She knew he had his

reasons for being angry—they both did. But she didn't want to talk about the Apostate.

She tried changing the subject to Hansel's past few months in Baptiste, but he felt there wasn't much to say. Everything was the same, aside from the Apostate's orders to funnel more students into the military. She wanted to know more about the war, but Hansel always managed to turn the conversation back to the Apostate. When he finally asked about the Mourners themselves, Elide was relieved.

She told him about how castle-like the academy was and how she'd wandered all over its sprawling grounds. Every course she had taken interested him, even her conversation with Starla's mother in Westerby and her arguments with her friends were considered noteworthy. There were moments in her story that Elide had thought would bore him, but he always seemed interested.

"I'm not surprised your friend's mother thought that. It's just like a baroness to push the subject of marriage onto a woman your age. I never even thought of setting you up with anyone," he said plainly. "Not that you never had any suitors," he explained, hastily correcting himself. "It's just they weren't suitable."

Elide smiled. She wanted to laugh but chose not to. Who she'd marry was the least of her worries at the moment. She just wanted to make it through the next few hours. There were plenty of dark thoughts stuck in her head, but she didn't dare sit on any one too long.

Finally, she had to tell Hansel. "Hansel, if something goes wrong," Elide signed, pausing for a moment. "I—"

"No," Hansel said, cutting her off. "I know what you're going to tell me, and I won't even consider it. If the plant doesn't kill you, it won't be me who does."

"But if the Apostate—"

"To hell with the Apostate!" he shouted, standing up abruptly. "That man won't define what sins mar my soul. And I sure as hell won't kill my little sister for him."

Elide hesitated.

"It wouldn't be for him."

Hansel's eyes narrowed. "Then who would it be for? Scopus?"

"And the Outlands," Elide signed.

He stepped away from her, walking to the edge of the hill, running his hands through his hair. Elide watched as he paced back and forth, shaking his head at the thought.

"No."

"He's planning to take the Outlands, Hansel," Elide signed. "There are innocent men, women, and children who will die if no one interferes. No one else has my power, and it could be hundreds—possibly thousands—of years before another Teller comes along."

Hansel shook his head. Elide got to her feet and grabbed him by his arms.

"You can't ask—I'm quite sure that God doesn't want me to kill my sister," Hansel told her, pulling away from her. "Ever heard of Cain and Abel? Didn't work out so well for them, did it? And I'm not even envious of you. I've missed you. And now that we're back together, you want me to kill you. Tell me, how the hell is that fair?"

He looked down at the ground.

"Please, Hansel," Elide signed.

Hansel shook his head.

"The Apostate won't be merciful. Not to the rebels or the Outlanders," Elide signed. "He'll use me to make the captive talk. Then, whatever comes next will be out of my control, but right now, this is in my control."

"I can't."

"Please."

He opened his eyes and stared at her hard. Then his gaze softened. Hansel gritted his teeth, but he nodded silently.

"Hansel."

"I will," he muttered.

Elide hugged him tightly, and she felt safe in her brother's arms.

"I will—but I'll also do everything in my power to keep that from coming to pass," Hansel said sternly.

When they let go, Hansel wandered away for a moment, staring out into the empty forest. And even at this distance, Elide swore she could hear her brother crying. She felt a twinge of guilt for the part she played in upsetting him. But she knew it was all for the greater good. And she considered that perhaps violence could be justified if done in the name of the divine. Their laws granted some leeway for it, and they couldn't know God's plans—but if laws had to be destroyed, could it not be done for the preservation of peace? Or was considering that blasphemy in itself?

# 25

At nightfall, they began their slow descent to the farm below. Elide stayed close to Hansel, matching his pace and using the trees as camouflage. By the time they reached the bottom, it was nearly the end of the guards' patrol shift.

"Your friend Fiona nearly got sent to the brothels," Hansel whispered, crouching down by a tree.

They were still a few feet away from the farm, but they could see the Enochs guarding the perimeter with their rifles in their hands.

"Is this really the time?" Elide signed.

Hansel shrugged. "Thought you might've been worried about her."

"I saw her in the newspaper, and she's married," Elide signed.

He scoffed. "Her association with the Timber name is all that saved her. If Gabriel wasn't so fond of her, she would've been shipped off to a bawd."

Elide shook her head silently. She knew what he was implying.

Juliette wasn't so lucky. There wasn't a reverend elder to speak as her character witness since she'd been married to one and chosen to have an affair. Though at the moment, Elide hardly felt Juliette was to blame. Their world was a mess, and love could make anyone blind.

Elide thought she'd understood everything. She thought the purest love could be found with their one true person, their soulmate. To the hopeless romantic girl within her, that was still true. But she was reconsidering love, to an extent, that there were different measures of love. The love she felt for her friends and that she felt for Hansel were different but the same. Neither was romantic love, but they were both pure and just as undeniable as the love she'd seen in movies. And what she felt for the Apostate, she couldn't begin to describe.

Her heart gave a miserable twist. Her mind was reeling; how could she have had it so wrong? She thought things between her and the Apostate would grow into something more, and then they would bring peace to Scopus together. But perhaps she had been too naive to see him for who he really was, knowing that her heart responded to him in ways that she couldn't control, and it pained her to admit it, even to herself.

"All right," Hansel breathed softly, pointing over the bushes, "they're going to switch guard now. We'll only have a few moments."

The Enochs walked slowly to the edge of the property where their replacements were emerging from a large white mansion, each with a rifle over their shoulder as they crossed through the grass, passing the farmhands tending the plantation. When they were clear of the plot in front of them, Elide and Hansel stood, their backs against the trees. Elide looked at Hansel, but he was focused on the marrowroot a few feet away. When she followed his gaze, she found herself staring at a white bud that was the largest of the bunch, its petals shimmering in the moonlight.

Hansel and Elide exchanged a look. He crouched down and crawled over to her, standing once she made room for him against the tree.

"You need to stay here, Elide. I won't be able to focus if you're out there. I'll grab it," Hansel said.

Elide went to argue, but he'd turned his back on her. And in one swift movement, Hansel leapt over the bushes and crossed to the marrowroot buds.

She looked back toward the mansion. Elide could see the Enochs smoking in front of the mansion while they ordered the farmhands around. The farmhands followed their orders without complaint, and luckily, they hadn't looked their way. Hansel had begun collecting the plant and sticking it into his pack.

As Elide watched him do it, she sighed in relief. *It's almost over,* Elide thought. She pressed her back into the tree and took a deep breath. For a moment, the world seemed to go silent and all she could hear was her breathing. *Everything is going to be okay,* she told herself when she took another deep breath. *Everything is going to be okay,* she thought again, but this time she heard someone yell at the other end of the plantation. She froze. *They're far away.* Her heart gave a painful twist. *It's too dark for them to see more than a shadow.* She could feel her heart hammering in her chest. *Probably just an Enoch whose command wasn't followed.* Elide shook her head at herself.

Then as she turned and looked toward Hansel, she heard someone shout, "Intruder!"

Elide felt her heart drop as she crouched down. What would Hansel tell her to do? *Don't move,* she told herself. Peeking around the tree, two farmhands and a tall blond Enoch had reached the plot. The farmhands forced Hansel onto his knees, and the Enoch stepped forward.

"Who sent you?" the Enoch demanded. His voice was familiar.

Hansel didn't answer.

The Enoch repeated the question.

No response.

The soldier's jaw clenched tightly. Then he took his gun from his holster and aimed it at Hansel's forehead. Her heart skipped a beat. *God, please don't do this,* she thought. *I can't lose him, not today.* Elide slowly moved around the tree, noticing the several Enoch gathered on the porch. *They aren't going to intervene.* She could feel tears stinging her eyes.

"I want an answer to that boy," the Enoch spat out. She swore she could see the man's shoulders rising and falling as he breathed, leering over her brother. "Nothing to say? Finally shut you up, have I?"

"What are you looking for me to say, Cain?" Hansel answered.

*Cain.* Elide felt her chest tighten. Ryder's father was here.

Cain let out a bark of laughter. "Let's start with that answer," he said. "Then you'll repent for that sister of yours's actions that cost my son his hand. *Don't look away,*" he hissed. "Keep your eyes on me, boy. Trust me, I find no joy in doing this. But we all have orders to follow. And any intruders are meant to be put down."

Elide gasped and felt a branch snap underneath her foot. As Cain turned, she hid behind the tree and held her breath. *Oh God, did he see me?* Elide felt a tear slide down her cheek. Then she heard someone grunt and another man shout. She peeked around the tree and saw Hansel fighting with Cain on the ground, exchanging blows. Beside them, one farmhand held his bloodied nose, and the other shouted for the Enochs at the mansion.

*You need to stay here, Elide,* she heard Hansel's voice in her ears again. But as she saw Cain get back onto his feet with his gun in hand, before she knew it, she left her hiding spot and started running at Cain. She could hear someone shouting as she jumped onto Cain's back, wrapping her arms around his throat, trying to choke him. Cain started thrashing wildly, trying to throw her off, but still maintaining his grip on the gun. Elide held on for as long as she could but was thrown off and landed on her back. She felt the back of her head just as she heard a gunshot. The first thing she saw was the blood on her hand, and the next was Hansel on the ground, pressing on the bullet wound in his stomach. She got to her knees and tried to crawl toward Hansel.

"Who the hell is this?" someone shouted.

"You little bitch!" Cain snapped, pointing the gun at Elide.

"Is that the Teller?" The voice came from far away, but when Elide tore her gaze away from the barrel, she saw Daegal Murik walking toward them.

Elide looked back at Cain. Staring into his eyes, they were cold, dark, and full of hatred.

"The world would be better off with one less of you," he said lowly as he pressed the barrel to her head.

Elide tried to back away.

Cain shook his head and said, "Say hello to your mother for me."

She held her breath. But before the gun went off, she turned again, and in that same moment, she glimpsed Daegal slash his arm through the air. Then a high-pitched whistling sound passed over the plantation.

Elide felt her chest rising and falling as she panted. Her eyes widened at the sight in front of her. The man that had towered above her moments ago had been beheaded. Cain's head lay a few feet away on the grass, his eyes and mouth open, and his body lay on the ground at her feet. As his soul departed, his eyes dulled and became lifeless.

"Glad to see you could join us, Elide," Daegal said calmly as he stepped forward and offered her his hand. His overcoat looked more silver than gray, but she swore the raven pin he wore was smiling at her. Instinctively, she looked at Hansel; he was barely holding his eyes open. "Angus, assure that the Teller's brother is taken care of. I'll be escorting her to Labrott," he instructed.

The Enoch nodded and bowed to him.

Elide grabbed her brother's hand but it was quickly pulled from her grasp. She felt a sudden sharp pain in her head as strong hands seized her, forcing her to stand. Elide tried to fight them, but her efforts were in vain.

She turned her head and saw them laying Hansel onto a wooden pull-cart pulled by a brown horse. But then her view was obscured by Daegal's coat as his hand reached the back of her neck, and the world went dark.

# 26

Elide opened her eyes and held the blanket over her close to her chest. It was cold, and she could see the fog of her breath in the air. Someone had redressed her in a white gown, and the wound on the back of her head had been healed. She could hear gruff, masculine voices coming from outside the door flap to her left. The flap itself held the Apostate's golden sigil. From the look of it, she was inside a tent.

Beams held up the black silk inner walls, which were dark and dense like curtains. It was dim, and of the seven candles on a table in the corner, only three were lit, leaving the pale fingers of light to stray in all directions. Elide was curious to know where she was but wasn't eager to peek outside the tent. And a full-length mirror beside the table didn't show much of the world outside the flap.

For a moment she hesitated, then she crossed to the other side of the tent and lit more candles, nearly screaming when she saw a sleeping bear inside a large metal cage. Its sides were rising and falling, so she knew it was alive. But that only made her more nervous. From the leather collar around its neck, she could safely assume it was someone's pet but couldn't help but wonder who it belonged to.

Elide picked up a candle and tiptoed closer to the cage, and the moment she stood beside it, the creature stirred slightly. She froze and then saw a small three-dimensional gold raven plaque on its collar that glimmered in the candlelight. *Of course, it's his,* she thought. Suddenly, the bear's eye twitched, and Elide's heart leapt in her chest. When the bear settled again, she took a deep breath and slowly backed away from the cage until her rear bumped into the table.

She sighed and shook off the feeling.

*You don't have time for this,* she told herself. *You have to find Hansel and get the hell out of here.* She set the candle back on the table and tried to calm her nerves.

*Where would he be?* Elide thought. *They took him away*

Elide could remember it all so clearly. But that didn't make her less afraid.

The door flap opened, and Daegal stepped into the tent. "It's time," he said sternly, as if he were commanding her to follow him.

"Time for what?" Elide signed.

Daegal sighed. "The tea is prepared. Your dear brother collected enough for several cups, however, we only need one."

"I won't drink it, Daegal," Elide signed.

"It wasn't a question," Daegal responded. "It was a command. And I would prefer it if you didn't make things difficult."

Elide didn't answer. She wasn't a soldier like an Enoch or Disciple any more than he was a novitiate. She was the Teller, and his threat was empty. Elide could feel her power, telling her he was lying. He couldn't harm her unless he wanted to be punished.

"Where is Hansel?" Elide signed. "You ordered an Enoch to have him taken care of. Where is he?"

Daegal heaved a heavy sigh and shook his head at her. He waited a few moments to see if she'd budge, but she didn't.

"Your brother is alive," Daegal said.

"Alive," Elide signed. "Where is he?"

"He'll only stay alive if you cooperate," Daegal answered.

Her breath caught in her chest.

Daegal held the door flap open, and Elide walked through it without another word. She shivered the moment the morning air licked her skin. Daegal took off his coat and wrapped it around her shoulders, shooting a glare at two passing Enochs. The soldiers bowed their heads toward Elide—with more respect than she'd expected— while leading their horses to a tent. As she walked, she wondered where they'd set up camp, as she was positive they weren't in Colchester anymore.

But before she could ask where they were, the answer struck her. *I'll take her to Labrott*, Daegal had said. So this was Labrott. She wondered how many camps they had stationed like this. Enochs and Disciples were drinking and playing cards in a few leisure tents. They seemed to be having a good time wagering and taking each other's money. When they passed the infirmary tent, she checked for Hansel but he wasn't there. Though, there were ten men with bullet wounds resting while medics tended their wounds. The first woman she saw was headed into a blue-colored tent, its door flaps held open with rope. She was wearing a gray beret and a matching coat with the Apostate's sigil on her chest.

*Scout*, she thought, as the woman entered the tent. More female soldiers were inside, gathered around a television set, watching some show. The sight made her miss her friends if only for a moment before Daegal led her to a much larger tent, where shouting voices clambered over one another.

When she entered, they abruptly stopped, and all heads turned to her. There were five reverend elders present, three of whom she didn't recognize, as well as the Apostate and his personal guard.

*Different cities*, she told herself. She glanced at the three other men. *But which cities?* Elide looked them over but couldn't find anything that gave it away. And when her eyes met Reverend Elijah Stone's, she swore he looked almost pleased.

*He's seen Hansel,* she thought. For that, she was relieved. But from the way Reverend Stone was smiling, she hoped he intended to repent after today's proceedings.

Then when Reverend Warner stepped forward, she could hardly breathe. He smelled like sweat, horse, and cologne, which the latter she guessed was meant to cover up the first two smells.

"You have caused a great deal of trouble, little girl," Reverend Warner said.

Elide cringed. His breath reeked of alcohol. She was amazed it wasn't seeping out his pores.

Reverend Warner scoffed. "Years of waiting for the Teller, and she runs off into the night with her brother. Off to indulge yourself in sinful pleasures, are we? What is it then? An incestuous plot?" A grimace spread over his pug face. "Perhaps that is why you were made a cuckold, Elijah. Hansel was abstaining from the lecherous wiles of his younger sister, and dear Juliette chose to assist him," he said while still looking at her. "Ever the generous one, that one. Perhaps it was not her we should've thrown to the wolves, but this one. It is no wonder God took away your ability to speak. You disobey the lord our God with the belief you are immune to punishment. Why, I bet if we checked her maidenhead, it would be gone. Oh, if I had a cane—"

Elide spat in his face, interrupting his tirade.

"You wretch!" Reverend Warner shouted, raising his hand.

Elide winced and turned away, but in the same moment, she noticed Daegal grab hold of the reverend elder's wrist.

Reverend Warner's eyes narrowed toward Daegal.

"That's enough, Zachariah," the Apostate said. "She is no more a temptress than I a demon."

"Yes, my liege," Reverend Warner said, bowing to the Apostate and backing away from Elide.

For a few moments, the tent was silent, and Elide's gaze stayed on the bearskin rug on the floor. Then she heard someone clapping slowly, and she gradually took in the room until her eyes settled on the Apostate sitting in a chair at the center. His expression was unreadable, but his eyes were hard, and the mocking clap stopped.

"Well done, Elide," the Apostate said. "You've single-handedly steered two platoons off course to guard this base. But I'm sure our soldiers will be able to make it another fortnight without reinforcements."

She glared at him, and his mouth quirked into a half-smile. The Apostate got up from his seat, his dark uniform nearly as menacing on his approach as the first time she saw him. But this time, as his shadow loomed over her, she looked him directly in the eye.

"I'm actually impressed," the Apostate said lowly. "You evaded me for so long, and yet all is as it's supposed to be. Everything you've gone through led you here—back to me. There's no negotiating it. God brought us together, Elide. We are meant to build the new world together. Why do you continue to resist?"

Elide didn't answer.

The Apostate's gaze met hers. His eyes were soft, but she could sense the rage behind them. Altair loomed in a back corner with another Disciple, standing on either side of a man with a sack over his head. The man's head hung low, and his clothing was stained in some areas. And the blood on the shirt made her heart lurch. Tears welled in her eyes as she recognized him.

*Hansel.*

"Bring him," said the Apostate.

The Disciples lifted him to his feet, but Hansel stumbled as he walked. They made it just a few feet before he collapsed onto the ground. Elide tried to get to him, but the Apostate pulled her back in front of him.

"No," the Apostate said, still holding her arm. "You stay here."

Elide did as he commanded while the Apostate removed the sack from Hansel's head. His face was bruised, and one of his eyes was swollen shut. Though he was breathing, each breath was labored, and he was struggling to keep his other eye open.

"Now," the Apostate said, staring down at Elide. "You're going to drink this." He took a vial from a tray that a red-haired Scout woman was holding.

Elide stared at the vial.

She didn't need to ask what it was. She knew. It was bronze like the book had described the concoction would be, glimmering in the sliver of sunlight that passed through the door flap. The marrowroot's pollen was already crafted into a heady brew in that vial. Elide wondered how long he'd been waiting to give it to her. And how long she'd been asleep.

The Apostate snapped his fingers, and Altair punched Hansel in the jaw. Hansel screamed as his shoulder slammed into the ground. The other Disciple kicked him in his stomach. Hansel gasped, and Elide grabbed onto the front of the Apostate's coat.

"Enough," the Apostate said, and Hansel wheezed as the men stopped.

Elide stared up into his cold, cruel eyes. *How had I ever given myself to you*, she thought, hoping he'd hear her. But his expression didn't change. She released his coat and stepped back.

She took the vial from his hand and removed the top.

"No use dropping it," the Apostate whispered. "We have plenty. But I'm not sure how much your brother can take."

Elide took a shaky breath in and took a sip, but as soon as the liquid touched her lips, it burned. She stopped and gasped. She knew she had to finish it, but even that small sip had made her chest feel like it was on fire. The Apostate sensed her hesitation, and she felt his hand on the back of her neck.

All her thoughts seemed to vanish except for a soft, unfamiliar voice: *Everything is okay*, it told her. *You have nothing to fear.* She recognized it but didn't know who it belonged to. *Drink. You'll feel better.* Elide wanted to argue with it, but she was somewhere deep inside her mind. Somewhere where she felt warm and safe. She felt the vial against her lips again. *It is like medicine, but sweeter and better for you.* Again, the vial came to her lips, and the liquid coated her tongue, but the voice was right. *It tastes like the sweets of your childhood.* Elide could taste the chocolate she'd eaten days ago in her mouth again, salivating at the memory as the brew traveled down her throat. *It is your warmest memories spreading through every nerve of your body, and all that you need can be found in its final drop.*

Elide tried to shake the feeling as the last drop hit her tongue and gasped as the Apostate took his hand away. The warmth slipped away from her, and she could hear someone screaming. Then she realized they were her screams.

Nothing could stop the pain. Nausea seized her stomach, but she couldn't vomit it back up. Elide crumpled down to the ground on all fours, the rocks biting into her knees as she continued to cry out. Hansel reached out for her, but she couldn't reach his hand.

"Take him," the Apostate commanded Altair. "Make sure you keep a close eye on him. I don't want any more mistakes."

The Apostate crouched down beside Elide. He stroked the back of her head, shushing her as he did so. But then his hand grabbed a handful of her hair, and he lifted her gaze to his as she gasped for air.

"I know the change is rather painful, as I've been through it myself," the Apostate told her lowly. "But once it's over, you'll thank me." Then he moved closer to her ear. "And when we return to Prana, I'll repent for my sins, and we'll be wed."

Elide wanted to refuse. To deny him herself, but the most she could do was try to grab him. And as she did, she fell onto the ground.

~

The pain came in waves, subsiding only to begin again seconds later. Elide shut her eyes tightly, gritting her teeth as pain surged through her body, though she couldn't stop herself from crying out time and time again. Originally, the intervals were shorter, only five seconds, but after some time, it became fifteen seconds and then thirty. And for those thirty seconds she was able to rest, but every time Elide tried to concoct an escape plan, the thought slipped her mind once the pain took over again.

Daegal had taken her back to the Apostate's tent, carrying her like a bride in his arms as she thrashed uncontrollably through each wave. She wondered why he wouldn't help her. But then she'd remember the Apostate's words, *I know the change is rather painful, I've been through it myself*—the marrowroot had given him that power. She'd only been at five seconds then.

Now, she was at thirty and her lungs were on fire, if not due to the pain then due to her screams. Each time it came, she found herself longing for those thirty seconds and even once for the Apostate. She hated to admit it to herself, but she wanted him to take the pain away. He'd already gotten what he wanted, there was hardly any need to torture her, this was enough. And perhaps that was why he hadn't shown himself yet. Though the bear was gone, the cage was not. And Elide assumed that perhaps the creature was moved to prevent it from being alarmed by her screams.

And as if he had heard her, the door flap opened, and he entered the tent. He glanced at her panting on the bed, and she knew she was quite the sight, her brow covered in sweat, chest heaving, waiting for the pain to come again. The Apostate adjusted his coat in the mirror, and as she could feel the pain snaking up her spine again, she thought, and thought hard, a single word: *Ares.* He turned toward her just as a scream escaped her lips.

She clenched her eyes shut, but then the pain dissipated, slipping away from her body, replaced by a familiar warmth. He sat beside her, one hand on her back and the other cupping her chin. As she lifted her gaze to his, she thought to hit him but knew that she wouldn't be able to endure the change without him. His dark gaze focused on her, and she felt her heart lurch. Though, she restrained herself from moving away.

"Why did you do it?" the Apostate said softly, staring into her eyes. "Why did you betray me?"

Elide shook herself.

"Calliope said—"

The Apostate scoffed. "Calliope, of course," he said, and Elide could hear the warning in his voice. "She got into your head. But I suppose that's her talent, isn't it? Not a Hamle, but so very persuasive when she wishes to be."

"Do you intend to give the marrowroot to the academy?" Elide signed.

"Yes," the Apostate said, leaning back into the headboard.

Her instincts told her he was telling the truth, and even with her completely at his mercy, she could see that he wanted them to speak. He wanted her to feel as if they were equals, and if she pushed too much, he would take his hand away and leave her writhing in pain until the change took her, or death did.

"Then what Calliope said was true," Elide signed. "You intend to take the Outlands."

"I intend to unite a divided nation," the Apostate said. "I intend to rebuild that which was lost and bring lasting peace to our people and theirs—"

"If they obey you," Elide signed, interrupting him.

The Apostate let out a bark of laughter. "What would you have me do? Allow their president to carry on?" he said, a hint of a smile on his face. "You haven't seen the state of things, Elide. You've only heard stories. I intend to end the war by any means necessary."

Elide took a deep breath. "And what about Hansel?"

"What about Hansel?" he repeated, cocking his head to the side.

"You don't need him," Elide signed. "Why can't you just send him away or let him go?"

The Apostate stared at her hard, his piercing gaze suddenly filled with rage.

"You would like that wouldn't you," the Apostate said as his fingers laced into her hair. Then a grim smile came over his face. "You think that if he's free, you'll find a way back to each other. How *sweet*." His tone was filled with disgust as his grip tightened in her hair, and she tried to pull away.

For a moment, she did, but then he grabbed her jaw tightly. "You're hurting me," Elide signed, trying to remove his hand from her jaw.

"Hurting you?" he repeated. "Did you ever consider

how your people would feel when you abandoned them? How frightened they'd be if they knew?"

Elide hesitated.

"No, of course not," he said harshly, and his voice dipped lower. "Why would you ever plague yourself with such thoughts when you were so quick to believe Calliope? It always comes down to me to see reason. I'm the one that mends the weak and broken with speeches about our bright future. I protect them from the endless evils outside our borders. I make the difficult choices for the nation—perhaps I was expecting too much of you. Without a strong will, you are nothing. You are too afraid to see it through to the end. The people need someone fearless."

"Fearless," Elide signed. "Is that what you tell yourself when they're murdering innocents in the Outlands?"

He released her chin. "It's a shame, really," he said as though he hadn't heard her speak. "I had seen such promise in our future." He leaned in close, studying her face, but pulled away. "Whatever you think you know now, soon our people will know peace."

Elide felt tears welling up in her eyes.

"So you'll get the rebel to speak, put an end to the rebellion, and then what? What happens afterward?" she signed. "More war? Days filled with horrors with no end in sight?"

He gazed down at her, bringing his hand to her cheek, tilting her head up to him, his thumb brushing over her lips. Then the expression on his face changed, replaced by something like confusion, but somehow also looked like desire.

"Tomorrow," the Apostate said as if it were a word to be savored. "We return to Prana, and we'll be wed." He dipped his head down and kissed her, and for some reason she let him. Rage, shame, and desire were fighting for dominance inside her. She hated him. But she still felt something that was alarmingly like longing when she looked at him. Her own power betrayed her by connecting with his, and in ways she couldn't describe, she knew his connected with hers too. Every time his skin came in contact with hers, he overpowered her with such ease, so much so that she wondered if she would ever be able to do the same. *Though I could never be as cruel or manipulative*, Elide thought to herself.

When he pulled away, his gaze was dark and filled with an emotion she didn't recognize.

"And after that," the Apostate said, brushing her hair out of her face. "We'll deal with the criminals you so desperately wish to protect more than your own people."

He pulled away from her, taking his hands away, and Elide winced, preparing for the pain to come, but it didn't.

"Altair will ride with you back to Prana," he said, standing from the bed. "I've given him permission to do what needs to be done if you try to escape. So do yourself a favor and don't try anything stupid."

Elide didn't answer. She felt as though she should respond with something brave but thought better of it. She wouldn't test her chances tonight. So she swallowed the lump in her throat and bowed her head. She caught a glimpse of the Apostate leaving the tent as she began to

pray. She prayed for a solution, perhaps even for punishment, but in time she fell into a fitful sleep.

## 27

They set out for Prana before dawn. The carriage horses' hooves roared like thunder as they rode, passing streams with flying fish, leaping and bounding out the water, drawing nearer to Prana by the mile. Elide stared at the gun Altair held, which was pointed at her legs, two limbs he could wound without any consequence. And though it took some time, Elide began to spot familiar landmarks and considered what she would do once they arrived.

Elide thought twice of going directly to Mother Superior and telling her the Apostate's plans. If Mother Superior believed she was telling the truth, the elderly Kedeh might rebel against the Apostate, and with the Mourners at her command, they'd have a shot at subduing him.

But she might not believe Elide, and she may call Elide blasphemous for questioning the Apostate's authority as he was endowed on them by their Creator to lead them. Still, Elide hoped against hope that the woman could see she was telling the truth; surely at her age, Mother Superior wouldn't need a Teller's ability to know a lie. However, Elide couldn't see herself convincing many that he—the Apostate—was in any way tyrannical.

It occurred to her that this wasn't something she could do on her own, but the situation was looking more bleak as they passed through the academy's gates.

"Out," Altair said, opening the carriage door with one hand while keeping the gun aimed at Elide.

Elide eased herself out of the carriage, landing on the ground outside and staring up at the dark double doors of the academy. She felt the gun press into her back and began to walk forward, spotting a new statue of a gargoyle at the entrance hall before feeling some relief at seeing Starla waiting for her inside.

"You have a few hours to get her ready," Altair said to Starla. "Ambassadors will be present. Make her look presentable."

Starla nodded and gestured for Elide to follow her. Elide followed her in silence, studying her face, seriously pondering what her friend knew. Though, her expression gave nothing away.

When they were out of earshot of Altair, Starla finally spoke, "Running was unbelievably stupid."

Her tone sounded both hurt and harsh.

"Do you have any idea what the Apostate has planned?" Elide signed.

Starla rolled her eyes. "Does it matter, Elide? You ran from your future, from your people, that's unimaginable. Possibly even *damnable*."

Elide gaped at her words. They walked up the stairs and arrived at Madam Cumming's shop, where the kind-hearted woman stood, giving her a sad smile upon their arrival. Then she went through a door that led into the back.

"She's just fetching your dress," Starla said, turning to Elide.

"I need you to understand what I'm telling you," Elide signed.

"What you need is a bath," Starla retorted sharply, pulling a twig out of Elide's hair. "Madam Cummings, you have got a bath, haven't you?"

"Yes, dear, come on back," Madam Cummings said, her chipper tone bouncing off the walls.

But before Elide could respond, Starla dragged her into the back, which was much larger than the store itself. Though as they navigated their way through the aisles of shelves filled with fabric rolls, she glimpsed the seamstress sewing a white gown, which Elide was certain was hers, though she'd only had a moment to see it before Starla forced her through a cracked door that had a bathroom behind it. The bathroom itself was all white though the wallpaper had swirls of gold on it.

Starla began to prepare her a bath. Her friend stuck her palm under the spout, checking the temperature before plugging the drain and commanding her to undress. After the bath was mixed with holy oil, Elide climbed in.

"Honestly, Elide, what were you thinking?" Starla said, pouring water over her hair and removing more leaves.

Elide narrowed her eyes at her. "I can bathe myself, you know," Elide signed.

"Yes, you can," Starla responded. "You could also run off again, and I can't allow that. Not for my sake or Calvin's."

Elide took a deep breath. "Starla, I need to meet with Mother Superior. She needs to know what the Apostate is planning. I can't just sit here and—"

"Mother Superior is dying," Starla said abruptly, "She was in the room with the Apostate when they learned you'd disappeared. The old woman had a heart attack."

Elide felt a pang of guilt.

"Calliope couldn't give her anything for it?" Elide signed.

"They tried to summon Calliope for a draught of some sort but couldn't find her either. I imagine it's rather unnerving for a woman of Mother Superior's age to learn the only hope of saving Scopus has disappeared. She's been in such distress, screaming in pain."

Elide's guilt suddenly became anger. *He gave it to her first.* She knew what marrowroot did to the body.

Then as she looked at Starla, though her mind had been racing with other thoughts, recognition suddenly struck her. Starla was no longer wearing novitiate burgundy. Nor was she wearing Mourner black. Her gown was gray, as was the coat she'd hung up when Elide had entered the bath. But on her breast pocket, a small raven was embroidered in blue just above the Hamle's bear.

Elide's heart sank. Her eyes met Starla's and only one

word came to mind: *Why*. When had she been brought into the Apostate's inner circle?

"How long," Elide signed.

"You're too sentimental," Starla said weakly.

Elide stared at her. She could hear Calliope's words: *He can manipulate feelings better than any Hamle.*

"The Apostate trusted me to watch over you," Starla explained. "He assigned me to your suite. He ordered me to befriend you—which wasn't easy. You weren't very trusting when you arrived, so I latched onto your feelings of kinship toward your brother—and found a way."

"A way," Elide signed. She nodded slowly as tears welled up in her eyes. "Is that what you tell yourself? That manipulating me was just a means to an end."

Starla looked away, gathering the twigs and leaves she'd collected from Elide's hair and throwing them away in the trash can. She smoothed the skirt of her gown. "You are a very kind person, Elide," Starla said softly. "And while I believe the world would be a better place with more kindness, I am not willing to risk the nation's fate over your fear of change."

"The Apostate is going to murder our people, *his* people," Elide signed. "For what? Honor? Glory?"

"If that is true, I am sure that he has already considered all other options," Starla said sternly, clearly unwilling to change her opinion on the subject. "Honestly, you can't be that naive. Have you never read a history textbook? People die during war. The needs of the many outweigh those of the few." Starla took a deep breath. "You'll see in the end once everyone is converted. Everyone will be saved, and we'll all be rewarded in heaven for playing our part."

A part of Elide wished that she could convince Starla otherwise, but instinctively, she knew that it might just as well be the remnants of the trust Starla had built with Elide. And trust built on a lie could hardly be worth trusting at all.

Starla fixed her hair in the mirror and put back on her gray coat.

"Madam Cummings has spent quite some time on your dress," Starla said after she was satisfied with how she looked. "I advised her on certain aspects of it, and I'm sure it will look lovely. I'll wait outside."

She turned and left the bathroom, and Elide stared after Starla, wondering how she'd ever been fooled.

The seamstress had truly outdone herself. The wedding gown was champagne colored and beaded with crystals; it proved to be one of the most beautiful dresses she'd ever seen. From the beaded pattern on the bodice to the tiered skirt and beading on the veil. It looked like something out of a fairytale and certainly what Elide would have wished for on her wedding day. But this *was* her wedding day, and her expression couldn't have looked bleaker as she stared into the mirror outside the church. She had wondered which ambassadors would be present, though she was certain before she had entered the entry hall that she had seen Mrs. Coin entering the church. Prospero's leadership was there at the very least, and she'd wager some, if not all, of the men that had been in attendance when she'd been caught would be as well. To make matters worse, she hadn't seen Hansel. Didn't know if he was dead or alive. Though the more she pondered it, she doubted the Apostate would kill Hansel. He wanted to control her, and he couldn't do that with her brother dead.

She was staring at the floor through her veil, wishing she were anywhere else. The Mourner orders' creatures emblazoned on the academy church's double doors looked more fearsome now as she stood before them. Elide had refused a bouquet despite Starla's insistence on appearance and natural proceedings of weddings, to which Elide replied that there was nothing more unnatural than her wedding. In some ways, she hoped to hold onto what little dignity she had left, grasping at whatever power she still held.

"I'm surprised your mentor never taught you to close your mind," his voice caused the hairs on the back of her neck to raise. The Apostate came to stand beside her, though he stared straight ahead at the doors. Elide stared at him. He wore a black suit, his beard was neat and complimented his sharp jawline, and his hair was combed back. His eyes were filled with what looked like determination.

The Disciples that had come with him entered the hall first. Each was dressed formally, though they were notably armed, as divine violence waited for no one, surely even in what was meant to be a house of God. She swallowed down her tears and took a deep breath.

"What do you gain from this?" Elide signed.

"Our situation is unique," he answered, staring down at her. "The possibilities that lie ahead are limitless. Like us." His voice was softer now and almost kind. "One day, you will tire of being angry with me, Elide. And you will give me an heir that will rule over a new world. A better world."

"How can you know that it will be better?"

"Because after the rebirth of the nation, comes the rebirth of the world," the Apostate recited, sounding prophetic and confident in his reasoning. "As it was given, so it is promised. We were chosen for something greater, Elide. When you remember that, there will be peace between us."

The Apostate turned away from her and waved his hand at the double doors before them. Then Elide watched as they slowly opened, revealing a long wedding aisle. And as she walked, a few things happened as expected; she saw a few familiar faces in the pews, including the entire Coin family in one pew, from the reverend elder to Cyrus—who nodded at her—Reverend Warner and his wife, and the Howlers. Starla didn't make eye contact with her.

Once they made it to the front, Elide felt her heart sink as she knelt before the altar with the Apostate, and when she looked past his shoulder, she half-hoped she would see Hansel, but he wasn't there. Daegal sat in the first pew with a brown-haired woman in Mourner black, cooing and cradling a smiling baby. Then the ceremony began.

Elide could feel her eyes watering. She was choking back tears by the time the priest began speaking to the attendees and was trying not to shake.

But as the Apostate stood up for their vows and took her hand, her spirits lifted. She knew it was her groom's grasp, his power washing over her in familiar warm waves, but she didn't want to fight it. Whether it was self-preservation or pride, the last thing she wanted to do was cry in front of an audience. But as she held his hands, she felt such certainty flooding her body—though it was fabricated —she wanted to hold onto that feeling for a moment. It nearly matched the feeling she had when she called on her power successfully. It had been the first time she hadn't felt alone. But at the same time, she was revolted by the fact that it could be just as easily wielded against her as the Apostate was doing now.

Elide looked up into the Apostate's eyes and searched them for answers. Though all she saw was a power-hungry man.

"I, Ares, take you, Elide, to be my wife," he repeated with such confidence, his hands firmly holding hers. Elide feared him. How easily he could instill that same confidence into others around him and make them reliant on him. "I promise to inspire greatness within you and protect you from those who would bring you harm." The words sounded romantic. Likely even were so to the elite present. "I promise to always hold you in the highest regard." He spoke the phrase calmly, but his eyes communicated a warning, clearly a veiled threat. "I pledge my undying love to you. Though one lifetime could never be enough." In that same moment, his pupils seemed to darken, though she hoped she imagined it. "This is my sacred vow to you, my equal in all things."

Elide was sure she would have fainted if he were not holding her there.

She found herself looking past the priest at the tapestries on the wall by the piano, but specifically, the beautiful woven rendering of Rudolphus and Lysandra on their wedding day. Lysandra looked remarkable, though the eyes of the tapestry looked particularly sad. She wondered if this was a common theme for the men in his family; marrying women who didn't want them.

The priest bowed his head toward her. And she took a deep breath. She pulled her hands from the Apostate, and suddenly dread filled her once again.

"I, Elide, take you, Ares, to be my husband," she signed, trying desperately to keep herself from fumbling. Elide hardly wanted to make a fool of herself in front of the ambassadors, much less be on the other end of the Apostate's rage. "To always hold you in the highest regard . . ." She was nearly finished. She just had to make it through the last part. "My equal in all things."

Then they exchanged rings. And as the Apostate slipped the wedding ring onto her finger, Calliope's words found her again: *The Apostate is your only equal.* That part still reigned true. Her only problem was that she'd let him in.

The priest spoke again, but she didn't quite hear him. And before she knew it, the Apostate tilted her chin to meet his gaze and his lips met her own. For a few moments, she was lost to the kiss, only faintly hearing the applause and excitement from the pews. And while her mind and body were flooded with artificial certainty, she had some semblance of a plan of action forming in her mind.

# 28

Last spring, she wouldn't have imagined she'd be wed or even thought marriage was an option until she'd graduated, and yet here she was. A year ago, she was just starting to study for the LAT, and now she was shut in her nation's leader's bedchamber in an elite academy as his wife, awaiting him to consummate a forced marriage brought on by his feigned repentance. But she had been too naive to see the type of man the Apostate was before giving him her virginity.

Elide lay with her head on the pillows, staring up at the ceiling. She'd changed into a white nightgown and let her hair loose, trying her best to relax. *At least it will be on a bed this time*, she thought. The desk hadn't been particularly comfortable, though she could remember the feeling of him. But she didn't blush at the thought of it. She was trying to think of more important matters like closing off her mind to her bridegroom, something she'd read about in the beginning of her Secular Evocation textbook but hadn't thought to master. Had Daegal had them read it intentionally? Was he trying to help her, and she'd been too late? She wouldn't know now that she was wed to the Apostate. And no matter how hard she racked her brain, she couldn't remember exactly how to do it.

The front door opened, and the Apostate swept into the room. He was wearing his black uniform—but was far from dressed for bed. She sat up, eyeing him dubiously. He turned to her. "We needn't consummate our union so soon," the Apostate said, looking at her. "I have no desire to bed an unwilling woman."

Elide hesitated. She wasn't sure what to say. She mostly was glad his character wasn't completely compromised; the fact remained that she hadn't read him entirely wrong as he wouldn't force himself on her.

"Here," the Apostate said, wrapping a coat around her. "You're needed in the war room."

She nearly asked what for, but the answer hit her almost immediately. She thought to refuse but decided her efforts would be in vain. He opened the bedroom door and waited for her to move.

Elide took a deep breath, got up, and stepped into the hall. When the Apostate was by her side, the Disciples flanked them as they walked, escorting them safely to the war room. The Texan ambassadors waited, dressed in reverend elder garb or mart violet. Reverend Coin stood shoulder to shoulder with a bronze-skinned man with a strange sun crest embroidered on his teal coat. The Apostate introduced her to him as the newly minted Mart of Colchester, Kenneth Parker. Beside him, in a purple overcoat, the new Mart of Baptiste—her heart sank when she saw him. She tried to manage a smile, which came easier when the Apostate gripped her arm behind her back, and his power flooded through her. Enochs flanked their city leaders respectively and a group of Disciples dragged in the prisoner. Her face was dirty, and her hair was short, she was scrawny like she'd been starved, and there were bruises on her skin.

The sight of her would normally make Elide cry if the Apostate weren't gripping her arm so tightly. Elide knew he was warning her, and no matter how silent it was, a looming threat was enough to make her cooperate. He released her arm and took hold of her hand, taking her over to the prisoner. The curious ambassadors followed close behind her.

*So that's why they're here,* she thought as they stopped in front of the prisoner. *To prove I can perform.* Or that he had control of her.

"Now," the Apostate whispered into her ear, "I will ask her where they are, and you will make her answer."

Elide felt her heart lurch with pain as she caught sight of the look on the girl's face. The girl was younger than Elide, likely a teenager. Elide wanted to protest, but the Apostate turned away from her.

"I will ask you this again, Danielle," the Apostate said, standing in front of her. "Where is the base you came from?"

The girl spat on the ground in front of him.

The Apostate turned to Elide and nodded toward her.

But Elide just stared at the girl. She wouldn't. No matter what he did to her, she couldn't do it.

The Apostate clenched his jaw and narrowed his eyes at her. Then Elide felt overcome by a pain in her heart, as though an invisible hand had wrapped around it and begun to squeeze. She gasped, staggering for a moment before she steadied herself. *Will her to answer you*, a voice inside her head demanded. Elide refused to obey. She felt the pain in her arm this time, and it was like her arm had been stuck into an open flame. The voice came again: *Make her tell you their locations.*

Elide felt as though something reached inside her, pushing her power forward, focusing her gaze on the girl, and the teenager screamed. Danielle thrashed in her seat, squealing like a frightened piglet. Then she could hear all the girl's thoughts, racing words from different foods to her family's names—and then. *Demand the truth*, the gruff voice shouted at Elide.

"U-underground in B-barcombe, Stamford, Leeside, W-willowdale . . ." the teenager stammered out, her body shaking as she spoke. "Mount Orion and Berxley." Tears fell from the girl's eyes. "Those are all I know. I-I don't know anymore, I swear. P-please stop."

The invisible hand pulled away, taking the voice with it, and Elide collapsed to her knees. She held her head, feeling dizzy, but her power settled once more.

Elide could faintly hear applause and some laughter coming from the ambassadors. Though one looked particularly sour by the girl's answer. In the corner of the room,

Elide saw Cyrus staring down at the floor and when his eyes met hers, she saw what looked like pity.

"Berxley? You mean I've had those bleeding hearts under my nose this entire time?" the enraged mart snapped. "I swear on my honor, my liege, I will execute every rebel that I find there. You have my solemn promise."

"Easy, Mart Parrish," Reverend Warner said with a bark of laughter. "We'll handle those abominations in time. Now is the time for celebration! Shame the Mother Superior has had to miss it—"

"May God rest her soul when the time comes to pass," the Apostate said calmly.

Reverend Coin shook his head sorrowfully. "Who do you have in mind to take her place?"

The Apostate smiled. "Well, after Calliope's untimely absence, Professor Chandra Murik will be taking up the position as soon as she is able."

"But she's just had a babe, hasn't she?" Mart Parker said, tilting his head in confusion.

"Indeed," the Apostate answered. "But her husband has agreed to help her with the task until she is well enough."

Elide felt nausea seize her stomach. What had she done? Dear God, what had she just done?

She heard footsteps approach her and felt two strong arms lift her to her feet. Then she was leaning against something solid and looked up into Cyrus Coin's eyes. He steadied Elide on her feet, quickly turning his attention to the Apostate.

"Ah, my boy, ever the gentleman," Reverend Coin said, patting his son on the back.

The Apostate smiled. "Indeed."

His eyes flickered over to Elide, but at the moment, she was too exhausted to fear him.

"Altair, help Cyrus escort Elide back to the bridal chamber," the Apostate ordered. "She is more than deserving of some rest."

She hobbled along with the men, trying not to trip over her own feet. The moment they were out of the room, Cyrus took her arm and slung it over his shoulder, eliciting a scoff from his companion. Elide was grateful for the support; she wasn't sure how much longer she would manage on her own. She could feel her power inside her, pulsing through her with every heartbeat, reminding her that it was there. But it being there reminded her that at any moment, the Apostate could control her, and she would be helpless to stop it.

When they re-entered the bedchamber, Cyrus helped her out of her coat and even took off her shoes.

He started to say something, but she couldn't quite hear him as she slipped into a deep sleep that she hoped she'd never wake from.

Elide woke the next morning frightened but not alone. Beside her, the Apostate lay sleeping peacefully, and she began to shake at the sight of him. In his sleep, he looked like the man her treacherous heart desired, the one who'd sought to bring peace to his people. But she knew the truth, he wanted power, and it didn't matter who he had to hurt to get it. Yesterday had proven that.

She looked around the room and saw a silver dagger sitting on the dresser across the room. Elide looked at the Apostate again. For a moment she could see herself taking the knife and plunging it into his heart, ending him and possibly the war. Then she would find Hansel and get to the border as fast as she possibly could. And somehow, she found herself standing in front of it and picking it up. But when she turned back, the Apostate was awake. He sat upright in the bed, fully awake. She wondered how long he'd been awake.

*Of course, he'd been awake the whole time*, she scorned herself.

"Going to kill me then?" he said, standing from the bed. "Are you sure you want to do that?" The Apostate took a few steps toward her, and she grabbed the dagger, pointing it at him. "Tell me, have you ever taken a life?"

He took another step toward the dagger, and she aimed it at his heart. She could feel his power emanating off him, tugging at her own. But she continued to point it at him, trying to keep her hand steady.

"Kill me then," he said, standing in front of her now. Leering down at her. "You can't do it, can you?"

She glared up at him. But something in her couldn't do it. *He's inside your head*, she told herself. She could hear the sound of her breathing. But he was completely calm. Then she thought better of it and thought of something worth more to him.

Elide turned the blade and pointed it at her chest. *I'll do it*, she thought, and his gaze focused on her. She knew he was listening. *I'll kill myself. If not today, then I'll try again tomorrow. And I'll keep trying until I succeed. You will never use me to hurt anyone again.*

The Apostate's eyes narrowed, and suddenly he arced his hand. The dagger flew from her grasp, skittering across the floor and smacking into the wall.

But then for a moment, she remembered standing with Calliope underground—the memory so vivid that she swore it was unfolding right in front of her again.

Elide glared at the Apostate. If they were equals, then he couldn't control her. Marrowroot amplified their divine powers. Her power belonged to her—not the Apostate.

She had drunk the draught under duress, but now she was sure. The Apostate couldn't control what he wasn't given control over. She could hear a familiar voice whispering to her as the invisible hand began to wrap around her heart, and then she felt the same certainty fill her, but this time, she fought back. She scratched the Apostate's face, and he slashed an arm through the air, but Elide did the same. Then their powers collided, and Elide flew back into the wall.

As she rubbed her head, she saw the Apostate unconscious against the wall across the room, his shoulder impaled by wood from the bedpost. Elide got to her feet, shaking off a dizzy spell as she steadied herself. Then she ran, stumbling out of the bedchamber and finding her way to a staircase that she had no idea where it would lead.

Elide found herself trapped in a haze of confusion as her eyes adjusted to the sunlight. She was staggering around the back of the Thanatos Institute. Peering around the corner, she saw a civilian carriage, though she was unsure how far she would make it in her state. Her stomach was growling, and she hadn't had water since the wedding, but she couldn't go back inside. From the look of it, there weren't any Disciples searching for her, though she wasn't sure how long she'd been gone. And her leg had been giving her some trouble since her brief fight with her husband.

But she defiantly took a deep breath and limped her way to the carriage in her nightgown. The driver cocked a brow when she made it around to him. He looked in his thirties, wore a crimson coat and reading glasses, and appeared to be solving a crossword puzzle. His dark hair kept falling into his eyes. His companion was an older man in a black waistcoat with a rifle, reading a book and high-lighting parts.

"Is everything all right, Miss?" the driver asked.

Elide nodded. Then she heard shouting coming from the back of the Institute. She eyed the large gray building, and her heart leapt to her throat when she saw Altair running by one of the windows.

"*Psst* . . ." Elide turned to the driver. "Elide, is it?" he signed to her.

Elide hesitated. She looked back at the Institute.

"I'm Clay Bracken," he signed, flipping open a passport quickly.

Elide stared at the name quickly and could feel tears coming into her eyes as understanding flooded through her. *Dorran Bracken*, Calliope had said. He was meant to help her. So who was this?

"Calliope thought you might be here," Clay signed.

Elide looked back at the Institute.

"I'm Dorran's son, I swear," Clay said aloud. He was beginning to sound nervous. "Well, come on! We haven't got all day. Logan and I don't have as many bullets as the Apostate has men."

She stared at Clay blankly. Her instincts didn't tell her he was lying. But Elide was worried that she was too tired to tell.

"Get in!" Clay demanded, opening the carriage door as the old man slid into the driver's seat.

Elide wasn't sure if she could trust him, but she figured wherever they would take her would be better than here.

Elide climbed into the back of the coach as the old man cracked the reins and they pulled off. When she shut the door behind her, she looked out the back window, watching as several Enochs made their way out the back of the Institute, and she settled into the carriage seat across from Clay. A complete and utter stranger with a gun, that for once, wasn't aimed at her.

# Epilogue
## Hansel

Hansel Hester's head was bowed but not in prayer. He wasn't sure God heard him anymore. After everything that had happened with Juliette, and the countless beatings he'd endured over the past few days, he was sure he wasn't favored by God and that the title of Mart had befallen him by mistake. He would sometimes be tested by temptations beyond his control, knowing to refuse them. More than anything, he reflected on his time with Juliette and how much he loved her. And knew that she had loved him in return. But at twenty-three, Juliette was married off to Reverend Elijah Stone, a man five years her senior, two weeks before Hansel was honorably discharged from the Seekers. He had a sister to look after, so he took the title of Mart at twenty-four and the money that came with it. Taking care of Elide after their father passed wasn't easy, nor was his career change. No sooner than he'd taken up the title, Reverend Warner tried to have him removed as Mart of

Baptiste, on the grounds of his beliefs not aligning with the old ways. The issue of marriage being brought up time and time again. Hansel showed no interest in the eligible women of Texas or arranging a marriage for his eighteen-year-old sister. He was met with an ultimatum; marry or marry off Elide. As he loved his sister, he'd chosen the former rather than the latter. And despite his near removal from office, he didn't miss being a Seeker for even a moment. When he'd first listed it as a preference, he had no idea that the career was so gruesome; the administrators had only spoken of the honor that came with serving one's nation.

In his time during training, he'd received many letters from Juliette. She had been the brightest student in their year; she was training to be a lina in Prospero and always sent him perfumed letters. They'd gotten him through for some time, he could survive for months on one, and he'd often write back when he wasn't in the field. The honor of receiving her letters lasted longer than the honor he felt as a Seeker. It was the raid on a farming village in the northern Outlands; after that, he'd lost sight of what made them so honorable. He hoped to return to Juliette, but he'd spent most of his life unlucky. Two weeks and three hours were all that had stood between him and Juliette. She had agreed to marry Reverend Stone hastily—she'd told him in a letter after. She'd thought he'd died. But the marriage remained unconsummated. Juliette was a virgin, and her husband was always too busy to consummate their marriage. She believed that perhaps he was uninterested, but Hansel knew Reverend Stone was merely too preoccupied with visiting brothels in Kirekwall with the likes of Berxley's Mart Parrish. But still, he tried not to fixate on the idea of being with her. The way her voice trembled when she saw him for the first time in years. He wondered how he'd ever left.

Even now, in the back of this godforsaken metal transport trailer, he could still remember the feeling of her skin. Though he was trying to hold his breath as at least one of the other marked criminals had soiled himself. There was one man on his knees in the corner, mumbling to the wall as the carriage jostled. He assumed it was a prayer, though he didn't know the language. Though he knew the scars peeking out from the top of his shirt had come from a Disciple's whip.

"You're a mart, aren't you?" a gruff voice asked. Hansel turned to his right to look at a brown man with a scar running across the bridge of his nose and loose-fitting white clothing with a thirty-three on his chest pocket.

But Hansel didn't get a chance to respond.

"He ain't a mart anymore," a thin bronze man holding onto the barred window said. He took a deep breath of the fresh air. "He's wearing the same chains as the rest of us."

"I wasn't talking to you, Cross," the man said, and Cross scoffed. "But you were a mart?"

"Yes, of Baptiste," Hansel answered.

"Yeah, that's right, Baptiste!" he repeated. "You bought my wife's cupcakes at the market!"

Hansel thought back, faintly remembering the taste of the cupcakes. Mostly relieved to have the memory instead of tasting the rank air.

"That meant the world to her," he told Hansel, with a large grin on his face. "Tell you what, you and I are going to be friends."

"Ain't no one want to be your friend, Rusty," Cross shouted from the window.

Rusty looked hurt by the comment. "Everyone can use friends, Cross. No need to be rude," Rusty retorted harshly. He turned back to Hansel. "I promise you, I won't be any trouble as a friend. My mom used to say that I'm as bright as they come. I can think myself out of any situation."

"No use lying to him, Rusty. You couldn't think yourself out of a paper bag," Cross told him.

Rusty started arguing with Cross. The two were going back and forth, trying to outmatch each other. In the skirmish, Hansel couldn't help but take in how much more frantic the man in the corner's prayers had gotten.

Hansel sighed. "Honestly," Hansel said, drawing Cross and Rusty's attention as if they'd forgotten they were talking about him. "I'll take all the friends I can get."

Hansel heard horses neighing loudly out front and a loud bang on the trailer door. The door shrieked open, and three Enochs entered with keys and electric batons. And his breath caught in his throat as the familiarity of the world outside sank in, the sunlight beating down unforgivingly as they were dragged out into the heat in chains. Far ahead, he could see the rows of gray brick buildings that housed bunks for the workers. The electric fences that surrounded the camp as they were led through it. Above them, on a hill in the west, were white farmhouses that overlooked it all; the residents were elites commanded by the Apostate. The watchtowers were manned by Disciples. The labor camp itself was controlled by the man who supervised the training of the Seeker cadets from Baptiste—and by far the one man Hansel didn't want to face.

He was back in Whiteridge again, where there was no escaping his past, and whatever lay ahead was far worse than what he left behind. And if he were to make any plan of action to escape, he would have to do so carefully—as he'd only get one shot.

The adventures are just beginning!

If you'd like to follow along  sign up for my newsletter  at www.aminahfox.com/newsletter, where you'll receive updates as new books in this series are released and much more!

I also hope you'll consider dropping a quick review at the retailer and book review site of your choice.

Thank you and happy reading!

TURN THE PAGE FOR

# THE MOURNERS

## THE DEADLY ELITE

### BONUS MATERIALS

# THE MOURNERS

## *TELLER*

A telepath marked by their power to induce excruciating pain through the projection of vivid and realistic pain illusions. By delving into the thoughts and emotions of their target, they can manipulate their perception, making them experience intense physical or emotional pain. This unique ability can be used for various purposes, such as interrogation, defense, or even psychological warfare.

Among telepaths, Tellers are a rare and enigmatic anomaly. Some researchers claimed that Tellers occasionally displayed the uncanny ability to mimic the abilities of other telepaths, further deepening the mystery surrounding their true potential.

# THE
# MOURNERS

ALL MOURNERS ARE CAPABLE OF MASTERING THE POWER TO READ MINDS. THEIR CLASS IS DEFINED BY THEIR ADDITIONAL POWERS.

## *LETA*

A telepath that can manipulate and control the elements. Advanced Letas can control and influence the weather, creating storms, hurricanes or bringing forth clear skies. the mastery of multiple elements is an extraordinary feat. They have a profound connection with the elements of fire, water, earth, and air.

The mastery of multiple elements is a rare accomplishment. The most prevalent combination is a mastery of air and water. Those who possess these dual affinities can manipulate these elements with grace and precision.

It is exceedingly rare for a Leta to master more than two elements. Those who can are revered for their unparalleled prowess. Mastering all four elements is a skill that very few have achieved.

# THE MOURNERS

## *RAPHA*

A telepath with the power to heal others by empathizing with their pain and channeling their energy to mend wounds and ailments. Intermediate raphas can communicate with and understand the thoughts and feelings of animals, forging a deep connection with the natural world. Advanced raphas can bring back the dead.

Raphas are known as both "Death's Hand" and the "Healing Hand." In times of war and conflict, they are sent onto battlefields to tend to the wounded and dying. Their touch can close fatal wounds and alleviate the suffering of those on the brink of death. They also possess the ability to cause internal organs to fail by amplifying the emotional and physical pain they sense in others.

The emotional toll of absorbing and alleviating the pain of others, as well as the burden of knowing they possess the power to end lives, can take a heavy toll on Raphas. They often require support and guidance to maintain their own mental and emotional well-being.

# THE MOURNERS

ALL MOURNERS ARE CAPABLE OF MASTERING THE POWER TO READ MINDS. THEIR CLASS IS DEFINED BY THEIR ADDITIONAL POWERS.

## *MIRAI*

Among telepaths, the Mirai possess the power to perceive all possible futures. They can tap into the vast web of potential outcomes and glimpse the myriad of paths that lie ahead. However, the future is often presented as a chaotic jumble of possibilities.

Intermediate Mirais can accurately predict the future. They can sift through the tangled threads of possibilities and pinpoint the most likely path to a desired outcome. They can also look into the destiny of a single person, gaining insights into their fate, decisions, and potential actions. This allows them to make informed choices that align with their goals or to aid and guide others on their chosen paths. but this predictive power is a double-edged sword, as it requires immense mental discipline.

Advanced Mirais can enhance the abilities of other telepaths. But they have a weaker amplification effect than Mancios. Their reliance on touch-based amplification makes them ideal for one-on-one interactions or for discreetly aiding a single telepath in need.

# THE MOURNERS

ALL MOURNERS ARE CAPABLE OF MASTERING THE POWER TO READ MINDS. THEIR CLASS IS DEFINED BY THEIR ADDITIONAL POWERS.

## *KEDEH*

Among telepaths, Kedehs are rare, but not as rare as Tellers. They possess the unique ability to detect the presence and nature of telepathic powers in others. They can discern whether someone is a telepath and often gain insights into the specific nature of their telepathic talents.

In addition to their other powers, they have the innate talent to track individuals by connecting with their thoughts and emotions. They can follow the mental traces left behind by a person's presence, making them invaluable in finding missing persons or identifying hidden threats.

Advanced Kedehs can access and retrieve memories from a person's mind. This allows them to view the past experiences and recollections of others, providing valuable insights into their history, motivations, and secrets.

# THE MOURNERS

## *LASKA*

Among telepaths, Laska are common. These individuals have the ability to generate and control electricity. They also have the extraordinary power to interface with and manipulate electronic devices and technology.

Intermediate laskas can breach security systems, extract information from digital databases, and disrupt or manipulate electronic devices to their advantage.

They are commonly believed to have a tactile disadvantage seeing as they must make physical contact with their opponent.

# THE
# MOURNERS

ALL MOURNERS ARE CAPABLE OF MASTERING THE POWER TO READ MINDS. THEIR CLASS IS DEFINED BY THEIR ADDITIONAL POWERS.

## *HAMLE*

A telepath that possesses a multifaceted set of powers that revolve around perception, dreams, and emotions. Their abilities include: illusions projection, dream manipulation and emotion control.

Hamles have the remarkable ability to project powerful illusions directly into the minds of others. These illusions can be tailored to create vivid, lifelike scenarios or manipulate sensory experiences. Another facet of their power is the capacity to enter and manipulate the dreams of others. They can venture into the dream realms of individuals, gaining access to their deepest thoughts, fears, and desires. This ability allows them to explore the subconscious, uncover hidden memories, or even influence the dreamer's waking thoughts and decisions.

Advanced Hamles can exert control over the emotions of others. They possess the power to influence and bend the feelings of individuals to their will. They can enhance positive emotions, such as joy or love, or induce negative emotions, like fear or anger, effectively becoming puppeteers of human emotion.

# *MANCIO*

Mancios are exclusively male telepaths with the powers of mind control and persuasion. Their abilities are exceptionally rare and are known to run in certain family bloodlines. To inherit these powers, a male child must receive specific genes from their parents, either from the father or the mother, making their existence a rare occurrence.

Mancios are renowned for their innate charm and persuasiveness. They possess the uncanny ability to influence the thoughts and actions of those around them, bending them to their will with a mere thought or glance. Their powers of persuasion make them adept at negotiation, diplomacy, and even manipulation when necessary. But the true extent of their powers is a closely guarded secret among their kin, and they are often taught from a young age to understand and harness their powers. But at their most powerful, their only equal is a Teller.

Tellers are known to have the same amplification abiltiy; Mirai have a weaker amplification ability.

Elide, now branded a traitor, must confront dark forces
intent on expanding the regime and discover the true
extent of her power…

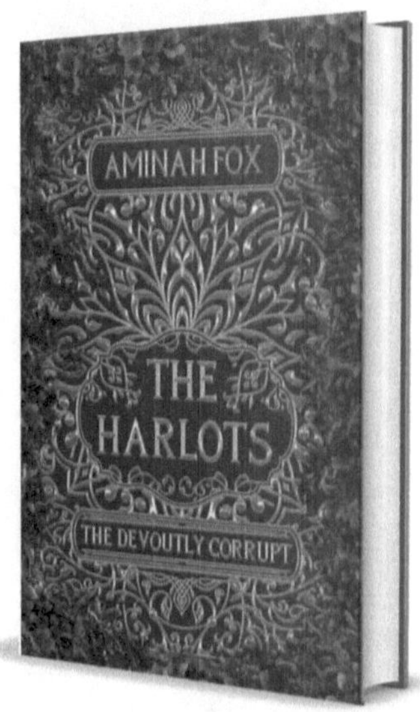


Return to the war-torn world of Scopus in

# THE
# HARLOTS

## THE DEVOUTLY CORRUPT

READ THE FIRST 2 CHAPTERS

# Prologue
## Cyrus

In the tapestry of war, destinies are woven in blood and steel. There is no place for forgotten oaths or the maelstrom of questions that clawed at every fiber of his being under the weight of his newfound responsibilities, but luckily he had maintained his persona admirably.

Today, however, the commander's gaze faltered upon the chilling absence of a particular individual—a woman—the last hope of Scopus. A chorus of frenzied cries woke him during his afternoon respite, announcing her disappearance through the use of an unmarked carriage. A carriage that had materialized out of thin air, bypassing the watchful gaze of paperwork and protocols, leaving no trace of its entry or departure.

*How could this happen?* Cyrus thought.

The guards had been handpicked for their unwavering loyalty and discipline. Disciples were trained to emanate an unyielding presence, one that conveyed the gravity of their responsibilities as protectors of the Apostate and the sanctity of their charge. But they were more than mere sentinels—they were the embodiment of an impenetrable shield, ready to defend their charge at any cost. Yet the 35th Regiment had failed. Their failure was his failure, and he—Cyrus Coin, commander of the 35th Regiment, a man adorned with countless accolades for his unmatched valor, bravery, and gallantry—now had to reckon with the fact that in one afternoon, two elite academies had been compromised due to his failure.

Despite Prana Academy's seemingly impenetrable nature, a phantom vessel had breached their meticulously plotted defenses, navigated to their front doors, and taken away the lone hope to end the war—the Teller. At the moment, his best bet for an explanation was the two men in front of him, Lieutenant Giles of the Disciples and Sargeant Reynolds of the Enoch.

Giles was a broad-shouldered tan man in his late thirties, bald with a close-cropped beard and weathered face marked by battle scars. He shared a history similar to Cyrus, having left the Seekers to become a Disciple. Reynolds was a boy on the cusp of manhood, at twenty-two years old, more adamant about proving himself. Tall, dark hair, well built, and ambitious—ambition was good. He was more likely to be honest and perhaps reveal which, if any, Enoch showed any signs of waning faith in their cause.

"I find it rather coincidental," Giles said, scratching the bridge of his nose with his forefinger. "Wouldn't you say, Reynolds?"

The young Enoch beside him continued to stare at the ground. "Not wholly unpredictable." Reynolds agreed with a clipped northern accent as he turned to straighten his green uniform in the mirror beside him.

"How about we move past who orchestrated it for a moment," Cyrus said. He had meant to say it sternly, but he sounded positively hostile. "We must focus on finding the truth. Where could the Teller have gone?"

His thoughts were scattered. Between upholding an air of confidence and masking his failed attempts to renew his faith—which were made more prominent after watching his superior torture the Teller—he was at his wit's end.

*Elide*, he thought, remembering her name.

He'd watched their head of state bend her will to his own, and men cheered. It was barbaric, the likes of inhumane torture he'd only been exposed to in his time as a Seeker.

Giles straightened up, his voice tinged with frustration, darting a glare at Reynolds beside him. "To the west, perhaps they're heading toward Apana. There is a hidden tunnel beneath the city that leads to a rebel hideout. It's possible the Teller learned of this and intends to go there," Giles stated. "I sent four of my men on horseback after them. They won't make it far."

"That is *if* they're going to Apana," Reynolds said. "After all, it was your men's negligence that started this mess. Their lack of vigilance allowed her to slip away undetected."

Giles bristled, his eyes narrowing at the young Enoch in response.

"Don't be so quick to deflect, boy. My men were monitoring every entrance to Thanatos and Prana, until *you* and *your fellow* Enoch relieved us. Perhaps they were the ones who let her escape."

Cyrus interjected, his tone demanding their attention. "*Silence.* Speculation and accusations will lead us nowhere. We need answers, not finger-pointing."

Reynolds, eager to assert his own theory, spoke up. "It's more likely she had help from someone inside, someone like Calliope," Reynold stated, countering Giles's suggestion. He moved closer to the desk Cyrus sat at. "We have several informants who have heard whispers of the intention of moving the Teller to the west but to *Kirekwall.*"

"Nonsense!" Giles said, shaking his head. "Kirekwall is a home to sodomy, belligerence, and brothels. Why would she go there?"

Cyrus listened intently, weighing their arguments. Kirckwall or Apana? Where would their resources be put to better use? He knew that time was of the essence and a decision had to be made.

"Both theories have merit. Giles, as your investigation is already underway, assure your men reach Apana. Reynolds, you will deliver my instructions to your superior for him to give me any information regarding your informants."

Giles and Reynolds nodded, their disagreement momentarily set aside in the face of their shared mission. As they hurriedly departed, Cyrus knew he would need to resolve the issue between the Disciples and Enoch before it descended into chaos.

The moment he was alone, Cyrus shut his eyes and took a deep breath. When he opened them again, he stared up at the domed ceiling, counting the cracks in the concrete walls. He considered returning to bed but still needed to report to the Apostate. He still owed him an explanation. A meeting with his superior that could potentially dissolve his mask of certainty, and leave his faith in ruins.

The fireplace crackled at the far end of the room, and he straightened in his chair. The room was warm, but if he were any closer to the fire, he'd be sweating. When he heard footsteps, he sighed, ready to turn around and dismiss whoever had arrived. But when he saw his visitor, he sprang to his feet.

The flickering fire cast an ominous glow on the man's grim face, illuminating the lines of frustration etched deep within his sharp features. Pale skinned, inky dark haired, and currently looming over Cyrus.

"Dismissing your men so easily, Cyrus? Is that how you handle such a catastrophic failure? Is that how I should deliver the news to millions? With no sign of remorse or empathy? As if the realization of the Teller's betrayal doesn't dash their hopes of a brighter future?"

The Apostate glared at Cyrus, his voice laden with rage as he spoke.

Cyrus met the head of state's eyes, trying to keep his anger at bay.

His jaw set, and he forced himself to answer. "My men acted swiftly. Their report offered a few leads on where she might have gone."

He'd controlled his tone, but the defiant nature of it was evident.

The Apostate narrowed his eyes. "A few leads?" he repeated, and his voice rose slightly. "The Teller slipped through your men's fingers, and you're defending their incompetence?"

Cyrus's frustration mounted. "With all due respect, *sir*, those same men have shown unwavering dedication and saved countless lives throughout their careers. Most have perfect records. This event is an anomaly, and I assure you, we will rectify it."

The Apostate leaned forward, his anger seething beneath his composed demeanor. He and Cyrus stood close to one another, sizing each other up in silence, but neither man backed down.

Then his superior laughed.

"Anomaly or not, Cyrus, the responsibility lands on your shoulders as their commander. This breach tarnishes not only their reputation but also yours. If news of this reaches our enemies, they will use it to their advantage," the Apostate said grimly. "You have failed me, and you have failed Scopus."

Cyrus squared his shoulders but didn't let his superior's words deter him.

"I understand the weight of this failure, and I will bear it alone," Cyrus stated as a solution dawned on him. "I implore you to grant me the opportunity to search for the Teller alone. As a Seeker, I became accustomed to navigating and surviving in different types of terrain. If you refer to my previous commander's recommendation, I'm sure he'll have mentioned my tracking skills."

The Apostate regarded Cyrus with reluctant admiration.

"Cyrus, while I understand your resolve, this task is perilous for a man of true faith in our cause," the Apostate said, his voice measured yet bearing a hint of resignation. "At this moment in time, we cannot risk losing our most decorated commander."

"I do not wish for any of my men to be punished," Cyrus stated. "Nor do I wish them to be tempted to sin in a city that's claimed others before it. They may falter, but I will not. If you trust in my skills and experience, I will make amends. And upon my return, I will fortify the defenses to ensure such a breach never occurs again."

He hoped his voice sounded confident and laced with determination. But the room fell into disquieting stillness as the Apostate considered his plea.

The silence stretched to every nook and cranny of the chamber to the extent that Cyrus could hear the pipes banging in the walls. The quietude reminded him of the calm before a tempest, that brief moment on the battlefield where decisions carried the weight of life and death.

But Cyrus had already made up his mind. His resolve took shape, forged in the crucible of doubt and determination.

He would embark on this solitary quest, driven not only by duty but also by the lingering whispers of uncertainty that lived in his nightmares. A quiet questioning of purpose that remained even under the Apostate's gaze.

*The penalty for desertion is death*, he thought, scorning himself.

But if he wanted to continue playing his role, he had to confront his wavering allegiance and decide whether to march forward with the cause he had sworn to protect all those years ago or to leave it behind for an unknown future. The decision weighed on him, but it was his alone to make.

Suddenly, the Apostate sighed, breaking the silence. Then he studied the commander, his expression one of reluctant agreement.

"Very well, Cyrus, I will grant your request," the Apostate said. "Find the Teller, bring her back to me so she can be dealt with accordingly, and you will be redeemed."

With a firm nod of acknowledgment, Cyrus left the room, knowing that the path ahead would be fraught with danger and that the consequences of his actions would ripple far beyond the walls of this fortress.

# 1

## Elide

When Elide emerged in a glade alone, she stood there in silence, trees towering above her, the ground beneath her feet blanketed in snow. Rays of sunlight filtered through frost-laden branches, casting a gentle glow on everything around her. She wore a heavy brown coat she couldn't remember putting on, and every breath she exhaled came out as a puff of fog. It was quiet. Perhaps even serene.

But her heart gave a miserable twist. The thought of her brother, Hansel, suffering somewhere far away for helping her was more painful than the memory of him being taken from her.

And now she stood in the middle of nowhere, unsure of how she'd gotten there. She'd catch herself wondering if it had all been worth it, out of habit, a bad habit she'd developed, because she knew what the Apostate had planned, and every single time she tried to ignore that nagging thought, her mind doubled down on it. Was she really any use now? Here?

She sighed.

Then, a soft rustling resounded from a distance, disrupting the silence.

Her heart skipped a beat. She turned her head as heavy footfalls, muffled by the snow, grew louder.

Her eyes widened as a creature emerged from the trees. She gulped.

Its stature commanded respect, standing tall and proud amid the snowy landscape. A thick coat of silver fur enveloped its massive frame, gleaming in the sunlight. Its paws crushed snow underfoot, each step heavy and deliberate, infused with a silent power that rippled through the crisp air.

A surge of panic gripped Elide, instinctively urging her to flee from the potential danger.

*Wolf*, she thought, looking left and right in search of an escape route.

But when she looked back at it, the wolf's eyes held her captive, dark and penetrating. And as it moved closer, she sensed they held a depth of intelligence, a knowing that went far beyond mere instinct. It was as if the wolf had journeyed through the annals of history, collecting tales and wisdom in its wake.

The wolf stopped just a few feet from her, towering over her as it craned its head. In that moment, the fear melted away, and the creature straightened its back. But it didn't run. Instead, it looked as though it were waiting for something.

On an impulse, she closed the distance between her and the beast, stopping the moment she stood in its shadow. As she stared up at it, the creature lowered its muzzle toward her. Elide reached out her hand to touch it, the fog of her breath escaping her lips as its nostrils flared. When it decided she wasn't a threat, it began to move its muzzle closer, but just as her fingers grazed the creature's wet nose, she was jostled awake.

Her breath caught in her throat as she took in the sight of the man on the red upholstered seat opposite of her and sighed. She was still in the carriage, Clay Bracken across from her.

The man, with his dark, untamed hair, lay undisturbed, a peaceful expression gracing his features. His chest rose and fell in a steady rhythm, completely at peace with his life. Elide guessed he was in his early thirties and seemed accustomed to using his crimson coat as a makeshift pillow. His clothing was faded and adorned with patches, but from what little she knew of him, his father was a brothel owner, meaning he was wealthy, and therefore, his outfit was a disguise. Clay wore it pretending to be of a lower economic class, and clearly, he was clever. Or at least clever enough to get in and out of Prana undetected.

As the soft glow of the passing gas lamps filtered into the carriage, it cast shadows upon his pale face, revealing the contours etched with the resolve of a warrior. In the stillness of the moment, she watched over him, her heart heavy as she worried what lay ahead.

After they rounded a corner, the carriage glided to a halt. A sharp knock reverberated against the window, pulling her from her thoughts.

Elide's heartbeat quickened.

"We're here," Logan called out from the other side of the door, his tone infused with a mix of authority and impatience.

Clay stirred, his eyes fluttering open as he rubbed his face. He blinked, appearing momentarily disoriented, before a sense of awareness settled across his features. Sitting up, he adjusted his clothes and cast a quick glance toward her, acknowledging their shared presence with a small smile.

"Everything's going to be all right now, Elide," Clay told her.

Elide gave him a tight-lipped smile.

Clay rose from his seat, his muscled frame commanding attention in the confined carriage space. He pulled on his coat and reached for the door handle, pausing for a moment to study Elide's face.

"I'm fine," Elide signed.

With a nod of assurance, he pushed the door open. Cool air and the sounds of their destination rushed in. Elide followed suit, stepping out onto the streets.

"Take my arm," Clay ordered. "It's not too far from here."

Elide's cheeks burned as she remembered she was still in her nightgown. Then, a weight settled over her shoulders, and she looked up into two kind eyes behind round spectacles.

"Thank you," Elide signed to Logan as she pulled the coat tightly around her body.

Clay cocked a brow at her, and she didn't respond.

"Take my arm, it'll be safer," he said. After a moment, he added, "Trust me."

Elide nodded silently. She slipped her hand into the crook of his arm and walked beside him. She wanted to pretend she had been here before but couldn't help but take in the city around her—on the off chance she needed to run.

Shadows danced along the walls of sandstone buildings, lending an air of secrecy to the bustling thoroughfares. The scent of exotic spices and sizzling meats mingled with the delicate aroma of perfumes worn by the courtesans who roamed the streets.

Her stomach growled, reminding her she hadn't eaten in quite some time. She considered bringing Clay's attention to it but knew more pressing matters were at hand. As they traversed the labyrinthine streets, the sounds of Kirekwall enveloped them.

The raucous laughter of revelers spilled from taverns, blending with the melodious tunes of street musicians. Logan notably stopped to drop money into a musician's hat. Clay seemed more adamant about getting to their destination.

Wooden food stalls lined the avenues, their sizzling grills and aromatic concoctions captivating the senses. The sizzle of skewered meats and the crackle of flames intermingled with the siren-like calls of vendors, tempting them with their delectable wares. In the heart of the city, gambling dens sprung to life, their entrances guarded by brutish men whose eyes narrowed as they passed. But not before the clatter of dice and the shuffling of cards punctuated the night, competing with the laughter and cries of both victorious and disgruntled gamblers.

Navigating through the chaos, Clay pulled them into a back alley, hidden from the prying eyes of those who lumbered along on the main streets. Yet, even the shadows teemed with life. An enormous rat scurried across the ground, bread clenched tightly in its jaws, and Elide noticed a drunken man being tossed out of a dimly lit tavern. The man appeared unperturbed as he propped himself up against a wall and sang a slurred song. Only to be interrupted by the jingle of coin purses exchanging hands as transactions unfolded between patrons and courtesans lingering in back alley doorways.

Their footsteps echoed against the stone beneath them, and Elide knew they had moved deeper into the heart of the city as they stopped at an unassuming wooden door.

Clay eased her hand off his arm and knocked.

A small panel on the door opened, dark and empty.

"What do you seek?" a male asked with a stern voice.

"The only question that you ever need to ask," Clay answered.

"What lies at the heart of a world consumed by darkness?"

"Behind closed doors, the truth finds sanctuary."

"Humph . . ." the man behind the door said.

Then the door, weathered and worn, creaked open to reveal a dimly lit corridor, its stone walls adorned with murals depicting Apolitian lore. The bulbs on the walls flickered, each light near death, as they stepped across the threshold. When the door shut behind them, the guard stared down at her curiously.

He stood tall and imposing, clad in a sleek black uniform adorned with red trimmings. The fabric seemed to meld seamlessly with the shadows, camouflaging him. His warm brown skin was taut as he gritted his teeth. The guard's posture suggested years of training and unwavering dedication to his duty.

"This is her?" the guard grumbled.

Clay scoffed. "Yes, this is her, and I'm sure she'd like some rest. So if you don't mind, Vexx, I'll show her to the upper quarters."

Vexx muttered something. "Go ahead. I'll send word to Hollowdenn that you've returned unharmed with the—" He hesitated as he gave her a once-over, appearing unimpressed. "Teller."

Elide felt a surge of annoyance.

Eventually, the passage gave way to light, revealing a surprisingly well-lit lobby adorned with worn-out carpeting and flickering ceiling lights. The air hung heavy with a peculiar mix of decaying wood and the faint aroma of stale coffee.

Clay strode up to the receptionist casually. "Evening, I've made a reservation?"

The receptionist, a man of at least thirty, with dark hair and square glasses, raised an eyebrow. "Checking in, then?" He pulled out a worn-out green ledger with what Elide presumed was the name of the place.

*Karthik Hotel. Home of the Karthik Gardens.*

"Name?"

Clay leaned in slightly. "Clay Bracken."

The man appeared more curious then. He scribbled something in the ledger and said, "Welcome back, Mr. Bracken. I'm afraid you'll have to take the elevator at the end of the hall. The other elevators are out of service."

The concierge scribbled something down on a piece of paper and tore off what Elide assumed was a receipt.

Clay smiled. "Thank you."

Clay gestured for Elide to follow him down the hallway, its threadbare carpet muffling their footsteps as they walked. The numbered doors lining each side nodded to this being a functioning hotel, but the subtle vibration beneath their feet betrayed this reality.

At the end of the hall, they stepped into a vintage elevator with brass buttons and swirling patterns etched into its metal frame.

The concierge's voice echoed from behind, "Enjoy your stay, Mr. Bracken . . . *and guests.*"

The elevator doors slid open with a soft chime, revealing a small compartment adorned with flickering bulbs. Elide stepped in, the doors closing with a mechanical hum.

Inside, the panel offered a range of floors, mostly numbers beside two mysterious designations: KG and SRL.

"Sub Rosa Lounge," Clay muttered to himself, raising his eyebrows as he found the button.

He pressed the button, and the elevator jolted to life, descending with a rhythmic clunk. As the numbers on the dial decreased, so did the sounds of the hotel, replaced by the distant hum of machinery and muffled conversations somewhere down below. The elevator came to a stop, and the doors opened, revealing a hidden corridor far removed from the hotel above.

When they reached a stairwell crafted from weathered stone, Elide slumped her shoulders. For a moment, she closed her eyes, begging the Almighty for the strength to climb them. Luckily, Clay didn't leave her side. Their footsteps echoed as they climbed, as if acknowledging the significance of their arrival. They reached the landing, which was adorned with tapestries that depicted Apolitian history and what she assumed were names of the resistance's dead. Those names told stories of sacrifice and hope, serving as a reminder of the collective purpose that propelled them forward.

At the top of the staircase, a corridor stretched out before them, leading to a series of doors that were private quarters. The doors were crafted from rich, dark wood, each one bearing a unique symbol, likely personalized to reflect the individual behind it. When they stopped in front of a door that was barren with a key sticking out of it, she hesitated.

"This one is yours," Clay told her. "I'm right across the hall if you need me," he said, gesturing toward the door with a silhouette of the scales of justice on it. "There should be clothes and toiletries inside the room already. You'll meet the others in the morning," he told her softly, and she nodded. "Can I get you anything?"

"Food," Elide signed.

"All right, I'll send for some food," he said and nodded at Logan, who was standing down the hall. "Logan! Grab Elide here some food, will you? Make sure it's a balanced meal."

Logan nodded, then wandered away.

"You don't have to stay out here," Clay said turning back to her.

Elide blinked. She looked at the key in the lock and unlocked the door, then stepped inside the room and flicked on a light switch.

Turning back to Clay, she signed, "Thank you, Clay."

Clay smiled. "Not a problem," he said, and he went inside his room, closing the door behind him.

With a sigh, Elide shut her door and locked it behind her. Her eyelids grew heavier, urging her to sleep.

Half-awake, she faintly registered the room around her: a window, a desk, a wardrobe, a bathroom, a flickering bulb in a lamp on the bedside table, the bed. But Elide forced herself to shuffle over to the bathroom and peel off the coat and the rest of her clothes as she turned on the bath. She watched the water gurgle out of the tub's faucet before plugging the drain and slipping into the soothing embrace of the steaming bath. Submerging herself under the water, she wet her curly hair and then rose again to detangle it with her fingers. With a loofah, she scrubbed away dirt from her brown skin and was relieved the moment she was clean. Afterward, she dried herself with a towel and shuffled back to the room.

By the time she climbed into bed, the room was dark, save for the soft glow of a single lamp in the corner. Elide sat on the edge of the bed, trying to wait for the much-needed meal she'd been promised. As the minutes stretched into what felt like hours, betwixt the warmth of the room and the thoughts of her brother being tortured somewhere far away, she found herself in a drowsy state. Unable to resist, she lay back, intending to rest her eyes for just a moment, but instead fell into a fitful sleep.

# Acknowledgments

I have been lucky to have many amazing people in my corner cheering me on and supporting me throughout working on this book. I could not have written *The Mourners: The Deadly Elite* without the support of countless friends and family members. It has been my privilege to work with many wonderful people throughout this process.

My editor, Jeanine Harrell, whose keen eye and expertise made this story better. She has terrific instincts, and a knack for spotting flaws in my prose that I would have missed.

My cover designer, Gabriella Regina, who created a magnificent cover for this story. From the moment I saw this cover, I knew it captured the humble beginnings of Elide's story.

And, of course, many thanks to my family: my father, Kevin Fox Sr., who encouraged me through early drafting stages, and was still excited even when I wouldn't tell him the title. My older brothers, Kevin and Stephen, for their endless enthusiasm and heartfelt advice, and who have always been there for me. And my kind-hearted, loving mother, Bridgett Quarles, who was very understanding of my long hours of editing, and stayed up for late-night movies (and binge-watched series) with me.

Last but not least, thank you to all those that I have not named, who cheered me on throughout the writing process. You helped me more than you know.

And many thanks to my wonderful readers who continue reading my work.

# About the Author

Aminah Fox is an American author, born in June 1998 in Oakland, California. She is an alumna of the University of Toronto (MI in Library & Information Science) and Hofstra University (BA in English, Creative Writing & Literature). Her sophomore novel, *The Mourners: The Deadly Elite,* was published in 2022. She lives in Texas (USA) and Toronto (CAN).

www.aminahfox.com

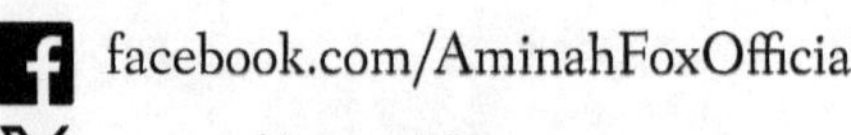

facebook.com/AminahFoxOfficial
x.com/AminahFox
instagram.com/aminahsfox

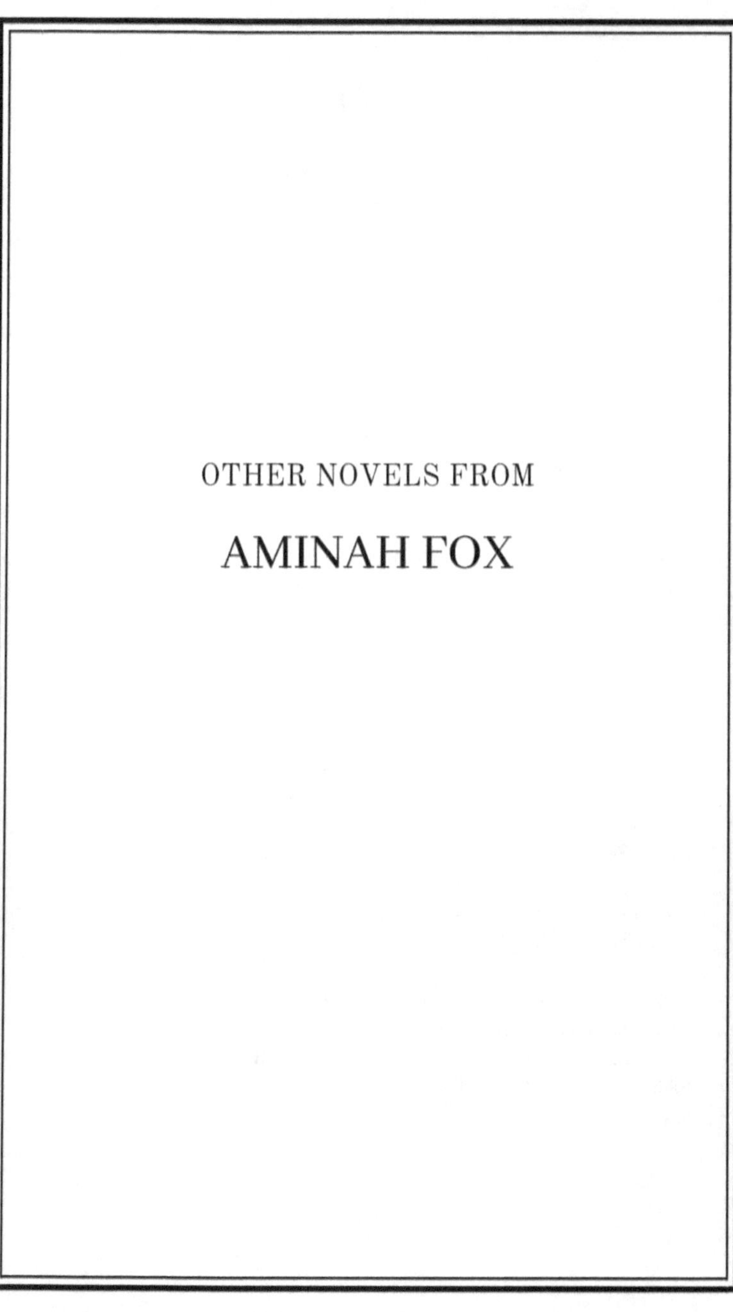

OTHER NOVELS FROM

# AMINAH FOX

# THE
# HARLOTS

## THE DEVOUTLY CORRUPT

AMINAH FOX

**The second novel in an adult dystopian fantasy
series where a voiceless young woman must
confront dark forces intent on expanding the
regime and discover the true extent of her power...**

Haunted by guilt and grief, Elide finds herself torn between her past and an uncertain future. Branded a traitor after her daring escape from Prana, she seeks refuge with the enigmatic rebels known as the Crimson Thorns, a group determined to overthrow the oppressive regime gripping their world.

But Elide's resolve is put to the test as she struggles to conceal her true identity as the Teller, a role that could change the course of history. With her newfound allies at her side, she embarks on a perilous journey to reclaim her destiny and liberate her world from the clutches of the Apostate's tyranny.

Unfortunately, Elide faces a dual threat: the Apostate's sinister plan to expand the regime's dominion beyond Scopus' borders, and the relentless pursuit of his disciples. Bereft of her mentor's guidance, Elide must learn to wild the untamed power within her.

Amidst the chaos, Elide finds an unexpected ally in a tracker, who harbors his own doubts about the regime. Together, they navigate the treacherous landscape of a nation teetering on the brink of civil war. As tensions mount, Elide realizes that the fate of Scopus hangs in the balance, and the time to act is now...

# THE ELEVENTH HOUR



**The first novel in an adult dark fantasy series following where a young woman from a wealthy magical family must travel back in time to prevent a horrible tragedy, when growing conflict threatens to destroy her world—even if she doesn't know what she may lose by doing so.**

*The past is always present...*

On a brisk summer's night, in a state of mundanes, a peculiar train leaves the station, its heading, a hidden borough of magic—and magicks. Hampshire, New York—a borough divided into three counties, each controlled by a magical noble family—Mandrake (County of Merlin), Dimitri (County of Morgana), and Bane (County of The Fates). After a treacherous plot unfolds, Alfred Mandrake, Head of the Mandrake family—who maintained decades of peace in Hampshire—is dead. But when his eldest son plots to wage war against the family responsible, his sister Hermione intervenes.

Hermione is a 21-year-old witch, and luckily, she was left her grandfather's final magical invention: a pocket watch that uses memories to travel back in time. With the trinket in her possession, Hermione and her half-brother intend to go back to March—four months before the massacre, that killed thousands, including their father.

Unfortunately, when their plan goes awry, they land thirty years in the past, with the trinket suddenly inoperable. Now, they must repair it, but navigating the past is no easy feat. As Hermione explores this dark, unfamiliar world, pursued by murderous villains, she soon learns to save her future, she may have to destroy her past.